JERK,
california

jonathan friesen

speak
An Imprint of Penguin Group (USA) Inc.

other books you may enjoy

An Abundance of Katherines	John Green
Defining Dulcie	Paul Acampora
Looking for Alaska	John Green
Paranoid Park	Blake Nelson
Restless	Rich Wallace
The Rules of Survival	Nancy Werlin
Speak	Laurie Halse Anderson
Twisted	Laurie Halse Anderson

SPEAK
Published by the Penguin Group
Penguin Group (USA) Inc., 345 Hudson Street, New York, New York 10014, U.S.A.
Penguin Group (Canada), 90 Eglinton Avenue East, Suite 700, Toronto, Ontario, Canada M4P 2Y3
(a division of Pearson Penguin Canada Inc.)
Penguin Books Ltd, 80 Strand, London WC2R 0RL, England
Penguin Ireland, 25 St Stephen's Green, Dublin 2, Ireland (a division of Penguin Books Ltd)
Penguin Group (Australia), 250 Camberwell Road, Camberwell, Victoria 3124, Australia
(a division of Pearson Australia Group Pty Ltd)
Penguin Books India Pvt Ltd, 11 Community Centre, Panchsheel Park, New Delhi - 110 017, India
Penguin Group (NZ), 67 Apollo Drive, Rosedale, North Shore 0632, New Zealand
(a division of Pearson New Zealand Ltd)
Penguin Books (South Africa) (Pty) Ltd, 24 Sturdee Avenue, Rosebank, Johannesburg 2196, South Africa

Registered Offices: Penguin Books Ltd, 80 Strand, London WC2R 0RL, England

Published by Speak, an imprint of Penguin Group (USA) Inc., 2008

5 7 9 10 8 6 4

LIBRARY OF CONGRESS CATALOGING-IN-PUBLICATION DATA
Friesen, Jonathan.
Jerk, California / by Jonathan Friesen.
p.   cm.
Summary: Plagued by Tourette's syndrome and a stepfather who despises him, Sam meets an old man in his
small Minnesota town who sends him on a road trip designed to help him discover the truth about his life.

[1. Identity—Fiction. 2. Fathers—Fiction. 3. Tourette syndrome—Fiction.
4. Automobile travel—Fiction. 5. Interpersonal relations—Fiction.]
I. Title. PZ7.F91661Je 2008
[Fic]—dc22 2008007922

Speak ISBN 978-0-14-241203-9

Printed in the United States of America

acknowledgments

I'm so grateful for special people placed on my journey. Like signs along the road, they pointed me in the right direction. I especially want to thank the following:

Wendy: You are an amazing woman, both for who you are and what you endure! I love you. Emma, Isaac, and Si, you also have sacrificed, and bear the burden of "writer's children" with poise and patience.

The circle of friends around my family who provided support and encouragement while I was "away": You made this book possible.

Angelle and all the great folks at Penguin: Each of you has blessed my trip.

As have my parents: Your generosity allowed me to meet deadlines, and know my three blessings were in good hands.

Joel: Our walks mean more than you know.

Word Servants and advance readers: In the early stages, your encouragement kept the project moving forward.

Lauraine and Deidre: You believed in me long before I believed in myself. You are gifts to me.

Cec: My mentor and friend, you've touched my life in ways I can't express on this page. Thank you for letting me fail, and for telling me the truth, no matter how wonderful it was.

Most of all, I'm grateful to God: I see your fingerprints on everything. You turn tears to joy, and curses into blessings!

dedication

To Wendy, who chooses to stay

part one
sam

chapter one

"SAM HAS IT. QUESTION IS, HOW BAD?"

The pediatrician smiled. Like he got off on destroying a kid's life. Like children frequently went to sleep normal and woke up monsters who couldn't keep their damn bodies still.

He stared at me, waiting. My right hand twitched. He pointed and continued. "The disease has seasons. One day he'll flail like a windmill in spring. Then the wind'll die and you won't see anything for months." He turned to my mom. "There are some experimental drugs—"

"Who the hell is supposed to pay for those?" my stepdad said.

The doctor rose. "I can see you need some time, Bill." He shook my six-year-old hand, gave my stepdad a pat on the back, and slipped out of the examining room, leaving the three of us to stare at my jerking hands and shoulders.

"What'd he say, Mom? Bill? When's it gonna go away?"

Bill stood and paced the room. "Go away? Your twitches won't ever stop." He cursed and kicked the doctor's swivel chair.

I stared at Mom. "Never? Not even when I'm older?"

Mom scooted her chair in front of mine. "He says you have Tourette's."

I mouthed the word, and she leaned forward and stroked my arms. Gentle at first, then harder and harder and mixed with tears. I knew she was trying to rub that bad word out of me.

"What does that mean?" I asked.

"It means," Bill said, "you can forget about ever running my machines."

My hands squeezed the jacket Bill gave me, the green one with Tar-Boy on the front and a cement mixer on the back. I pulled free of Mom and grabbed Bill's pant leg.

"I can stop it. Please, Bill." I started to cry. "I'll be still. Promise!"

Old Bill turned his back, Mom closed her eyes, and even at six years old I knew I was alone.

chapter two

"YOU'RE QUIET IN GROUP TODAY."

Leslie, the social worker, stares at me. I look around at the others. Eight guys rest their heads on the table.

"Everyone's quiet," I say.

She places her young elbows on the table and rests her young head in her young hands. "But you're somewhere else, aren't you, Sam?"

Bryan snores from across the circle, and I point at him, but this woman's eyes won't go away. I glance at the clock—ten more minutes.

"I *wish* I were somewhere else. How many more weeks do I have to come?"

Dumb question. I know exactly. Ten. In Old Bill's barn hang fourteen sheets of paper covered with smiley-face suns. Ten of those sheets aren't yet blasted through with BB-gun pellets.

Leslie smiles the smile people use at funerals. "One of the

ways we build friendships is by answering questions. A good way to do this is through small talk. You respond with something cheery about your day or your family."

Room 14 is a morgue. Powder-blue walls and no window. Only the tick of the clock and the buzz and flicker of the fluorescent light remind me I'm still alive.

I slump down in my seat and cross my arms.

Socially maladaptive. According to the special-ed teacher, that's what I am. Sentenced to a semester in Leslie's "Sunshine Club," I'm one of the lucky ones up for parole at Christmas break.

I glance at the lifers. Ken and Kerry, autistic twins; Larry, who slugged a cook. Not sure how cramming in a tiny room for an hour after school will turn any of us into charmers.

The word *maladaptive* scrawled in invisible ink across my forehead just stole another hour of my life. Today, I don't have the time.

"I can see you're defensive, but look around you, Sam." Leslie's eyes plead. "These boys are here to be your friends."

Another snore from Bryan.

"Let's try a role-play. I'll pretend I like you." She perks up and clears her throat. "Remember, small talk. Answer with something general and light." Her smile widens, so do her eyes. "I'd love to hear something about your family."

I check the clock, look back at her, and nod. "My dad is dead. Don't worry about it, because he was a loser drunk who dug holes for a living. But he was generous. Kind enough to leave me this damn disease as my inheritance."

Leslie's smile is gone, her face frozen.

I push back from the table. "He left my mom for some other gal and then got himself killed." I stand. "And his replacement, Old Bill, is almost as bad. Any other questions?" I pick up my backpack and walk to the door. "Do appreciate the small-talk lesson."

Bryan's snore catches on something ugly, and he wakes with a "Huh!"

Before the door closes, a quieter Leslie goes to work on another victim. "You're quiet in group today, Bryan."

I jog to my locker, drop to the ground, and change into running shoes. I push through the front doors of Mitrista High. Outside, air hangs heavy, full of October mist. My lungs suck in the soup.

I stand and stretch and jog out of town. It's quiet. Birds, frogs, crickets—thick air smothers them all. The paved road ends and shoes hit gravel. My pace evens. My brain clears.

Shouldn't have come down on Leslie. Ain't her fault.

I jog through Bland—population sixteen—past three houses and Crusty's Coop, and reach tiny Pierce. It's only a minute's run from our farm on the near side of town to the Shell station here.

Two cars filling up? Today's 10K must be a bigger race than I thought.

Behind me, gravel pops and crackles, and I glance over my shoulder. Three school buses approach. I drift to the road's edge as they rumble by. A minute later, a string of twenty more overtakes me. I reluctantly fall in line behind them, and we all turn left into the Northwoods Wildlife Refuge.

The race won't start for an hour, but already a crowd gathers. I dash through the parking lot and join the onlookers beneath a string of colored pennants. I weave through the people until I reach the rope cordoning off the runners' starting area. The grassy field is littered with athletes from all over Minnesota, and above them stretches a large banner.

NORTHWOODS 10K OFF-ROAD CLASSIC

Kids wearing numbers small-talk easily. They laugh and stretch and check the sky.

I lean against the rope that separates me from them. I glance up, too. It will rain. It will rain hard and fast and their running shoes will stick in the mud. The sloppy path through the woods will make for a slow race. But it will be a race, and I don't have a number, and I'm on the wrong side of the rope.

A woman hands me a program with the list of runners. I scan the schools, the names. Over two hundred numbers today. I trace the list with my finger and locate the Cs. Sam Carrier would have been number thirty.

"Carrier?"

I look up. Coach Lovett approaches. Mitrista's new running coach weighs in at over three hundred pounds. But for an extra thousand a year, I guess a shop teacher will do most anything.

"From what I hear, you'd win this race. What's holdin' you

back, son?" I look over his shoulder at Mitrista's four entrants. Two shove each other; darn near a fistfight. Coach follows my gaze. "Lord knows we need ya." He turns back toward me. "Mailed you off a sports waiver. You get that signed?"

I exhale slow and kick at the dirt.

"Just need *one* of your folks' signatures," he says, and taps my shin with his shoe. Coach steps nearer and whispers. "Your stepdad never has to see it."

I blink hard, and my mouth gapes. Coach smiles.

"When I took this job from Coach Johnson, I asked him for the name of Mitrista's best runner. Don't you think that runner should be on the running team?"

"He told you about Old Bill?" I ask.

"Told me a lot of things about you. Didn't understand the half of them."

I stare down at the rope, feel the first drops of rain on the back of my neck, and nod. "Farm needs work, and he don't want me doin' extras. Besides, keepin' a secret from him ain't that easy."

Coach steps back. "Reckon not. But it's a shame to see all that speed go to waste. Think on it." He turns, takes one step back toward the team, and stops. "When it rains, that trail will be either grease or quicksand. Bad footing takes a runner down. Sure'd like to know where the slick spots are." He faces me, smiles, and leans forward. I lean in, too.

"How'd you like to give the trail a quick run? We could use a scouting report." He pats my back. "Don't need a waiver signed for that."

I straighten.

I'd be running for the team.

My hand clenches, crushes the program, and my shoulder leaps three times.

Coach takes off his cap, runs his hand through thinning hair. "What in the world is that?"

He saw. He asked. Coach Johnson must not have told him. Probably seconds until he takes back his offer. I lift the rope, duck under, and dart past him toward the trailhead.

The sky dims. Moments later, rain falls straight and hard. It lands with giant, soaking glops.

Runners dash for cover beneath the race tent. Spectators race to their cars. I stand and let water bounce off my jerking shoulder, stream off my sniffing nose. I'm in nearly constant motion. Today, like every day, seven seconds of still is all I get.

A megaphoned voice fights through the storm. "Due to weather conditions, the Northwoods 10K Classic is postponed! Race postponed!"

Whoops and groans go up from beneath the tent, and numbered kids streak back into the rain, hurdle the rope, and thunder toward waiting buses. I give my head a violent shake. I'm left alone.

Minutes pass, maybe more. Soaked cotton suctions onto my skin, but I don't want shelter. I want to feel the chill. I want to feel *something*. I spin around, watch raindrops dance in the puddles, and think how close I was to running a race.

I slosh into the starting area. The clearing is a small lake, and water licks my shoelaces. A number floats by. I scoop it up and put it on—stretch and smile like a numbered kid should. The downpour eases for a few seconds, and I can faintly make out where the course bottlenecks and disappears into the woods. With the tree cover from there on, it'd be a drier run.

In the first grouping, Sam Carrier. He holds the fastest time of any senior this year—

A splotch of red shifts against the trees. A figure stands near the entrance to the course.

I look around. Shadows mill about the tent, but that's all.

"Hey," I holler. "You probably didn't hear. They called it!"

The kid doesn't move.

I walk nearer. "You can't run this course in this rain. It washes out. Ten more minutes and they'll cancel it for today!" I squint toward the road. "Your team's probably waiting for you in the bus!"

I turn back. The guy in red is gone.

I blink hard and splash through the clearing.

Late afternoon with skies this dark? Kid'll get lost for sure.

"Hold up!" I dart in after him.

Can't be more than a few steps ahead.

I run my hard, angry run, but fifteen minutes pass and I haven't caught anyone. No way he's still in front of me. He probably never started in—

A flash of red rounds the next bend.

I push harder but don't gain.

Use your head, Carrier!

I duck onto a footpath that snakes through dense tree cover. Sticks and brambles crunch beneath my feet, and tree limbs gouge and scratch my arms. I pop out of the woods and rejoin the trail as the kid passes. He screams, startled, and races by me. It's not a boy scream.

Can't be.

I grit my teeth and pull alongside her on a straightaway through a field.

"What are you doin'?" I huff.

"I'm running a race." She speaks easily, her breath barely audible.

I'm quiet except for the squeak of my waterlogged shoes. I pick up my pace, glance to my left. Our arms bump and we reenter the woods.

"You know nobody else is?" I say.

"What?" she asks.

"Running a race."

She pulls up. I try to stop and turn, but my feet slide on a tree root. Both feet flip up, and I land on my gut in a puddle of mud. I groan, push up to my knees, and look up at her.

I watch raindrops trickle down her cheek; see them kiss her lips before continuing their path down her neck. The drops disappear behind the red shirt and shorts that cling tight against her, before they emerge and trail down her legs, drip off her body. *Lucky raindrops.*

Her body is beautiful and she runs fast and I can't remember who spoke last.

"Weren't you racing, too?" She looks at me, all of me. I wish I were covered with more mud. My opponent cocks her head, gently bites her lip.

I look down. "The sky is dark. I thought you might get lost."

She moves close. I glance up, but I'm still on my knees and I can't find an appropriate spot to put my gaze. I drop my eyes to her ankles.

Even her ankles are pretty.

"So you ran through the woods to make sure I'd stay on the trail?"

I nod.

She laughs. It's cute. "Where do you go to school?"

"Mitrista."

"Well, Mr. Mitrista, I run for Minnetonka, and I don't need your help. But I am training, and I do need these miles." She whispers, "Thanks for the push."

She reaches out her hand, but when I don't shake it, she brushes soaked hair off my forehead. My eyes close, and when I open them she's looking at her smeary brown fingers. She smiles and leans forward. Her breath is warm against my ear.

"You're muddy."

She straightens and takes off running.

I turn to watch. She stops and looks back over her shoulder. "Are you going to make it home?"

I nod my mud-caked head and point toward the ground. "I live here."

Again, she smiles.

I look down where my finger points at the mud puddle. *I live here? What kind of stupid line is that? And get up off your knees, Carrier!*

I grab a nearby limb and haul myself to my feet. "I meant that I live near here."

She's gone.

I glance around. My muscles don't jerk, and I close my eyes. I breathe deep, and like the third runner who finally catches up, the disease overtakes me. Slowly at first—a hard eyeblink. But that's not enough; there's more that has to work its way out, and my teeth grind. Movement spreads to my shoulder, and soon my whole body springs to twitchy life.

Good thing she ran off when she did.

I run through our imagined conversation start to finish.

"Hi, my name's Sam. What school do you run for? What's your name? Do you like muddy guys who talk to you from their knees?" I exhale long and hard. *Shouldn't have bolted out of that small-talk lesson.*

I stare one last time down the path where the most beautiful girl in the world had run. Then I take off my number, turn, and trudge back the way I came.

chapter three

THE NEXT MORNING, BABY LANE'S CRY REACHES upstairs and wakes me from a hard sleep. I dress, slap on strips of reflective tape, and tiptoe out of the house. The sky is dark as tar, and in the blackness I breathe deep.

I stretch and fall into an easy pace on my regular route. Ten minutes in, my skin tingles, and I U-turn. Breaking into a run, I turn off the road and slop into the wildlife refuge.

My shoes crunch fallen sticks and slop over the washed-out trail until I reach the spot. Her spot.

I stop and catch my breath and try it over—try to say the words I should have said yesterday. In my mind, she smiles and takes my hand and we walk home together. But not to my home, another one—where I speak well and act normal and nothing jerks unless I tell it to.

My shoulder leaps and I open my eyes, stare at the root that sent me to my knees. The tingle is gone.

"Give it up, Carrier." I sigh and jog out of the woods. Each step brings me closer to the stares and whispers of Mitrista High, and though I'm not tired, my legs turn leaden.

Forty minutes later, I drag into town. I duck inside the school and scamper to the locker room, where I shower and change. The bell sounds.

It's Friday. You can put up with homeroom for one more day.

Muffled voices fill the halls outside the locker room.

On second thought—

I join the crowd, slip back out the front door, and skip homeroom. It's only fifteen minutes long, but the room is gray and cinderblock and feels clean like a mental hospital. Ms. Espe sets chairs in a circle so that we can share. I don't want to share.

Ms. Espe loves to place me in the center of her "circle of humanity." She loves giving the other kids a chance to be human; to watch me jump and twitch while they shower me with kind words.

She loves turning me into a freak.

My muscles will not dance for her this morning. I don't feel freakish. I haven't since my rainy run with a beautiful girl who touched me.

Instead, I stand outside the school and watch headlamps zip by on Highway 23. Tires moan and leaves dance in their wake. I shiver and smile.

Fifteen minutes pass, and I turn and reenter. I will go to English, chemistry, and geometry before lunch. I'll eat and sit through Spanish. I'll walk back out this door without having heard anyone say my name. But it'll be the weekend, and I'll be out of this school, and I won't care.

By the time I reach geometry, I'm a twitchy mess. I step late into class, scan the back row, and curse. Row four is filled, too. I plop down in the center seat in the center of the room and my neck jerks violently. From the desk behind mine, Heather Tailor chuckles. She's new. Doesn't yet know the rules. Stare, roll your eyes, shake your head; it's all fine. I'll pretend not to see.

But please, don't ask. Don't make me say what it is, or I'll shrivel into nothing.

"Snap quiz." Mr. Doe's nasal voice slices through student chatter. "Happy Friday. Clear your desks."

The class groans, Heather swears, and my shoulder jumps. My elbow knocks my textbook to the floor with a thump.

"What's with you?" Heather asks.

"Samuel." Doe adjusts his glasses and peers up from his desk. "Come up here, please. Bring your things."

I don't move. I feel the stares. "You heard him," Heather whispers. "Move." I take a deep breath, reach down for my book, and rise. I close my eyes.

Please, let me be still this one time.

I walk toward the teacher's desk, aware of every muscle. Four more steps. Three. My right shoulder flies upward at the same moment my head cocks down. The shoulder smacks the ear so hard it rings. Not loudly enough. I hear murmurs.

"Yeah?" I whisper, and lean forward, my gaze fixed down on Doe's desk.

"You're too distracting today." Doe smiles one of Leslie's funeral smiles, the sympathetic one, as if he's doing me a favor and putting me out of my misery. "Take your quiz in the hall."

"Damn!" I blurt. My hands shake—they want to grab Doe's stupid yellow-and-green necktie and yank and yank until he takes it back, until he grabs his eraser and wipes what he said out of everyone's memory.

My fingers tense; they have to do something, and I drop my text on the floor, grab the quizzes off his desk, rip the pile in two.

What am I doing?

I turn and glance at the class, silent except for a voice from the back. "Freak."

I want to crumple onto the floor and cry. I'm so tired of the words, the looks. My knees buckle. *Not here.*

I make it to the door and push outside into the hall.

Somewhere alone. The auditorium.

I stumble through the hallway. Steps quicken to a jog, and a sprint. I pound into the foyer and throw open auditorium doors. They bang against doorstops. I spread my arms, hold them open, and stare. Inside it's dark and lonely and perfect. I swallow hard, let my arms drop. My breath eases as I step into coolness. I walk up the aisle toward the stage.

One chair rests on it, and I climb the steps and plop down. Silent and out of sight, my muscles still.

"Why'd he have to announce it to the class?" I whisper.

I lean forward, rest my head in my hands. My gaze jumps

to each of three auditorium doors. I wish I could lock them and stay here forever. Out there, my act will be the talk of the school, again.

The side door rattles.

"Crap." I'm not ready for a heart-to-heart with Leslie. Not yet. My gaze scans the floor, catches on the handle of the stage's trapdoor.

I reach for it and slip down beneath the stage. The crawl space reeks of cigarettes and dead things. I feel around my head for the pull chain that hangs from a solitary lightbulb. I find it and yank. Light flickers, and then steadies. I glance around my feet and wince. A dead rat.

The bell rings, but I make no move toward the lunchroom. Hallway shouts mute and disappear. I breathe deep. It's just me, my jumping muscles, and the rodent.

Minutes pass, and doors rattle again. Girls' laughter fills the auditorium. Sounds like two. I crawl forward through thick layers of fabric toward the black curtain that separates the underground stage from the orchestra pit.

I'd hate to mess up and poke my head out. I stop and lean backward against a support post.

"How about Jane and Donovan?"

Heather.

"The Velcro couple? They're still together, always. It's enough to make me sick."

"I miss Minnetonka so much." Heather groans. "Tell me more news. About anybody."

"I think I covered everyone in the whole school last night. Sorry I crashed on you. That off-road race wore me out."

Their footsteps get louder, until it sounds like they're right in front of me. Probably sitting in the front row. Only a curtain between us.

"Why'd you want to talk to the shop teacher?" Heather smacks her gum.

"He's your cross-country coach. After I ran your track this morning, I thought I'd check your roster."

"Whatever," Heather says. "Wait. You were looking for this Mr. Mitrista guy, weren't you?" She laughs. "I still can't believe you called someone that! You have to tell me the whole story. Start right after I dropped you off at the race."

A beautiful laugh fills the auditorium.

"I was running and he jumped out of the woods. The guy ran beside me for five minutes. He was really strong."

"Oh my gosh, Nae. He was probably waiting for you the whole time."

"No. He was a runner. He wore number seventy-eight, I think. But it was hard to read. He fell in mud and leaves."

I smile. It's her.

"Anyway, I must have gotten it wrong, because your coach just showed me the listing. Seventy-eight was a guy from Monticello."

"You're in the wrong town," Heather says.

"He said he went here."

"That's more proof he's a wacko. I've checked out the guys

on our team. Definitely nobody worth looking at. Except maybe Ryan. He's cute, in a short and skinny kind of way."

The girl who touched me laughs again. "This guy's strong. Brown, wavy hair. He's tall, too, at least he would have been if he would have gotten off his knees."

"He sounds like a nutcase. Maybe he is from here, because this school's full of them. While you were talking to the shop teacher, a kid in my geometry class flipped out. My teacher said it's some brain disease."

The girl doesn't answer.

My heartbeat pounds in my ears. *I have to see her.*

I crawl back to the lightbulb, ease to my feet, and place my head against the trapdoor. From my crouch, I push upward. An inch, then two. My eyes peek over the lip of the stage.

Nothing. Must be looking right over their heads.

I lower and head back toward the orchestra curtain. I can't see the seam.

"I can't believe it!" Heather says. I hear claps, and lots of chair squeaks. "How'd it end?"

"I finished my run. I waited around the finishing area, and walked to your place. And you know the rest."

"He didn't come after you?"

"No."

"Did you want him to?"

It's quiet for a time.

Then I hear Heather again. "You have Coach Andrew, who's gorgeous, calling you. You have Harvard and their track team and that medicine program—"

"Sports medicine."

"Whatever. Your life's all lined up. You're set to get out of here. Let this thing go," Heather says. "This guy's probably already with someone, right?"

She doesn't answer.

I grab the fold of the curtain that separates us and squeeze.

He's not, he's not.

A chair seat flips into place, and then another.

"Where you going, Nae? I have gym and homeroom left. That freak from geometry will be in there."

"No, he won't," I whisper.

I crawl out from beneath the curtain and peer over the chairs. In the dark and from a distance, my girl is still beautiful.

"Nae." *Is that ReNae or LyNae?* I lean forward, my arms resting on the back of a front-row seat. Maybe her front-row seat.

"Me? Mr. Mitrista? My name's Sam. Sam Carrier."

chapter four

"I SURVIVED."

I flip off the safety on my pellet gun and fill the last smiley sheet with holes. "You know, Leslie. I can't tell you how reformed I feel. And I owe it all to you." I check my watch. It's been eight hours since I walked out of Mitrista High and into Christmas break and freedom from the Sunshine Club.

I store the gun and jog out of the barn. It's a cold night, and the December wind cuts my face, howls on by. I run to the house in blackness, but inside I'm light and free for two weeks.

When I return to school, I'll be watched for signs of maladaptive behavior. I'll be "observed" and documented. But they won't see anything unusual—I won't let them—because if I'm sent back to Room 14, I'll die.

Not that Old Bill would care. I flop into bed and stare at the ceiling. The thought stays with me for several hours, but at

3 A.M. I screw up—again. I let her into my brain. I lie in bed and think of auditorium girl.

Lot of good this night is doing. Might as well work her out of my system.

I get up and dressed, light-foot it down the stairs, and grab sandwiches. I push outside into a howling snowstorm. Ankle-deep snow covers the yard, and I run to the machine shed, fire up the space heater.

More than twelve hours later, my hands are stiff and oily and covered with blood. I pull a shred of green jacket from the rag barrel, soak a corner in mineral spirits, and scrub. Rough skin appears, sliced and gouged and scratched.

"That's what I get for a day with screwdrivers."

I walk back to Old Bill's truck, to the newly rebuilt engine. I scoop up my tools and haul them toward the workbench. Carefully, each finds its spot on the wall.

Never, ever, mess up my tools again, you hear, boy?

I still hear.

I flick off the heat and the lights and lean in to the metal door. Nothing doin'. It takes three hard shoulder rams to force my way outside into a thigh-high drift.

Lungs fill with icicles. A shiver works through me, and my shoulder jumps four times. I blink hard. Haven't seen a snow-storm this bad in years.

I can't see our farmhouse—can't see anything—except for a faint glow from the center of the yard. I tramp toward the yard light, and the wind whips around me. Within the clearing formed by the barns, the shed, the listing silo, and the farmhouse, snow whirls like the white stuff in glass Christmas balls.

"Alberta clipper." I wince and cover my ears. "Guess we're due." Seems once a year Canada opens the hatch and shoves winter down our throats. I reach the light and grasp the post. Raw skin burns.

"Sam Carrier, get those lazy feet moving! I'm waitin' on that tree."

I squint toward the farmhouse where Old Bill fills the doorway.

I turn away, blink hard, and scowl. Since when does he give a rip about trees? About anything but his big, fat self. My hand fists, and I gently punch the light post. I want to smack it, dent it, take a sledgehammer and swing and swing until it lies in twisted pieces on the ground. But I can't. Don't know why but I can't, and my shoulder jerks again.

The wind blows harder, and I'm in the eye of a snowy cyclone. It whisks the blanket of white off our barn and sucks it back into the sky. I hear a creak and a pop. Ten paces off, an ice chunk thuds to the ground. I turn toward it and the windmill.

"Missed me."

I scan the tower and glare at the fins as if my eyes can set them spinning. But its gears are frozen, and unlike me, it doesn't move. I twitch again, and I'm jealous—jealous of a stupid windmill. Ice will melt, a breeze will blow, blades will turn. But not now.

Now they're still.

Old Bill hollers some more, but his words garble. I focus again on our windmill tower and begin to count. I'm aiming for ten motionless seconds.

. . . *Seven. Eight. Crap.*

"Hey, jumpy!" Old Bill roars, "You deaf, too?"

I'm not deaf. Or weak or mute or retarded. Just like he's not a counting lunatic, not really. His obsessive-compulsive brain never gives normal a chance. My muscles don't give me one either. Being like him sucks.

I leave the pole and notice how numb I am, how content I am being numb. I reach the porch and step inside. Snow coats my hair and flannel shirt. I brush it off, stomp the flakes from my jeans, and shiver. Inside our farmhouse it's cold. Cold and stupid and Christmas Eve.

Old Bill sits by the fireplace and stares at the smallest jacket I've ever seen. He holds it up with a satisfied smile. From where I stand, I see the side with the cement mixer.

He notices me, lowers the jacket, and nods toward the door I've just entered.

"Tree." Old Bill uses his nice voice—the one that still sneaks out when my muscles don't move. If he wouldn't stare so hard, he could use it all the time and we could talk or fish like we did when my tics weren't so bad. But these days, Old Bill glares until I flinch. Then the nice voice leaves, and I know he hates what he sees. And I think maybe *who* he sees.

"It's freezing out there. Let's just wait." I peek at the

peg-board where the snowmobile key dangles. "Didn't get any sleep last night, and I worked on your truck engine all day. I'll head into the backwoods first thing tomorrow morning."

Mom sneaks out from her bedroom. She looks from me to Old Bill and drops her gaze, exhales long and slow. She says nothing.

"You should hear your slacker, Lydia." Old Bill huffs and hauls his belly off our moth-eaten couch. The threadbare cover snags on one of the thirty keys looped around his belt and pulls up with him. Mustard fabric stretches from the couch cushion to his rear.

Fisting his precious keys in one hand, he rips free and begins a frantic count of them. If he comes up short, Old Bill will have a coronary.

"Twenty-seven, twenty-eight, twenty-nine."

What a gift that would be.

"Thirty." He sweeps blond wisps off his forehead, folds his meaty arms, and faces me square. "I saw what you were eyeing. You ain't takin' no snowmobile out in this weather. Some twitch of yours liable to wrap it 'round a stump." He glances down at the Portacrib where Lane sleeps and lays the tiny green coat over its edge. "Now, *my* son is goin' to wake to a tree his first Christmas. Clear? Start walkin'!"

I look to Mom, whose gaze falls to the floorboards.

A balled-up fifty bounces off my chest. "While you're out, stop off at Jensen's." Old Bill drains his soda can, crushes it, and lobs it toward the kitchen. It clinks off half-empty bottles of whiskey heaped in the wastebasket and rattles across the floor.

Old Bill clears his throat and walks to the counter. Beneath the cabinets, beer and soda cans neatly line the wall. He touches each one, starts his whispered count.

"Only twenty-six." Old Bill leans over the sink. "Four short," he whispers. "None in the pantry." He counts them again and whips around.

"I'm low."

My jaws tighten, and my hands burn. I stare at the crumpled bill, nudge it with my toe. I take a deep breath and kick it back toward Old Bill. "Already been there three times this week. Thirty cans on Monday. Thirty more yesterday. Maybe you could count something else?" I turn and look at Mom.

Her hands fidget about her face. She steps back toward the safety of the bedroom. As she shrinks, Old Bill moves nearer and grows larger. The next words will be his. Big, angry, ugly words.

Old Bill's eyes flash wild, and he licks his lips. He speaks so quietly I barely recognize the voice.

"I'm low."

In my mind I shout at him. Shout my no, because I can. Because I'm not mute or weak or retarded. In my mind Mom joins me, and together we scream at Old Bill.

But Mom doesn't speak up anymore.

chapter five

I HAUL TOWARD HOME IN MY ESKIMO GEAR. THE parka fits snug across my shoulders and chest—snugger over my forearms—and a half inch of frozen wrist sticks out the end of each sleeve. At six feet and climbing, I have Old Bill's peak in my sights. But my brown eyes prove that though balding Bill has height, the man has no genetic claim on me. I regrip the ten-foot pine dragging at my side and sling our tree saw over my shoulder.

I check Bill's prized cargo. The snow-covered case of beer rides in a red plastic sled roped around my waist and glides along a tree's length behind me.

"I'm crazy—this is crazy. Risking my life for booze so he can count it." I yank at wrist-hugging mittens and puff air across purple palms. "You're waitin' on a tree? Right." The two-hour trek has stolen feeling from my fingertips, and even with layered mitts, I can barely grip the pine.

I step onto an ice patch. Both boots slip forward, and I

know I'm going down. For an instant, I feel weightless. It's been years since my last winter fall. I was seven, and it was my birthday.

"Bill!"

The back of my head had struck ice with a dull thud. I opened my eyes but saw only red. I blinked and Bill's head appeared. It was fuzzy around the edges.

"Stay down, Sam. Take a deep breath." Bill's big hand rested lightly on my chest. "Look at me, son. I need to see those eyes."

I thought I *was* looking at him.

"Concussion, I'll bet." Bill scooped me into his arms and walked off Stacy Lake.

"No! You said we'd go ice fishing on my birthday." I wriggled, and he squeezed me to his chest. "That's today, Bill! We need to go today."

Bill had laughed. "There'll be plenty other chances."

There weren't—at least not for the two of us. At supper, my disease woke up and muscles started to jerk again. Five motionless months, the only ones since my diagnosis, came to an end that day—the last day Bill ever called me his son.

I fall onto the Christmas tree with a crunch and stare into the sky. White is the only color I see. It should be a cold white, but I can't feel it against my cheeks. I sit up quickly, shake pine needles from my mittens, and force memories of Old Bill out of my head. I stand, plod forward, and listen. Smothered in hood, I hear nothing but amplified breath. Steps quicken. Suddenly I'm afraid that a big vacuum has sucked all sounds and feelings from the earth.

I'm going to die. Plows won't clear this road for days, and when they do they'll find me stiff and clutching a tree. They'll ask Mom to identify her frozen son, and she might not recognize him.

Because for once, he won't move.

I face the icy wind, and my forehead aches. That pain, breath fog, and wind-whipped white—that's all there is.

Until I'm practically on top of her. Well, her car.

A helpless vehicle covered by an inch of snow hovers perpendicular to the road. I follow its tracks. The red sports car spun a good ten feet off the shoulder, plowed down into the ditch, and climbed its far embankment. Its belly now rests on a rise, which leaves all four wheels free-spinning.

I indulge a full body twitch. Limbs fire and brains rattle against the inside of my skull, but I'm numb and I can't feel and I jolt again.

Damn disease.

Hazards and headlamps light giant flakes in pinks and yellows. Those lights brighten and dim as the engine revs, falls silent. The crisp air fills with the scent of gas.

I drop the tree and stomp into the drift.

"Hey!" I rap on the driver's door. "Need help?"

The window lowers an inch, and a glob of snow breaks from the roof and blows inside.

"Oh, cold!"

A grunt escapes my mouth. I bend over, peer through the slit, and my frozen body springs to life.

"Heaven," I whisper. "We meet again."

"Get away!" The crack disappears, and a flurry of activity

fills the car. I straighten and wipe my nose and work the jaw grinds out of my system.

It's her. Can't believe this. Breathe, Sam. I gaze down through clear patches where snow has fallen from the glass.

If I could put this girl in my sled and whisk her away where no one could find us—away from Old Bill, from Pierce, from myself—she'd get over my twitches. I cough and reach for the blade slung over my heart.

"The saw! Probably thinks I'm some kind of psychotic—" I pitch the tree saw toward my sled and swipe the remaining snow from her window. I start to unzip my coat; to show her I'm not hiding anything, that I'm not a crazy nut.

Wild eyes peer out. More stunning than in October. Bare legs and shoulders typically don't appear in Minnesota until early May, but here they are—perfect. Around her middle, burgundy velvet hugs her tight and moves when she moves beneath auburn hair and angelic face.

She's some kind of princess. Just as pretty dry as she was wet.

The window lowers again, farther this time, and she smiles. Warmth ignites my fingers. The tingle works up my arms; my shoulders rebel, tense, and leap.

Concentrate, Sam. Be still.

Perfume wafts from inside the car. I bend in slow motion and press my nose against the glass. With a toss of her hair, she inches nearer. My head tingles, ready again for her touch. I gulp and gaze and hold my breath.

And she jams a tube of lipstick into my right eyeball.

"Ah!" I reel, crumple to my knees, claw at my face. "I'm blind, I'm blind—"

Smack! The door flies open and catches me square on the chin. Fells me like timber into fresh powder. My numb tongue warms and leaks blood that trickles down my lip with the cool consistency of molasses.

"My mout!" I ball into the fetal position and force open my lipsticked eye. Perfection leaps over my frame and bounds into the night.

I try to swallow, to speak, to see. Minutes pass, and beneath the storm's howl, my body stills and faculties return. I stumble to my feet, one big grunt and groan. So the rescue was unorthodox.

"Pummeled by my princeth." I spit into the snow and stare at the red spot. "How embarathing." I squint at the tree—now blown down the road—and massage my neck.

"Hey, wait!"

I spin, slip, and lunge for the open car door.

"You really just stopped to help?" I nod at the silhouette standing safely in the distance. "Where am I?" she asks. "Doesn't anybody live out here?"

I nod again.

"I left my cell at Heather's." She pauses and stares, and even though I'm hidden inside my parka, I wonder if she sees my muscles stiffen. I relax as her stare finally leaves my face and follows the rope to my sled and the half-buried saw beside it. Her eyes soften and she smiles, breathes deeply, and glances at the felled tree near her feet. "A tree saw. Rescues might go smoother if you leave that at home."

I shut the car door and face her and touch my swollen eyelid.

She nudges the pine tree with her boot. "Is your eye okay? Are you okay? I was scared, and I thought—" She shudders and rubs her bare arms.

I wonder what that skin would feel like against my rough, scarred hands.

"It's just that not every guy who stops wants to help. I mean, I can't trust everyone." She looks around, focuses on my face, and smiles. It's a sadder smile than before. "Why won't you talk to me?"

Because you're perfect and since smacking me you've been really kind, but that's only because you can't see me and you don't know me. Maybe if I had time to rehearse, I could come up with something to make her laugh. But I've got nothing, and I stand mute.

She exhales long and slow. "Okay, Christmas-tree man, looks like I need a hero."

A hero? Me?

"I've never met a guy carrying a saw and pulling"—she steps toward my sled and bends down—"beer." Straightening, she blows into cupped hands.

Why not me? And not just any hero. Her hero.

Those hands lower to her hips and my gaze follows.

"I jammed my jacket beneath for traction, but that was dumb because the tires—well, they ate it. Have any ideas? Maybe a push or something?"

I squint at her car. I know physics, and I know spinouts. It'd take five men to budge that thing in this weather. But heroes don't show weakness. I put on my thinking face and nod slowly. Maybe too slowly.

She stomps into the ditch, grabs my hood, and shakes. "Hey! Hello. I'm freezing out here!"

Of course, the cold. She's cold!

"Hee—" I clear frost from my throat. "Here." I whip off my mitts and cram them into her hands.

"No, you don't have to—"

Stiffened fingers unbutton the parka, unzip the inner lining, shred the drawstring beneath my chin, and throw off the coat. "Here!" I press the parka into her arms.

I pant in my flannel shirt, misbuttoned and half untucked, still tethered to my cargo of beer. Nose-flow forms frozen ridges and clings to my upper lip. Tears seep from the lipsticked eye, and my swollen tongue fills my mouth. I feel naked without my parka—naked and ugly—but we're standing so close, my insides burn, and I'm not cold. And after she vanishes into my coat, neither is she.

The parka never looked so good. To have her wearing my clothes, well, it feels like we belong together.

Just then, the chain-saw roar of snowmobiles cuts through the howl. My coat turns its back on me to face two oncoming beams. "Looks like company soon. Maybe they'll help?"

I nod.

She glances over her shoulder. "Do you have a name?"

Our eyes meet. I try to stay, to let her look into me, but my eyes decide to blink hard, and my gaze retreats to the safety of my boots. *We're a long way from October. She doesn't remember me.*

"Yeah," I say.

She waits for more, finally hinting a smile. "Well, that's good to know."

She waves her arms above her head. Sleds roar nearer, and we step onto the road. Both snowmobiles circle and settle next to her. Three visors raise.

Just my luck.

I don't mind the Dahlgren twins. Not at all. Doesn't surprise me to see them riding double tonight—they're always together, laughing and joking, making me wish Baby Lane was seventeen years older. A nod from Nils sends Lars jumping off their sled and tromping toward the car.

It's the other one, the lone rider on the yellow Polaris. One look at him and my stomach tenses. He rises, removes his helmet, and rubs the red pressure band formed across his forehead. He forces a hand through thick, hockey hair.

"Who have we here?" Jace Ryeson's snowsuit swaggers toward my coat; I no longer exist. "Name's Jace. Looks like you need a ride."

She stiffens—even through my Eskimo coat I can see it. She stuffs my mittens into oversize parka pockets and backs toward me, away from Jace. My heart swells.

"I'm Naomi. Thanks for stopping. I, well, we—" She points at me over her shoulder. "I think he's going to push my car out." She glances back and catches me in a teeth grind. Naomi bites her lip and cocks her head. "You have to be cold."

"Sam, what happened to—what are you doing?" Jace snickers at my plastic sled. "Boozin' Billy's got ya playing beer Santa, huh? On Christmas Eve. Pathetic."

My stomach turns. Why do I care what he says about Old Bill? I suddenly want to tell Jace the truth. That Old Bill's counting it, not drinking it. I want Jace to stop ripping Old Bill 'cause I know what it's like when a twitch attack comes, when everyone stares and whispers, and I fake a yawn or stretch. So what if Old Bill hides his habit? Why can't people leave the jerk alone?

"Shut up about Bill. He ain't a lush," I say. "Can't help it, is all."

My defense sounds weak, and my gaze runs to Nils's gentler face. He offers a tight-lipped nod.

"When Santa here jerks his face like that, it ain't from the cold. Is it, Santa?" Jace does his best jaw-tic imitation and rolls his eyes.

I swallow hard and shiver. Warmth I feel from Naomi fades fast.

"Wheels are airborne, Jace." Lars wades out from behind the car and mounts the sled behind his brother. "She'll need a tow."

"Hear that, Naomi? And that ain't happening tonight. But look here, two snowmobiles and three of us. Got room for you. Like it was meant to be." Jace eases onto his snowmobile and pats the seat behind him. "Second thought." He scoots back. "Ride in front. It's warmer." He stretches out his hand.

Naomi glances at Jace's glove and back at me. She looks confused, like she can't figure out why it's them against me, why they don't offer to help the guy without a jacket. She stares at me, I think, and wonders what they know and I know and she'll know, too, if she stares long enough.

"But you can't just leave him," Naomi says.

"She's right, Jace," Nils says, "It's rough—"

Jace silences Nils with a glare. "It's Santa's night. He's got work to do." Again, he reaches his hand out for Naomi. "Don't worry 'bout Sam. He ain't that far from home. Now come on, I'm getting cold."

"Go on. I got this stupid tree to lug." My whisper falls unheard into fresh powder.

Naomi still looks at me. She's been doing that far too long, and I start to squirm. The squirming leads to humming, the humming to grunting. I fight to stay calm, but her eyes are winning and there is nowhere to hide.

"No thanks, Jace. I'll stay with Sam."

"Hah!" The word fires from my mouth.

I purse my lips and bite my swollen tongue, but my vocal cords are locked and there's nothing I can do. "Stay with Sam! Stay with Sam!"

All turn toward my uncontrollable blurt.

Jace shakes his head. "Like a freakin' parrot."

The shouting urge returns and I spin away from Naomi as the three words have their way with me and cut into the wintry night. I slam shaking hands over my mouth, but the crowlike sounds keep coming, sharp as barbed wire. Behind me, engine gunning conceals the murmurs and chuckles.

"Might want to reconsider," Jace calls. "I ain't as much fun to listen to, but this sled moves a hell of a lot faster than Twitch's plastic one."

Naomi doesn't answer. I'm the only one who talks and, like a terrier out barking at snowflakes, can't shut up.

Please go! Now that you've seen me, heard me. Take your perfect eyes and go.

"Suit yourself! Stay with Sam. Stay with Sam." Jace's voice pierces through my back and lodges in my heart. "Hey, Naomi, be sure to give Sammy a cracker."

The drone of Jace's sled can't cover his laughter, and he rides into the night.

"Can't you two guys do something?" Naomi asks. "Doesn't he need help?"

"He's okay," Lars says. "I mean, he—"

Lars leans forward and speaks to Nils, and their sled roars to life.

"It's too cold for anyone." Lars says, "Hang on. Maybe we can come back with Dad's sled. Stay in the car, okay? You, too, Sam. Stay in the car."

They scream off in the opposite direction toward their Princeton farm.

"Hey." Naomi's voice is soft. "You heard what they said."

Salty wet reaches my cracked lips. Quickly wiping my cheeks, I turn to face her. A final whisper escapes my throat.

"Stay with Sam." My head droops and we stand in silence. I don't want to talk. I don't want to feel warm. I just want to disappear.

"I've seen you before," Naomi finally says.

"No, I—I don't think so."

Naomi pulls off my hood and gives a gentle squint. "You're a runner, aren't you?"

I don't speak.

She smiles. "Will those guys come back?"

"Maybe."

"Maybe's not good enough." Naomi looks into the sky, then back to her car. "My life's in your hands. What can we do?"

She said *we*. My back straightens.

"Um—well, I guess you can hop in and let me *try* and push."

"You think you can do it?" She gently bites her lower lip, steps through the snow, and climbs behind the wheel.

I untie my sleigh and tramp behind the car. I lean hard against it but a foot slips and drops me to my knees.

Naomi leans out the window. "Tell me when you're ready!"

I whisk snow off my shirt. Feeling stupid doesn't brush off so easily. "You know, Lars was right, this car—" She disappears and guns fumes into my mouth.

I cough. "Ain't moving."

I stare at curtains of white falling from nowhere. At my cranberry hands that match the paint on which they rest. My shoulders jump and relax. "Try and push? What a joke."

Through the glass, auburn flecked with white cascades over my hood.

My hood.

And from nowhere they come, words propelled with all the hope and fury I own.

"Oh God, give me Herculean strength!"

I dip my shoulder into the car, dig my legs deep, and launch. The car inches ahead.

"You're doing it!" Naomi's voice fills my ears and exhaust fills my lungs. I gasp and heave again.

Rear wheels teeter up until I'm staring at her muffler. The car swerves down into the ditch, while my momentum topples me onto my stomach. I hear wheels spin; the car's tires are now in fresh powder where treads have no hope. I lift my head and blink. The car still moves away from me. Grinding front tires find gravel and whip the car onto the road, as my nose fills with fumes of burned rubber and hot smoke.

My mouth gapes, and I stagger to my feet. *That can't happen.* I stumble to the driver's-side window.

"That was incredible, Sam! Hop in."

I shake my head. I can't explain why I can't, why what she saw and heard means I can't. So I stare at the road and mumble something about living close and feeling okay and having to go.

My lies hang there between us, all stupid like, and I want to run—run away from my words and the girl I've thought about every day since October.

She reaches out and brushes snow off the breast pocket of my shirt. "Well then. It was good to see you."

Stay with Sam. Please, stay with Sam.

Naomi leans out and whispers, "Thanks for the push. Again." She kisses my cheek.

My cheek.

With a squeal and a whir of rubber, she crunches over our fallen tree and fishtails out of sight.

I stare into the void as I stroke the sacred spot on my face. "Damn. She took my coat."

chapter six

"THERE'S NO WAY I'M GOING TO THAT GUY AGAIN. I don't need a shrink." I hoist the sledgehammer and bring it down with a crack. Chips of concrete ricochet around me. Outside, it's sunny and June, but inside this pit, it's dark and dank. Mom pokes her head back into the garage, where Old Bill banished me to pound out the cement floor.

"You're just being stubborn, Sam. And his title is 'psychologist.'"

"Round glasses?"

"Well, yes—"

"Wispy beard?"

"It's well groomed."

"Say what you want, he's a shrink." I nod toward the concrete. "Watch out."

Mom disappears again. My next blow fills the air with chalky dust. I cough hard, drop the hammer, and join her outside. "I got analyzed plenty at school."

"Maybe if you had a friend, that would've been different, but you didn't even try. Four years and not one person invited over." Her face softens. "I'm sorry. I'm just—"

"Embarrassed as hell at your twitchy son and trying to make it right." I rip off my goggles and toss them to the ground. I squint and shield my eyes from the sunlight. My right shoulder leaps and I blink hard.

Mom glances down. "You need to talk to someone."

"Ain't your job to decide who." I kick at the grass. "Like I'm gonna bare my soul to Skittles."

I had nicknamed the shrink Skittles after the bowl of candy on his table. Just the thing to keep hyperactive kids feeling the need for his services. From our first visit years ago, I remember only that colorful bowl.

Too bad other people don't fade from my childhood memory. Other people like Old Bill. His voice fills my head.

How the hell is he gonna drive the grader if he can't control his arms?

According to Mom, jumpy arms didn't rattle Skittles. "Simple anxiety," he had said. "Buy the lad some fish. They're so calming."

Calming, my ass. I had jerked, dumped the whole jar of fish food into the water, and the guppies Mom bought me leaped out of the tank. Darn near scarred me for life to see fish fulfill a suicide pact on my bedroom floor. I screamed a seven-year-old scream and Old Bill walked into my room.

"I guess those fish would rather die than live with you."

I watched them flop on the carpet and I knew he was right.

Now Mom wipes gray dust from my cheeks and biceps,

steps back, and smiles at me in a way she does only when Old Bill isn't around.

"My strong son." She folds her arms and shuts her eyes. "I already made the appointment. Paid for it, too."

"You did *what?*"

Mom winces and nods. She reaches up, grabs my face, and squeezes. "Next Saturday you get a two-hour chat with a shrink." Mom tries to laugh. But her smiles don't stay long or hide anything, and the sad sneaks out. She lets go and crosses and uncrosses her arms. I wonder what her laugh sounded like twenty years ago.

Mom places a hand on my chest. "With graduation in one week and the tough year it's been for your Tourette's . . ." She sighs and turns away. "I figured a talk might help." Her gaze skims the contents of the garage strewn across the driveway and snags on a pair of jackhammers with BILL'S BITUMINOUS etched into their sides. "I know Bill's been hard."

She says this as if he's in a phase that will pass like a kidney stone. As usual, I play dumb and pretend to believe her.

"Fine. I'll talk to the shrink one time. For you." I roll my eyes, wipe my brow, and retreat into the darkness. "Long as you know I have nothing to say."

The Malibu has no desire to see the doctor either. Our farm in Pierce sits thirty miles from Skittles's Princeton office, but halfway there, the radiator decides it's had enough. Steam belches from under the hood, and I ease off the gravel road.

"I reckon it's a sign."

I push out of the car and stare down the lonely road. I

scratch my head. "This'd qualify as a good excuse," I say to no one. "It's a long haul either way." Leaning against the car, I stretch my calves and shake my thighs. "But I promised her, you know?"

I face Princeton, take three big steps, and break into a run. Gravel crunches, cool air rushes, muscles relax.

Finally free.

For as long as I can remember, morning runs have brought peace. Limbs that spend the day meeting jerky demands submit to my will—my control. Dizziness leaves, balance returns. Before the world wakes up—before its eyes mock me—Sam Carrier is strong and stable and sound.

And fast.

I pound into Princeton, my breath slow and steady. There are no urges—my brain has gone to sleep and leaves me alone. There is only the road and the sound of my feet falling in beautiful rhythm. I cut the corner in front of SuperAmerica and slow as I approach the Dairy Queen.

I ease onto the crowded parking lot, but don't want to stop. The moment I do, my muscles will grab me and twist me and make me feel like I belong in a freak show.

But it's hot and a cone is irresistible.

I stagger toward the order window, my heart filled with postrun euphoria, and indulge in a victory jerk.

"What the hell is that?" A male voice sounds surprised and quiets to a whisper. I peek. A packed convertible rests a few feet away. Two guys, two girls, four chuckles.

"Watch this guy," he whispers.

My gaze locks onto my laces.

I buy the cone, linger at the order window, and wait for the sound of their engine, but my ice cream disappears before they do.

No matter. I'll stand here until they leave.

"Where I used to live, we had an ice-cream joint that—"

Crap. Heather's in the car.

Still talking about her old place in highbrow Minnetonka. Word is her family left a wealthy Minneapolis suburb in search of more land. They found it in Hicksville—Heather's name for her new home. My forever home. With her blabbing, they'll be there until tomorrow. No use waiting.

Brace yourself. I turn and jog past and peek again.

My gaze bounces off Heather and the two guys like a pinball and sticks on Heather's friend.

"Is that you, Sam?" Naomi says as I pass.

The gentle sound of her voice makes me feel human. My pace slows.

"You know that freak, Nae?" Heather says. "I had to sit behind . . ."

I pull free of Naomi's gravity and sprint away from the laughter left in my wake.

I glance over my shoulder.

Shut up, Heather. I practically saved Naomi's life last Christmas. Well, after she beat me up. My fingers touch my tingling cheek while Naomi thoughts dance in my brain.

Doc, maybe I do have something to talk about.

I was born to love you.

I was born to lick your face.

The second line of the country tune drawling in Skittles's waiting room catches me off guard and I bust a gut. I'm still laughing when the doctor ushers me in.

"Do you find our meeting amusing?" Skittles stares as I brush by into his office.

Doc wears his stern face, and I look down. My shoulders tremble. There's nothing funny about this rent-a-friend, but all the morbid thoughts I own can't stop this laugh. I flop down on the couch, which shakes beneath me. For once it isn't from a twitch.

"Sam, your mother said this may be difficult for you. Sam, I see you came alone. That took courage."

If he begins one more sentence with my name, I'll vomit.

"Sam, how do you feel about being here?"

My stomach turns. "It sucks."

I glance around the room. Lots of papers encased in glass and a few scraggly plants. Depressing. I lean toward the doctor and grab a handful of candy. "But we don't have much time, thanks to the Malibu. Since this is the last time we'll talk, I'll try to touch on all the stuff Mom worries about right up front."

"This is confidential, Sam, so you don't have to worry about what your moth—"

My hand shoots up. "Right there, again. You've said 'Sam' four times already. Do you know that ain't my real name?"

Skittles settles back into his chair, and a faraway look glazes his eyes. It's obvious I'm the only one in the room. He strokes his wispy beard. "Interesting. What do you think your name—"

"Jack, Jack Keegan. I used to think names were like enve-lopes. Your folks tuck you inside one, the state slams on a postmark, nobody messes. Turns out they're like diapers. If the first one gets stinky, they'll just whip it off and slap on another."

Skittles adjusts his glasses and reaches for a pad of paper. "And how do you feel about—"

"Tell you what; I'll make this easy on you. I'm an expert at this psychocrap. Don't worry about questions. I'll blab and you scribble." I clear my throat. "See, Old Bill, my step-dad, ditched both my names not one hour after changing my mom's. The man hates everything Irish since a brawl with Officer O'Malley landed him in jail."

My shrink scribbles something fierce. "Tell me about—"

"Idiot. An obsessive-compulsive idiot. Counting cans or keys is this year's thing. It'll pass. He'll go back to gambling or cleaning or touching stuff eight hundred times in a row. Why Mom married him is beyond me. I was only two at the time." I pause. "But from the stories Old Bill tells me, sounds like he's a step up from my real dad. Get this. My dad's tics went crazy when I was born. He blames me and stops looking at me. Old Bill says he even quit holding me 'cause once he twitched so hard, he dropped me on the floor."

My face is hot, and I exhale hard. "How am I doin'? Should be enough soul-searching for Mom. Besides, I'm almost fin-ished with this subject."

"This is wonderful. Don't stop. And again, I can promise you that what you share here stays—"

"Whatever. So Dad kicks, I start twitching, and Old Bill

gets all pissed. But now, with Baby Lane? Well, the new heir looks normal, and Bill has hope. And I'm a twitchy shadow his golden boy will soon eclipse." I sigh. "Don't get me wrong, I like the poor kid. Being the object of Old Bill's affection is no cakewalk."

Doc scribbles and smiles and nods like he can't get enough of my crap. Like he lives to uncover it and smear it all over his yellow pad.

I run both hands through my hair. "And Old Bill loves the little guy. Kid covers himself with spit, and it don't seem to matter. Lane screams and blurts like babies do before they turn into normal kids who stop screaming and blurting." I bite my lip and stare at the floor, while my throat burns. I almost lose it. Almost spill my guts to a stupid shrink who won't stop saying my name and only listens because Mom gives him money.

"To Bill, Lane's noise don't matter." I swallow hard. "He finally has a son he's proud of." I peek at Skittles, who doesn't write down the only thing worth noting in our entire conversation.

I stand and take a deep breath. "But I have no desire to talk about any of that." I walk over to one of his glassed-in shrink certificates. I touch the casing, turn, and catch him in a wince. What a pathetic, little man.

I spin. "Do you know I've seen Heaven?"

"Heaven." Skittles frowns, lowers his spectacles, and peers above the upper rim.

"Absolutely. Four times now, not counting all the mental replays. The sight flashing by my good eye last Christmas, not to mention today just down the road here?"

The doctor scratches his bald spot. "Good eye? I'm still—could we return to your father and the passing twitchy-shadow comment for a—"

"Hell, no." I grin and walk to the window. "My time, my topic. You ever see a sunset so beautiful it made you afraid?"

"No, Sam."

"Well, I have."

"You're afraid of sunsets?" He scratches in his pad.

"Talking about Naomi here." I roll my eyes. "You know, let's just leave her name out of it. I call her Heaven. When I saw her at the Dairy Queen, she stole my breath. I jerked. They laughed."

Skittles squints, and then cocks his head. "Naomi—I mean—Heaven laughed at you?"

I turn from the window and my shoulders slump. I stare at my tensing wrist and fingers and glance at the ceiling tiles.

"Heaven laughs at me every day."

I plunk back down onto the couch, stretch out, and close my eyes.

"That girl? Yeah, she chuckled right along with her friends. But I can almost imagine it wasn't as loud as the rest."

chapter seven

THE WEEK PRIOR TO GRADUATION BLURS DUE TO
Mom's need for "deep cleaning." A whole different animal than
general straightening up, deep cleaning is mysterious, and
only Mom knows when it's finished. My role is simple: I rush
home from finals and repair everything Old Bill busted the
previous week.

It'd been a rough seven days.

"Stair rail, screen door, lawn mower, wooden gate, shed
shelving. I think we got it all done." I fold the list into a paper
airplane and fly it into my bedroom wastebasket.

"Open up, Sam." Mom thumps my door. "I need to dump
these coats to make room in the closet."

*Room for what? You really think anyone's coming to my gradu-
ation party tonight?*

I glance from my unmade bed to my cap-and-gown-clad
image in the mirror. "It's an impressive gown, but if you ask
me, the square hat looks stupid."

"Sam!" Mom sounds annoyed, and by the time I open the door, her forehead glistens. A sweltering morning plus an armload of coats plus a dead air conditioner make for a lot of steam. She pushes past me and collapses on the bed. Mom rises from the coat ball, turns to me, and stares.

"You look handsome." She adjusts the robe at the shoulders and flattens the black fabric against my arms. "You *are* handsome."

A couple hard squints and a jaw grind erase her compliment. "What I am is late. When's Bill getting back with the car?"

Mom glances at her watch, and her eyes widen. "Said by now. But he wouldn't miss your big day." We lock gazes and she purses her lips. "I'll start calling around."

Ten minutes later, Mom's frantic. "The whole town is already there, probably to get a good seat. I don't know what—"

"Later." I whip off the hat and robe, stuff the dry-cleaned costume into a plastic bag, lace up my running shoes, and bolt.

Saturday mornings are usually active times in Pierce, but this morning the place is a ghost town. I blow through Pierce proper with its two streets and forty houses and sprint back into farm country. My feet know the gravel road, and my mind wanders. I've dreamed of this day. I will hear my own Emancipation Proclamation, and I will be free. When my name's called, the crowd will erupt, and so will Naomi. Bet she'll be there to watch her best friend, Heather. Yeah, the rescued princess will cheer for me, her hero. She'll remember our kiss and seek me out.

My legs churn faster.

Naomi, is that you? What a surprise. Yeah, I am sort of busy. Play it cool. *Kind of got this graduation party right after the ceremony. You probably have plans with Heath—you don't? It'd be great if you came.*

I cut across the Pizza Hut parking lot. The towering lights of Mitrista High School's sports complex are only minutes away.

Thinking about me? Really? Well, you've been on my mind day and night. No, too desperate. *Yeah, you've crossed my mind once or twice yourself.*

I crumple against the Mallard fieldhouse. My thighs burn, and I double over in search of breath.

"I'm here. I made it." Shoulders jump, then calm—until the music starts.

"Crap!"

On the far side of the football field, a large congregation fills one side of the bleachers, while a raised platform faces them from the opposite sideline. Sandwiched between, and covering the playing field, stands a host of empty chairs. One of them's mine.

I shake my bag, pick up my crinkled robe, and curse. "A twitchy six-foot raisin." I smooth it against my chest and over my thigh. Pointless. It'll take Old Bill's steamroller to flatten these wrinkles. I reach for the mortarboard lying funny in the grass.

"No, no!" One of the corners bends up, and I force it flat. I hear a snap as the corner flops down at the crease and hangs, shielding my view to the right. "Nice. What else?"

My heart pauses in its rhythm. I scour the ground, search the bag, turn it inside out. No tassel.

"Handsome Sam, reporting for graduation, sir." I salute and break into a gallop.

"Pomp and Circumstance" fills the air, and I streak toward the line of graduates snaked behind the stands. By the time I reach my classmates, the first rows of seats have filled.

"Where—where am I s'posed to—to be?" I huff at Lars. He looks at me—the raisin—from head to toe. His mouth opens, and then clamps shut. Lars lifts a finger and points to the third row, where an open seat glints in the sunlight.

Dahlgren, D. Carrier—oh no. They already seated the Cs!

I push in front of Lars, puff out air, and let loose with a violent head shake—one last free one before walking into the fishbowl. My right hand supports the limp corner of my cap and the left smoothes down my gown, and I saunter into the Colosseum. I glance at the lions around me and break into a cold sweat. My peers look hungry. I break free from the line, stumble over knees, and topple into my seat. Third-row center.

"Where you been?" Dave Cartwright whispers from the left. "Man, you stink."

"I know. Our car broke down. I had to run."

My body fills with deceit's tension and leaps. I stretch my neck, my shoulders, anything to mask the twitch.

"Whoa, horsey." Dave scoots his chair away from me. "You gonna be buckin' like that for two hours?"

The next lie comes so easily. So easily it doesn't feel like lying. "Just stretchin', you know? Got to get comfortable if

I'm going to sit here all morning. But I need a tassel. Mom jammed all my stuff in a bag and forgot it."

I reach beneath my chair and pluck three dandelions. After twisting the stems together, I wrap them 'round the button on my cap. "There!" A yellow bouquet hangs down, and the third row laughs. *Maybe Naomi is laughing.*

Dave seems to forget my horsiness for the time being.

I peek over my shoulder. Mom and Old Bill stand near the bleachers with Baby Lane's stroller. I face the front and swallow hard. It's just too much. The hype, the audience. Their eyes.

At first, I will my jumps to a few shoulder spasms, but as each speaker "inspires" me, tension leaps to my voice box. Coughs and throat clearings morph into hums and grunts. As the commencement address begins, I'm in rough shape.

But not as bad as Mildred Moury.

At 102 years old, she's to give the keynote. The honor is, of course, due to her age. I agree that triple digits are a noteworthy milestone. But the vision of her slumped in a wheelchair, fresh from the Mitrista Manor Retirement Facility, doesn't fill me with hope for my future.

Her introduction lasts forever, and by the time the valedictorian cranks the microphone to Mildred's level, my spasms are in full bloom.

"Teachers, parents, young people." Pauses between words could hold entire sentences. I bounce my knee. Anything to give the jumpiness a better way to express itself.

Never works.

"Hum. Hum. Hum-hum." Staccato sounds shoot from my mouth, but lucky for me, Mildred's hearing left a decade ago, and she continues unfazed.

"Each one of you can reach your dreams. Each—"

I don't know whose breath I feel in my ear. But the whisper floats in, lands in my throat's uncontrollable magnification chamber, and bursts out my mouth.

"Stupid!"

"—one of you can succeed."

The first three rows spin and stare while behind me a chuckle spreads. I fake a couple coughlike sounds but can't make it sound like the word. Mildred doesn't miss a beat.

"Now I know many of you young people think I'm old. A lot of you think I'm—"

Whisper.

"Pissy!" I bite my lip and stare at the ground. Three dandelions fall from my cap and I trample them into the earth as laughter erupts around me. My vision blurs and it's not from sweat.

God, please, make them stop!

I squeeze my eyelids tight and my body shakes. I lean forward. Far as I can.

"Now I have much more to say, but if I did, you might think I'm—"

The whisper strengthens. It's calculated, calm, hideous. And effective.

"An asshole!"

"Shut up, Carrier!" Dave elbows me hard.

I can't. I can't!

"And knock it off back there." Dave hisses at the row behind. "It ain't funny no more."

I cover my ears and rock until Ms. Mildred Moury is off the podium. Jerks, like popcorn, explode every muscle on my left side, but it no longer matters. Poor Mom. Having to watch the thing I've become.

Principal Rivers offers instructions about procedure and the holding of applause, but as Sarah Adington strides to the front, it's clear he no longer controls this student body. Parents and students erupt with whoops and shouts. Even unpopular kids get "sympathy claps." Some bleeding-heart parent wants everyone to feel special.

Everyone.

"Samuel Carrier."

Silence.

I tremble. Not a sound but the clearing of Principal Rivers's throat as I stand at the base of the podium stairs. I stare at him through tears, turn, and scan the crowd. Mom leans against the bleachers and cries. Old Bill hides at her side, his face buried in his hand.

And I run. I run away from the podium, from the school, from the town. I run and listen to the sounds of confused voices. I'm at the fieldhouse before Principal Rivers's boom restores order.

"Quiet, please. Quiet! David Cartwright. Come on up, David."

I pause, rip off my gown and sweaty T-shirt, and stuff them in the trash. But not the square hat. I hurl that tasselless cap as high as I can and watch it snag the top of a backstop. "It ain't graduation if you don't throw your cap."

Dressed in only shorts and shoes, I'm good to go. Out of Mitrista, away from home and my graduation party.

Nope. I won't be making that one.

chapter eight

I RUN FAST. AND THE FASTER I RUN, THE STRONGER I feel. Sweat pours down my chest and back, but my legs won't ease. Three miles outside of town I'm still in full stride. Desperate to run out of myself, desperate to leave my shell behind, I turn in to a field and race through wild hay. My feet stumble over the irregular terrain.

Doesn't matter whose land this is or who posted the three "No Trespassing" signs. Nothing matters but the number of miles I can put between graduation and me. Marsh muddies my sneakers, then my shins. I slosh into Crow Creek, the trickle that oozes all the way from Lake Mille Lacs. Herons take flight, and I thrash into the reeds.

Fly away, lucky birds.

Knee-deep water feels good, but I don't deserve the feeling and scramble up the far embankment. I fall twice before I stagger to the peak.

I cram four years of high school into two words: "Why me?" My roar bounces off an empty heaven, lands squarely on my quivering shoulders, and crumples me to my knees. For once, I can't move.

Humiliated in front of everyone. The whole school and the whole town and Naomi.

I mouth her name and replay the entire ceremony.

"Nope. She wasn't there. She would have clapped for me."

Minutes pass before I stand and brush off my knees. I wipe the sting from my eyes and lift my gaze.

"Yeah. Definitely she would have clap—oh, man."

Twenty acres of color stretch out before me. Colors I can't name and don't recognize. Except for green. It's not one green but a hundred different greens that all blend together like they're only one. It's a garden. The biggest one I've ever seen. It has to be Coot's.

I know the wacko keeps one near town, but this is the first time I've seen it. For good reason. The whole thing hides in a hollow. Only a trespasser like me would ever know it's here.

I track a winding bark-chip path. It dips beneath interlocking boughs, skirts the shores of small ponds, and circles a windmill in the garden's center. The whole garden feels wild, including the path, which looks like it uncoiled itself and might do it again.

The grade is steep, and I sidestep my way down to the trail. Butterflies flutter between plants that belong in my book on rain forests. Bees and hummingbirds zip around my head.

The garden looks different now that I'm down in it. Like someone planned the thing, and it isn't some overgrown weed bed. While it ain't like the symmetrical flower beds on the cover of the magazines Mom steals from the hairdresser, it seems to know what it's doing.

My feet shuffle over the path, and I duck beneath tree limbs. One moment I'm in a small wood, the next I'm not. The trail veers left. I look back, blink, and shin a red metal chair.

"Dang! Who planted you right there?"

I plunk myself down on it to rub my bruise and stare at a tiny grove of apple trees just off the trail. Feels good to be hidden. I lean forward, elbows on knees, and my chin falls into my cupped hand.

Click.

I jump to my feet, and my chair topples backward with a thud.

"Startled you, did I?"

Not twenty paces off, George the Coot stares at a Polaroid camera.

I frown. "You take my picture?"

"You in my garden?"

I'm quiet and still.

"Darn thing takes so lo—there, you're starting to come in."

What precisely made George into a coot was a mystery. Simply always had been. And not just to kids; adults called him that, too. No one meant harm by the nick. Heck, when Mom said it, it almost rang with fondness. George was the nearest thing to a legend we had in Pierce. He had a sordid past—that much we all knew—but what that sordidness entailed we hadn't a clue. This gave our imaginations plenty of room to operate. When that boy was found dead near Princeton? "Well, I hope they checked Coot's place. He killed a man once, you know." When vandals spray-painted the high school? "Bet Coot's givin' them scoundrels room 'n board." All this made it an occasion—something to mention at the dinner table—whenever anyone got a good, up-close look at the man.

I've never talked to the Coot. But now the graying, leather-skinned gardener holds my picture in front of his eyes.

"Reckon I'll name it *The Thinker.*" George hobbles closer and shows me the photo. Yeah, he caught me in the pose.

"Why'd you take my picture?"

"Why'd you bolt the ceremony, kid?"

He was there.

My shoulder bounces. "You must not have seen the whole thing, Coo—" I stop myself short, bite my lip, and stare at wood chips.

"Saw the whole show." George moves right in front of me. I feel his eyes. "From your late entrance to the last run-away part. Had my fingers in my mouth to give a whistle the moment your foot hit that first step." He looks up. "Hell, I wouldn't have missed Jack Keegan's graduation for anything in this world."

My gaze shoots to his, but the Coot's eyes slip free. He approaches the nearest tree and strokes an apple blossom. "Do you know this tree started with a black seed?"

Jack Keegan? News flash. Old Bill changed my name sixteen years ago.

"Yep. A black seed. I put it in brown earth, set it in with clear water, and let golden sun strike it." He bends a branch and sniffs pink petals.

And you got no business bringing it back now.

"It grew a green shoot that turned into brown bark surrounding milky-white wood and burst green leaves that popped white-and-pink flowers, which'll turn into red-and-yellow apples filled with white flesh and more black seeds. That's a lot of beauty come out from a hard little shell."

"How do you know—"

"Your name?" He faces me. "You should have been at your party. Good cake. And those cute little ham sandwiches? Mm, Mm."

"I don't understand."

The Coot scratches his head and strokes his stubble. "No way you could make sense of anything right now. I left a note for you. It'd be a good idea to take a peek at it." A faint smile cracks his strong jaw. It's not a happy grin, but I can't figure it out, so it must be sympathy, which I don't need. I scuff his bark chips with my toe and glance up for his reaction. The Coot is gone.

"But I didn't invite you to the party."

"You ain't invited me to nothing, Jack." The Coot sounds a long way off. "Your dad did."

Figures. Old Bill and an old Coot, partners in humiliation. Probably out drinking and making fun of my name.

I kick the downed chair, but the garden muffles the hollow clang. I whip around, retrace my steps, and pause at the edge of the garden.

"And the name is Sam!"

I slip inside our screen door. Helium-filled balloons, victims of the rattling box fan, bounce around the ceiling and scoff: CONGRATS GRADUATE. Red, frosted letters on a sheet cake minus one piece, smirk from the kitchen table—WAY TO GO, SAM!

Shut up, stupid cake.

An army of red plastic cups surrounds our punch bowl, each filled with a half inch of melted ice cube.

I glare at the cake's missing corner. "One guest. What a party. Should have invited Leslie and the Sunshine Club." I exhale long and slow. I thought Mom would invite a friend or two.

As I stomp toward the stairs, my gaze falls on the stool beneath the phone and the open guest book.

Mr. George Rankin.

He really was here.

"How embarrassing. The only person I can get to a party is the Coot." A basket for cards sits beneath the stool. One stained and dog-eared envelope looks up at me.

"A note from a Coot. What a joke."

I pick up the tattered letter, turn it over, and my breath catches.

To my son, Jack.

"Crap!" I whip it back onto the floor.

The envelope's old and I stand there frozen and wait for someone to tell me what the hell is going on, why the town crazy delivered a note from a dead man. I stare and wonder why my heart pounds over a piece of yellow paper. I nudge it with my toe, glance around, and snatch it off the floor.

That sure isn't Mom's writing.

I sprint up the steps, slam my door behind me, and attack one side of the envelope. My hand jerks, and I rip the letter in two.

Slumping against the wall, I slide to the floor and piece together the paper.

Dear Jack,

Congratulations, son. You did it, and I'm so proud of you. Wish I knew what you need to hear right now. Wish I was there to say it. I'm sure Lydia will choose a good man to follow me. But if it all goes wrong, I'm leaving you and this note in George's hands.

Remember whose you are.

You are loved,

Dad

I stare at the last two lines. I can read the words, but I've no place to put them and nothing to stick them to and they bounce off meaningless.

"The writing jumps around," I whisper. "One big scribble. There's Tourette's all over this thing." I ball up the letter. "Ain't for me anyway—my name's Sam. No one's putting me in the hands of that loser Coot." My hand constricts, crunches the note tighter. "Remember who I am? Looks like the son of a twitch. Great inheritance, Dad. I'll add it to the love I'm already gettin' today."

My head falls back with a thump, and I shut my eyes, leave them shut as footsteps in the hall grow heavy. Soon Old Bill's rasp grates through my closed door.

"Hey in there! You know how much gas I burned searchin' for you?"

"He's had enough today," Mom calls out.

My eyes shoot open. It's been years since Mom offered a word in my defense.

"Him?" Old Bill hollers. "What about me? Larry and Randy from the quarry couldn't stop talking about your son's little performance. Should've sold tickets, they said. So I don't want to hear no more about me canning his party or throwin' Coot out on his crazy ear. Boy's own dad left him nothing. Nothing! Now I'm supposed to pick up the tab. Kid's had enough fun at my expense without me giving him a party!"

"He can't help it. You should know about—"

"Enough!"

The fierce jingle at Old Bill's side disappears, and I can hear him count in the distance.

I flatten the note over my thigh, read it once more. *A good man to follow? If it all goes wrong?*

"Well, Dad, got that right."

chapter nine

I MISS MY MORNING RUN BY FOUR HOURS, UNDER-
standable after yesterday's postceremony dash. Aching legs
flop down the stairs and collapse into a kitchen chair. Breakfast
will be cake.

Mom clanks around the kitchen and doesn't slow to greet
me. She doesn't turn either, and minutes pass before she speaks.
"I'm so sorry about graduation. I can't imagine how that felt."

I address the back of her head. "Yeah." I stuff my mouth
with chocolate. "Least I get a lot of leftovers."

"You had a visitor yesterday."

"I know, crazy old—"

"A friend of Heather's. My, but she was a pretty girl."

Icing spews from my lips. A big glob clings to my chin
before it plops onto my lap.

"She seemed very nice. Bill spoke with her."

"Oh no, no." I push back from the table, stand, and start to pace. "She was there? She was here? You're kidding me! What did Bill say? What did she say?"

"I couldn't hear, and she wouldn't come in." Mom sighs. "You can imagine how frustrating that was for me."

"For you? What about for me? Great. Just—nothing? You didn't hear—"

"Relax. She didn't know about the party. Bill said she came to thank you for something or other." Mom plunges a dish beneath the water.

My hands race through my hair, and both shoulders jerk. "Words. I need her *exact* words." I lean over the table. "Bill won't tell me. You must have heard something?"

Mom slows, cocks her head, and leans against the counter on one elbow. "Well, now that you're talking, it seems I might have caught the tail end."

"The tail! Give me the tail!"

"Right. The tail." Mom takes a deep breath, but still doesn't turn from the sink. "She said, now I think I've got this straight—"

"Mom!" I pound the table.

"Okay. Yes, she said, 'Thank Sam for being my hero.'"

My heart clobbers my rib cage. "Go on."

Mom shrugs and scrubs a plate. "That's it. Then she and Heather left."

"Oh, what a stupid, stupid—" I thump my forehead with the heel of my hand. "And while she's here, I'm wasting time with the Coot." I slump back down onto the chair and bury my face in my arms.

"He stopped in, too."

"I know, I know." My muffled voice moans into the wood. "He ate your cute little ham sandwiches. He told me. I still don't understand why he came." I lift my head in time to see Mom's droop.

"I don't know why he waited so long. I do know you have a thank-you to write. He left you ten dollars."

"I have to write a thank-you for that?"

"You have to thank him."

Letter writing is a nightmare. With my jumpy arm, its two words forward, one word back, as I erase myself through a note. There are better ways to show appreciation. Besides, I have a question or two for the man.

I rise from the table, stretch, and gimp toward the door while my legs fire and complain. "Can't believe Naomi was here."

"And Sam. She . . . she brought back this." Mom holds up the coat in front of her face. Her eyes peek over the top.

"My parka." I step toward it, and Mom raises it higher.

"Hey, relax. I'm not that tall." I pause. "You okay?"

Her shoulders slump, and I catch a glimpse of her face.

"Looks like she had it dry-cleaned," Mom says. "I think these are new buttons."

"Move the coat."

"What happened is none of yours, Sam."

"Move. The. Coat."

She smoothes the parka onto the countertop, turns, and looks into me. She fidgets about her lip, puffy and yellowish blue.

I gasp and walk toward her.

"No, Sam! You go, you hear?" Mom's voice surges. She points to her swollen lip. "Don't make this for nothing."

"Tell me he didn't—"

"And so help me, if you look back, I'll whoop you myself."

I run toward the screen door and give it a kick. The rickety frame smashes against the house. Once outside, I grip Old Bill's oak porch swing and heave it over the rail. It lands with a crack.

If Old Bill had been around front, I would have cracked him, too. So he pummels me. Fine. Just more defects to tote around.

But not Mom.

Never again Mom.

I storm through Pierce on a fine Sunday morning. I smack a stop sign, kick a telephone pole. My feet pound past Pierce Church of Peace. Organ music floats out the sanctuary and ministers to the five cars in the parking lot. *Bunch of losers!* My jaws clamp together for a grind. Teeth catch the inside of my cheek and fill my mouth with the taste of blood.

Your God gave me a dad who left me this!

Old Bill's assault on Mom jars loose something deep and hot and ugly. By the time I reach Coot's driveway, I'm about to burst.

Because I know it's me, that if I wasn't a monster, Mom's lip wouldn't be swollen. No matter what anyone says about who smacked who and who's at fault, if I were motionless, Mom wouldn't hurt and that obsessive asshole would be proud of me.

I pace the road in front of Coot's drive and glare at his property. Located five minutes away on the far side of town, George the Coot's farmstead is as trashy as his hidden garden is beautiful. Rusted shovels and lawn mowers, rotted wheelbarrows, and wagon wheels litter the lawn. Overrun with weeds, it's a wasteland of junk. There's a windmill near the house. Two outbuildings—a barn with osteoporosis and a crippled machine shed straddle the gravel drive. Next to the road, visible to anyone who passes by, there's a painted shingle fixed to a stake and hammered into the earth.

HELP WANTED. APPLY INSIDE.

I storm down the drive. "Coot!"

I bound up the front steps and double-fist the door. "You crazy coot, where are you?"

I whip around. George the Coot grips the handle of a razor-edged scythe. Bushy eyebrows raise and form deep wrinkles that chisel across that leather forehead. Watery eyes lock my own stunned pair in a straight-ahead stare. Mine want to flit, to escape, but only my shoulders are free to jump and dance. He strokes his stubbly chin—sounds of sandpaper.

"Ain't got to holler, kid. You need something?"

Why am I here? He hasn't done anything to Mom or me.

"I—I came to thank you, I guess, for the money."

He turns his head and spits. "So that's a thank-you." Coot glances toward the clouding sky. "I'll consider myself thanked." He pushes by me toward the farmhouse. "Excuse me, Jack."

Jack.

"Wait. I mean, hang on. Please." George stops in the doorway but does not turn.

"Old Bill. Well, Bill. He didn't invite you to my party?"

"Nope, threw me out."

"So my real dad—"

"His name was James. He was a good man."

I shift my feet and tense my arms. "Right. He gave you that letter, and this isn't some screwball gag. I mean, the letter's for real?"

George glances over his shoulder. His voice is soft. "What did it say?"

"You should know. You gave it to me."

"What did it say?"

I pause. "Something about Mom and stuff going wrong."

George faces me and lays down the scythe.

"And some weird stuff about you," I say.

George the Coot folds his arms. Looks a different man now. Kinder, I guess. A few neck twitches escape in the strangeness of the moment, and my gaze falls.

"Do those hurt?" he asks. "When you really get going. Them jumps hurt?"

"I kind of need them to hit a pain point or they don't count." *Why am I talking to the Coot?* I fidget with my hands, and then look back toward the road. "I got to get going."

"*That's* the truth." The Coot rolls his eyes.

I frown and shake my head. "What do you mean by that?" He says nothing. Looks at me as if I should be talking. But I've already said plenty. Spinning, I shuffle past the windmill and almost make it to the road.

"So you want the job or not?" George's call grips me by the scruff of my neck.

I stop and turn. He digs in the back of his pickup.

"Job?"

"The one you came to apply for."

Now I know what he means. Every summer, it seems a drifter happens through Pierce. Some slimy character with no life. The Coot hires 'im and gives him room and board. I used to see them—the Coot and the loser—on my run. They take off toward the Twin Cities in that junky Ford pickup. Sometimes I see them come back. It's usually late—eight, maybe nine. At the end of the summer I guess the bum moves on because the next year it's some other scraggly face.

"I didn't come for any job."

"Grow up, kid. What else you gonna do?"

I open my mouth and let it slam shut. A quick peek into my future reveals precious little. No money for college. My right shoulder leaps. With this arm, no running machinery for Old Bill.

"There's work in town. I'll find something. I ain't no loser desperate for help."

"That so?"

No more. I shake the dust off my feet. "Later."

Dinner is late and Old Bill's in rare form: he smiles.

"Now that you're done with school, here's the deal, boy. Your mom and I have discussed it." Old Bill shoots a silencing look toward Mom. Bet this'll be news to her, too.

"You're useless to me on the job site and a load on us all. Time for you to pull your own weight."

I put down my hot dog and glance at Mom's face. I feel mine redden and my jaws tighten. Mom's eyes plead, and her lips form the word *no*. Taking a deep breath, I stare across the table at Old Bill's full plate. He stuffs beans in his mouth, gestures with his fork, and keeps talking.

"Its high time you pay rent. Since you're one-third the adult population, I think one-third the mortgage and bills. Comes out to five hundred a month. Plus an extra two hundred up front for my broken swing."

I glance at Mom and raise a napkin to whispering lips. "What do I get for a broken mom?"

"What, boy?" Old Bill's eyes narrow.

"Where am I supposed to come up with—"

Old Bill slams down his fork, and Mom jumps. "Will you listen to him? I feed that birth defect every day, and the free-loader wants to go on living off my generosity."

"That's too much money," Mom says softly. She stares at her untouched food and rubs her lip.

Old Bill hollers, and Lane begins to cry. I get up from the table and lift the little fella from his playpen.

"Shh, hey, now. It's okay." I let my twitches run free and bounce him gently. "This is about me, not you." Within my jerking arms, Lane settles and smiles and his head falls against my heart.

I stroke his hair and kiss him. "It'll be fine for you as soon as I'm gone," I whisper. "Long as you stay still."

chapter ten

THE NEXT MORNING ON MY JOG, COOT'S "HELP
Wanted" shingle is gone, but its replacement slows my stride
to a trot.

GROW UP, JACK

"What the—"

Dawn's pinks and purples normally get my attention, but
not on this run. As I churn past Coot's farmstead, the sign's
words hold my gaze and turn my head.

"That guy is nuts."

My toe catches beneath a dead raccoon on the road.

"Wha!" I tumble over the roadkill and sprawl face-first
onto gravel.

"Your fault, Coot! Your fault." I brush myself off and peb-
bles launch from my lips. "Grow up, you say." I rise, ease back
into stride. "You're the one playing a stupid game."

Grow up, Jack. The phrase echoes through my head all day, and I wake the next morning with one intention:

Don't look at the sign. Don't look.

But when I pass by I sneak a peek.

CAN'T WAIT FOREVER

I squint, and my eyes widen. I face front just in time to leap the flattened raccoon.

"Hah. Missed me. And get used to waiting. Ain't nothing you could hang out there that'd get my attention!"

JUMPY HANDS WELCOME

I grind to a halt.

"This has to stop."

I approach his door to the squeaks of fruit bats and wind-mill gears—sounds that do not soothe.

"Don't like this." I whisper, "Cripes, I know I'll wake the guy. He probably sleeps with that scythe. Liable to come out swinging."

I risk the doorbell. Nothing.

From behind, the crunch of gravel. I spin around and peer through morning mist. From somewhere a whistle approaches, breaks into song:

"Slam the flowers, slam the flowers, oh, my darlin' Clementine."

A hand squeezes my shoulder.

"Hey!" I jump.

"Sorry, Jack. Put these in my truck, will ya?" George presses a plastic tray filled with flowers into my palms and disappears. I escort the plants to the parked truck and place them delicately in the passenger side of the cab.

"What are ya doin', kid?" George stands right behind me and asks loud and I jump again. He yanks the tray off the seat. "First off, flats and pots in back." He nods toward a truckbed filled with flowers and slams the flat back into my hands. "Can't be so gentle. Take charge. Show 'em who's boss. Slam those flowers!" He shoves me toward the back of the truck. I spot an empty space, shrug, and slam them down. Four flowers break free from their molds and topple, splayed roots up, onto the plywood sheet lining the truck bottom.

"Oh, man! I—" I shove mashed flowers back into their little plastic containers. My hands twitch and crunch the holders like Old Bill crunches beer cans. "I could use some help here." I glance up, but George is gone.

"There! I killed four of 'em." I haul off and kick his tire. "You happy now?"

When George returns, he pushes a wheelbarrow with four bags of reddish bark chips.

"These go in the bed. Try not to crush those two pots. Not too worried about the rest—making a mess of my plants already? That's good."

I clap dirt off my hands. "Listen, I only came here because of your stupid signs."

"What about 'em?" He disappears again. This time I watch him vanish into the machine shed.

"Keep talking, kid! I can hear you. Ain't as deaf as Mildred Moury!"

"I'll wait!" I stare at the wheelbarrow, sigh, and hoist the bags into the last free space in the truck. Coot returns with a shovel and a pitchfork.

"That sign. Why are you broadcasting my life?" I ask.

He looks over the cab. "All set. Three houses to do today. Lots of flowers. So if you'll excuse me."

George slaps the passenger door above the faded lettering: GARDENS, BY GEORGE! He continues around the front and soon the engine sputters to life. "Needs a new battery is all," he calls out his open window. George hawks and spits. "Bye, Jack."

The truck pulls away, but I feel drawn to it and give chase and catch it at the road. George leans out the driver's-side window.

"You can stay at the house. Comes with it."

I scratch my cheek. "Comes with—"

"There's an apartment underneath. Plenty of room for you to move around."

"Why don't you ever answer me straight?" I ask.

"'Cause you don't ask what you need to know. The job don't pay much, maybe a hundred a week."

I thump his door with my fist. "Stop right there. I have to cough up five hundred a month for Old Bill."

He reaches two fingers over and taps my temple. "Not if you don't live there. I need someone now." George rolls up his window, guns the old engine, and lifts up two fingers.

"I'll give you two days." His gravelly voice forces its way out the cab, and with a shudder, his truck lurches onto the road.

I pound the truckbed and again he clunks to a halt, lowers the window.

"There's a time issue here, Jack. Got a hell of a lot to do today. What do you want?"

I blink hard and try to figure how to ask the question that worms around in my mind. "Why—why would you—" His gaze is too much, and I look past him into the cab at a ratty spiral notebook—at a graduation picture paper-clipped to the cover. At her.

"Why would I *what?*" George asks.

My eyes glaze, and my voice monotones. "Why would you have a picture of her on your notebook?"

George glances down at the heavenly image. "This her?"

I nod.

"Can't a man choose who he wants greeting him each morning?"

I wince. *You're too old to be thinking about that stuff.*

"Calm down. Naomi's mom's been a client for years. I've known Nae since she was a wee babe." He looks back to me. "She graduated this year, too. Though I reckon she stayed at her ceremony long enough to get her diploma." George smirks. "That it?"

"Yeah."

"Good." He revs the engine. "Two days."

I watch him disappear.

My urge to run is gone, and I shuffle back toward our farm.

Coot works for Naomi? Must see her all the time.

"Hey, Twitch! Just the guy I need. Well, Bill does."

Jace pulls his four-wheeler next to me. I don't slow.

"Stop, Sam. Serious here. I was on my way to your place." Jace gestures toward the back. "Your dad's in a mess."

I roll my eyes and straddle the seat. Jace's dad owns and bartends at the Corner, Old Bill's favorite hangout, and we speed toward it.

"So your dad comes in last night all upset," Jace says. "Two hours later he's upset *and* wasted. My dad cuts him off, right? Stop jerking that leg, will ya? Makes me nervous."

"Doin' my best here. I—Bill got drunk?"

"Guess it was a sight," Jace says. "And Dad says he's tired of him counting all the shot glasses when he gets hammered."

"I'll let him know," I say quietly.

"Anyway, your dad loses it, and then my dad loses it. Pretty soon Bill is hollering around the bar, and I mean, *around* the bar. Outside. He's swearin' a blue streak; I see where you get that little urge." Jace turns his head and smirks. "It quiets down. Dad thinks he went home. Then this morning I go over to get Bill's keys from the till—"

"Whoa. Wait. You have his keys?"

"Yeah." Jace pats his pocket. "Dad said wrestling them away's what set him off. But shut up and let me finish. So I lock the door this morning, and I see him in—"

We screech to a halt. I follow Jace's gaze.

"A tree?" I hop off and stare up the maple in front of the bar. Bulbous Bill drapes across three limbs a good fifteen feet up.

Jace shakes his head. "You Carriers got strange habits. He done this before?"

"Not in a maple. Usually goes for elms."

Jace chuckles, and my shoulder jerks twice.

"Guess I'll go up," I say.

"'Fore you go"—Jace slaps the cast-iron key ring into my hand—"*you* give him these."

My fingers have never touched them before. "Yeah, sure."

The climb isn't hard. I soon sit on the branch that supports Bill's vomit-covered head—Bill's vulnerable head.

"Bill?" I tap his cheek. "Bill?" I slap him lightly and think of Mom. "Bill."

My fist balls and I rear back.

"What are ya doin' up there?" Jace fights to see through the lower branches. "You gonna hit him?"

My hand relaxes. I shake my head. "Get some water, would ya?"

Jace disappears inside the building. I reach toward Old Bill's middle, where he clutches a bottle. I grab it and sniff.

"Boozin' Billy. Last night you lived up to the name."

I lean back against a limb, fold my arms, and stare hard into the man who smacked my mom. And even though I feel ugly, a smile crawls across my face.

"One. Two." Key after key soars through the air. Into the bar's dented gutter, down its chimney, onto the sidewalk.

You hurt Mom? Clank!

How dare you touch her. Pling!

Your key-counting days are over. Tunk!

"Thirty." I palm the largest key. It's heavy and old and on its shaft I see scratch marks. I look closer. The scratches become letters. *JK.* My initials—the real ones before he stole them.

"Hey, what do you want me to do with the water?" A confused Jace stares at the glass he holds.

"Keep it." I turn the key over in my hand. *Just keep it.*

I slip number thirty into my back pocket.

A half hour later, I have Old Bill seated upright. He thanks me Bill-fashion.

"What the hell am I doing in a tree? Huh, boy? Answer me!"

"Countin' squirrels, maybe?" I scamper down. "My job here is done. See you at the house."

His Saturday-morning curses fade as I jog toward home.

After making one more stop.

I unearth the stake that supports George's shingle and stride into his machine shed. Minutes later, I'm back outside, and I sink a new stake deep into dirt. I straighten to admire the freshly painted sign that will greet George the Coot after work today.

WHEN DO I MOVE IN?

"I've got to be crazy." I turn from Coot's farm and dash home, a cool breeze at my back.

chapter eleven

MOM SMILES AT ME OVER HER AFTERNOON COFFEE. I frown over my sandwich.

"'This would be your time to say, 'Wow, big step, Sam,' or 'I'll sure miss you.'"

Mom pauses and sets down her drink. Takes her way too long to think of something nice.

"Stop." I scratch at a dried glob of jelly on the tabletop. "Don't bother."

She reaches across the table and cups her hands over my fidgety pair. "I know I haven't always done well by you." The wind howls and the door creaks and Mom's gaze darts toward it. She checks the clock and looks relieved. Not Old Bill yet.

"I should've done so many things different," she says. "There are things I should've told you. Things Bill threw out that you should have seen." Again, she checks the door, and then lowers her voice. "I'm talking about your father." Mom keeps confessing, but I don't want to hear this now and tune her out. I only want to pull my hands away from hers, get up, and walk away from the table, where she now cries. Can't stand hearing Mom cry.

"Forget it," I say. "Old Bill told me all I want to hear."

Mom breathes deep and squeezes my hands. "Promise me something?"

"Yeah. Whatever you say."

"Ask George about your dad."

I lean back. "That was sneaky."

Wednesday morning arrives, and Old Bill is AWOL, probably stuck in some maple. It's moving day, and I wait for Coot on our porch. The Coot's Ford sputters into our turnaround. I wince and scan the street. Good thing I told him to come early.

Coot steps out and stretches. "Beautiful day for a move!" He slams the driver's door, reopens it, and slams it twice more. "Crazy door. Startin' to stick."

"Okay, okay." I whisper, "Can you leave it for now?" Down the road, there are lights inside the Severs' farmhouse. "Maybe you could help me inside. I need to carry more things down."

Coot descends steps like Mildred makes graduation speeches, slow and full of pauses.

"Can you move faster?" I hiss and bump his back with a box of clothes.

"Yep." Coot hesitates, and then takes another lazy step.

I rush past him as soon as we hit the floorboards. Pushing

out into morning, I dash to the truck, dump my load in the truckbed, and race back inside. Coot still hasn't reached the door. I hold it open, tap my foot, and exhale as loud as I can. But he grins big and dumb and I know he didn't get the hint. Coot shuffles on by and whistles his way to the pickup. Through the screen, I watch his slow meander.

Keep going. Keep going.

Coot stops, stares at the sunrise before he tosses my pillows into the truck with another stretch and a yawn. His frame lightens as headlamps approach. He squints and smiles at the oncoming car and gives a big wave.

"Damn! Now everyone will—"

"Easy." Mom's reprimand, along with the smell of fresh-baked Danishes, floats from the kitchen. "I know they pop out, but try to hold that tongue."

I'm speechless. Twelve years of uncontrolled blurts and tics. She says nothing. Twelve years of Old Bill rips. Ignored. Then the day I leave she decides to get into my life. I stare at Mom. She stares at me. And I realize all her shame is about to walk out of her home.

I turn back toward the crackpot set to take me away. "Let's go, George." I motion for him to come inside. "Lots more to get."

Another car slows in front of our place, and Coot hollers to the driver. I retreat into the house and give a few furious head rattles.

"What's wrong?" Mom asks, and wipes her hands across her apron.

I can't look her in the eyes. "He moves so slow."

"Just his way." She turns back toward the oven.

Like you know the inner workings of a crazy coot.

"See that sky out there?" Coot appears in the doorway. "What smells so good, Lydia?" He turns to me and I grab his arm, yank him inside, and slam the door behind him.

"Might want to think twice." Coot pats me on the back. "Don't be expecting this kind of cookin' at my place."

"Don't sweat it." I plod upstairs, full of grunts and sniffs. "She only makes those on special occasions." *Like when they finally get the creature out of the house.*

Everything I own fits in the back of Coot's run-down truck. We both climb in.

"You want to say good-bye?" he asks, and starts the engine.

"No."

Mom stands on the porch and waves and dabs her eye with a tissue. I can't tell if she's happy or sad to see me leave, so I peek at her through cracked fingers and waggle my head because this feels so pathetic.

All across Pierce, my classmates will soon hop in their cars and turn back for that last look at smiling, sobbing parents. Then they'll fix bright eyes on a brighter college future. Ahead of them, the open road and dorms full of crazed freshmen.

I give Mom a feeble wave and turn toward my destination: the junky farmstead of George the Coot. I let my head fall against the window. What a proud mom she must be.

◆ ◆ ◆

We reach the entrance to George's driveway, and he pulls onto the shoulder. I straighten, rub my eyes, and gasp. The signs are gone. In their place sits a rusted bulldozer with a headstone painted on the blade. Anyone passing can see it—see the name on it.

SAMUEL CARRIER

1989–2008

IT'S TIME FOR HIM TO GO

"What the—" All I can think of is his scythe.

"We turn in." Coot stares straight ahead. "It's Jack—no more Sam. That ain't your name. Never was. Clear?"

"Clear? No—no! You are some kind of crazy. This ain't funny!" I reach a quaking hand toward the door handle. "My name's Sam."

Treadless tires squeal as Coot throws the truck in reverse.

"Where we going?" I ask.

His voice is calm. "Taking you back to Sam's place."

Minutes later we skid back into my turnaround. George gets out and pitches my clothes into a heap on the lawn.

"He's crazy," I whisper.

A hand slaps my window and I jump, slowly lower the glass.

"You don't mind if I leave your stuff on the grass. Figure you can take those steps faster than I can."

Coot doesn't wait for an answer; he reaches into the truck-bed and launches pillows. My knee bounces, and I stare at the farm that no longer looks like home. Then I hear The Laugh.

Oh no.

Alan Glenn on the way to Lowell's Construction. Don't need to look up. Nobody has a double snort-cackle like Alan, and it's getting nearer. A junior at MHS, he's positioned to take Jace's place next year as the obnoxious senior everybody likes. He's already chosen his wimpy sidekick, and Bobby Harris walks with him now.

"Wait." I leap out of the truck, reach down and scoop an armload of shirts, and hurl them into the truck.

Coot flings the shirts back onto the ground. "We'll never get anywhere like this, Jack."

I grab a fistful of magazines from his hands and push him toward the cab. "Get back in."

He shrugs and we sit in silence. Snorty and friend laugh, and I slump down in my seat. Coot straightens.

"Go!" I hiss from my balled-up position in the bottom of the truck.

Coot looks down and whispers back, "Where am I going?"

"To that tomb thing! To move it before anyone else sees."

"Sorry. I like it." Coot and I listen to Alan's laugh fade into the distance. "'Sides, it's on my property, mine and Jack's. And only me or Jack can touch it."

"You bet I'll touch it." I lift the door latch, tumble onto the lawn, and bolt toward George's place and my tombstone. I'm almost out of earshot.

"Reckon you'll be wantin' the dozer key?"

I skid, stumble, whip around.

"Stupid, Sam!" I pound toward Coot's truck and nearly reach it. The pickup lurches ahead.

"You asshole! Give me that key!"

The truck spins onto the road, and I chase after it. George the Coot drives into Pierce and turns down Main Street. He passes the service station. He chugs by the post office. He rounds the Corner, Scurvey's Superette, Bill's Bituminous.

"Stop the truck, Coot!"

Morning faces line Main Street. Faces on bodies still in pajamas. Faces with forks frozen inches from mouths. Through windows and porch screens, through the glass of Al's Diner. No need to read the *Mitrista Times* today. I am the news.

Coot waves to the faces as if he leads a parade, and the truck slows. I lunge, miss, and flop on tar.

"Ouch." A woman feels my pain, but I don't have time to look. I roll, rise, and churn on.

"Tell you what." Coot pokes his head out as he U-turns on Main Street for the second time. "I'll fork up this here key, and you wait to move your headstone until we discuss the matter."

I clench my teeth and run harder.

"We'll shake on it at my place." A blast of green exhaust fills my lungs, and the truck speeds around a corner.

"Coot!"

I cut across Melvern's yard, leap a fence, and surge onto 2nd Street. The truck is just ahead of me. A salty sting stabs my eyes, and I rip off my drenched T-shirt. It catches on my ears and creates a white blindfold. I yank and . . .

Smack!

My knee bashes metal. I topple forward into a truckbed,

where I writhe and moan. My sweaty shirt clings to my face, but my smiley-face boxers ring my elbow, so I know I'm in the right truck. I twist and moan and sink deeper into my clothes. *The Coot will pay.*

I've worked my way down to the plywood that lines the truckbed, and my tailbone rests on a hammer. I wince and reach for it. *Just what I need to dent my name on that headstone—*

"Nae!" Coot's voice calls out, and I freeze. "That you? Reckoned I wouldn't see you till tomorrow."

"George? No way!" Footsteps get louder. So does her breathing. Heavenly breathing. I can hear her, feel her. I press my backside into the truckbed and pull my pillow over my face.

"This is awesome," Naomi says. She's right by the truck. "I spent the night at Heather's." More beautiful heavy breathing. "Needed fourteen miles this morning and she said Pierce was about that."

"That it is," George says. "Still serious 'bout that running?"

"Andrew, well, Coach, wants me to do the TC marathon. It's a big one. He thinks I have a shot in my class." She pauses. "If you met him—he's so different than Mom. He listens. Everything isn't, 'When you get to Harvard . . .'"

No one speaks for a time, but Naomi's feet shuffle.

"Don't like that man, Nae." George exhales loud and slow. "But what do I know? I'm just the gardener."

"No, you're almost family."

I hear lips. *Better be on the cheek.*

"I need to keep going. I can't believe I ran into you."

"Yep. Say, before you go, I got someone you should meet."

Dammit, Coot. Haven't you done enough today?

"From the thump," George says, "guessin' he's in back."

"Thump?" Naomi asks.

My fingers tense and clutch the hammer, and my mouth finds the neck hole of the shirt. I bite my pillow in case she tries to move it. Sure enough, I feel a tug, but my jaws won't let go.

She yanks. I yell. I shoot up. She screams.

"Naomi!" I say.

I can't see her because of my T-shirt. But standing in the truckbed, hammer in hand, I hear her voice a little ways off.

"Sam? Why are you—what are you doing in George's truck?" I reach up, rip off the shirt, and jump onto the street. My throat clears by itself.

"I—I chased his truck. He calls me Jack. It started with my tombstone."

Naomi slowly nods and looks at George, who shrugs and turns away. She smiles, looks at me again, and bites her lip. It's a long look and doesn't stay in one place and I don't know what her eyes mean. Suddenly I feel very naked.

"Would you mind putting down the hammer?" she says.

"No!" I drop the tool and stare at her waist. I don't want to speak to her navel, but I can't help it. "I mean, no, that's fine." Naomi glistens in her green tank and running shorts. We stand there a long time, I think.

"Missed you at your graduation," she finally says.

"You were there," I say quietly as I stand there in the street.

Naomi walks to George's window. "I'll look for you tomorrow, then?"

"Bright and early."

She jogs down the road, stops, and turns. "So neither of you is going to explain how you know each other, or what Sam was doing in the truck."

George whistles.

"Best not," I stammer.

Naomi nods. "Best not." She smiles, shakes out the muscles in her thighs, and soon disappears around the corner.

I walk after her, make it ten paces, and stop. *She saw my graduation? Oh, man.*

"I don't understand." I turn and call to George.

His truck is gone, and so's the dozer key.

I hobble onto George's property, stagger up the drive, and throw open the door to his truck. No keys.

"I never leave them in the truck." George walks out of the house.

I look at him, hate him, and my bruised knee buckles. My face accelerates toward the gravel and arms don't respond. I brace for impact.

It never comes. Two arms catch me and place me firmly against the truck. Two eyes stare into mine. George's face blurs, doubles, blurs again, so I can't be certain, but it looks like his eyes hold tears. My head falls back against the wheel well.

"Why are you doing this to me? What did I ever do to you?"

George doesn't answer. He just keeps looking. Soft looking. I blink hard. Only an idiot would move in with a wacko
like this. Of course, crazy men fall into two categories—those
who know Naomi and those who don't.

My mind returns to the tombstone. "You did say I could
move it?"

"Yeah. Waitin' on you, kid. Need you to agree to the name
change."

I squint and my vision clears. George crouches, his head
rests in his hand. Very much *The Thinker*. He seems smaller,
and though minutes ago I wanted to pummel him, now I can't
work up an ounce of anger.

"Fine," I say.

He looks up.

"As long as that headstone ain't the start of some psycho
thing." I think of my rampage through town and groan. "Call
me Jack. Why do I care? I get called a lot worse."

George offers a tight-lipped smile. "You want to go get your
headstone?" He jingles the key in front of my face.

"Will you?" I chew my lower lip. "It freaks me out."

"Yep. And we'll get you to your room. But first, the tour."

chapter twelve

WE WALK GEORGE'S PROPERTY FOR AN HOUR. HIS instructions meander like his steps and include lawn-mower operation and hornet-nest warnings, but I'm too exhausted to care. I perform my own search for quiet spaces—breaks in the shelterbelt, dips in the land. Places where others' words can't reach me.

His ten-acre strip stretches down to a creek, which, if followed, leads to his other hidden parcel. The Garden Bowl.

"Why plant a garden miles away from your—"

"Our."

I shake my head. "Whatever. Your, our, property."

"Them plants needed the right soil. Needed the right valley." George looks over his overgrown slope. "This wasn't it, is all."

Little else noteworthy about his grounds, except for the windmills. Behind the shed lay about ten dismantled models. Fins and shafts and rotted posts. Ten upright mills surround the heap. The towers are too short to catch wind, and they stand there like frozen midgets.

"Imagine you want to see your bed," George says at last.

"Do I ever."

I follow George around the side of the farmhouse and stop. He pats me on the back and points down.

"That's a storm cellar," I say.

"Yep."

"You expect me to—"

"Yep."

My shoulder leaps, calms, and jerks again. I take a deep breath, bend over, and lift rickety doors. I cast a glance at George, who nods toward descending steps. I kneel and peer down and feel like an idiot.

"Never been in a storm cellar?" George asks.

"Never lived in one."

"Fair."

I stand and step down into dank cool. Sunlight streams in from where I just was and want to be again. George's outline casts shadow around me, but I make out plants and rakes and mousetraps.

"This is my apartment? I ain't sleepin' with rats."

"Calm down, Jack. Keep going."

Keep going? I look up at the foundation—at a wooden door with a brass knob, a peephole, and an address. And a name— *Keegan 115.* I brush dirt from my knees, and reach toward the door hewn into solid block.

"What kind of—oh."

Light and warmth pour out of what should be, given the age of the place, rough dirt-floored crawl space. But the ceilings are high and furniture modern. A kitchen with an island is on the left, a large family room with couch and La-Z-Boys on the right.

"Bathroom is in the hall yonder, the bedroom across from it." Behind me, George plunks down one of my duffels. "And those stairs straight on lead up to my place. Ceiling door."

Polaroid photos of windmills cover every wall except the one in the living room, where family pictures dominate. Grandpas and grandmas. Husband and wife with baby. Just happy baby.

"Photos okay?" George says.

I twitch hard near the eyes.

"Take that as a yes." George motions around the place. "Come and go as you please. Cover your own meals. I don't cook." He walks to the freezer. "Couple TV dinners to get you started. Questions?"

I spin a slow circle, still, and rap a few times on the table. "I get all of this?"

He don't say anything. He just stares at me like I'm supposed to say more. I want to thank him big. Tell him this is the best gift I've received since my green cement-mixer jacket. But I don't want to screw it up and say something dumb and watch him yank the gift away just like Old Bill.

"Sorry for hollering that day. I did mean to thank you for the money."

George cracks a smile. "Yep. You get the apartment." He hobbles over to me and stares at my jumpy shoulder. "That money came from your dad's wallet. That was all he had on him when he died."

My stomach sinks.

"Ain't much, but ten dollars bought a lot of medicine sixteen years ago."

I spent Dad's money on shoelaces and Mountain Dew. Feels wrong, and I turn and walk toward the wall and stare at a windmill. *Don't worry. Got your twitchy inheritance tucked away safe in my brain. Really appreciate that.*

It's quiet for a while. "You know," George says, "I once had two mills settin' side by side, and their fins whipped in opposite directions." I glance back over my shoulder. "What do you make of that?" he asks.

I shrug, turn back to the wall. "Maybe one of your mills was screwed."

"S'pose." George's footsteps shuffle to the door. "Or maybe the wind was confused."

I think on that with no success.

We have the rest of my stuff inside by midafternoon. "Get sleep tonight," George says, and knocks his knuckles on the door frame. "I'll be pounding early. Missing work today means twice as much tomorrow and morning comes soon." He smiles and opens my door to leave.

"Hey, the pictures are fine." I point at the portraits. "Looks like a nice family. These your grandparents?"

He doesn't turn and disappears into the storm cellar. "Nope," he calls, "yours."

The door shuts behind him, and I tremble. Biting my lip, I move nearer to the display. *Mine?*

Both grandpas and grandmas look pleasant enough. They wear the old-person serious look, but the grandma on the left has a twinkle.

"Nah. Coot pullin' one of his—"

I see Mom. Nearly unrecognizable behind her glow, her arms circle the neck of a tall, good-looking guy. It's not Old Bill. And the baby in the stranger's arms isn't Lane, the Golden Child. Stepping closer, I stare into the man's face, blink hard until the urge passes. He has my eyes.

So does that baby.

"Crap." I step back, trip over a box, and land on my rear. My heart races.

I should get up off my butt and settle it, stare harder at my father until I can see the embarrassment in his eyes and the sneer around his mouth. 'Cause I know it's there, it must be, he's holding me.

But I rise and tremble and look away because that's not what I saw. He looked like the same guy who wrote the letter. The proud one.

Your old man was so ashamed. I shake Old Bill's words from my mind.

See for yourself. I try to peek.

"Can't do it. What if he's laughing at me?"

I rip the pictures off the wall, stuff them under the sofa, and stare breathless at the space.

"Who cares what you thought anyway?" I run hands

through my hair. "Just my dumb, dead—" I wipe the sweat from my forehead. "Just leave me alone."

Suddenly I'm tired, and my knee aches. I plod into my bedroom and fall diagonally onto the king-size mattress. "What a bed." I close my eyes, and then shoot them back open. Dad's photo is stuck on my retinas. I rub them hard and try again. Still there.

"No way I'll sleep."

For four hours, I stare at the ceiling. But I must have given in, because the next sound I hear is a woodpecker above my head. The bird takes voice, gravelly and loud.

"Wake up, Jack! Hey, down there. We got a drive ahead of us."

chapter thirteen

"NOBODY HOME." GEORGE TRIES THE DOORBELL. "Be right back." He leaves me in front of the largest door I've ever seen. I turn a slow circle and gawk at the mansion. "This is insane."

I faintly recall a sunrise stumble from my bed to George's truck. The two-hour drive to the Twin Cities lulled me back to sleep. Not sure exactly when I woke next—my head is still thick—but I know I've a good case of morning face, and I hope this big door don't open.

I squint at George's beater. Looks ridiculous parked in the beautifully landscaped cul-de-sac that forms the owner's cobblestone turnaround. I dig sleep from my eyes and look down at the ketchup stain on my white T-shirt. Heather's right about us—hicks from Hicksville.

"Go see the lake." George presses a keypad on the six-car garage. "Lake Minnetonka. 'Round back."

It takes a while, but I finally reach the backyard. Waves splash gently against a private beach. Manicured gardens dot the lawn and surround a tennis court, and a swimming pool shimmers in the sunlight. I scurry back around to the front of the house. I don't belong at a place like this, and the way I look, neighbors will think I'm breaking in.

"Never seen anything like—what are you doing?" I ask.

"Ripping." George digs up one of the nice-looking flowers that line the front walk.

"You supposed to do that?" I glance up the drive and toward the neighbors. "I mean, you do work for these people. Don't you?"

"Nope." Plunge. His shovel head vanishes into earth. "Figured I'd come out here and steal a few." Step. His boot drives the shovel deeper. "And since those cameras out back took a shot of your face, reckon I'm in the clear." Curl. He twists the tool and the ground releases its grip—the stalk with all its roots rises and topples beside the hole. Near twenty already lie dead, and he moves on.

"You're joking, right?" I bend over, try to catch his eyes.

George smirks but doesn't look up. "Relax. You don't look so bad. Those cameras don't do anyone justice."

"I'm on film?" I straighten and twitch hard and try and remember if I let loose while in back. *Man! One full-body job right by the pool.*

"Hold up, George. Do you work here?"

"'Course I do." He swears, and I feel really stupid. He kills another pretty flower.

"So . . . what do I do?" It strikes me that the only plant I know is a Christmas tree, and then only if cut and decorated.

"Find the line of hosta on the far side of the garage."

"What's a hosta?"

George points at a clump of green with racing stripes.

I hurry to the side of the garage but can't find a match. "There are green plants here," I holler, "but no stripe thing."

"That's them. Back of the truck are thirty plastic pots. Lift 'em and stick 'em."

I stare at the plants. "You sure the owner wants this?"

"Shovel's in the truck. Big hurry today."

I jog to the truck, find the stack of pots, and jog back. I breathe deep. The first green clump gives me a mean look. He's big and happy where he is.

"Hang on, plant. I'll ask him again." I poke my head around the corner. "Why—"

"We're gonna slam them somewhere else," says George.

I bite my lip and jab at the dirt. "And if I kill 'em?"

"Can't." George hobbles toward the backyard and disappears around the corner.

It takes twenty minutes to uproot the mean one. I stare down at my defeated enemy. I'm still staring when George rounds the corner. He glances into the crater I dug and nods. "Ever done *anything* with plants before?"

"Cut Christmas trees."

He smiles. "Yep. Got the job for you."

I hold up my shovel. "Will I need this?"

"Hell, no."

He leads me to a small grove of trees near the lake. "This one." He whips out a knife from somewhere on his pant leg and flicks his wrist. The blade missiles into a slender trunk. "And, this one." George winces out the blade, spins, and flings it into another tree, narrowly missing my nose. His eyes scan, widen, and squint as they find their target. George wrests the knife from the trunk and fires it circus-thrower style. It embeds in a tree thirty feet away. "And that one. Gone. An ax and a tree saw are in the garage."

George heads toward the house, but I stand motionless and stare at the knife.

"How'd you learn to throw like that?" I call.

"Didn't. It was luck. Bound to hit one."

I step toward the blade. I tug once, twice. That thing is deep, and straight, and dead center, and heart level.

"Bound to hit one." I leave the blade and run toward the garage.

By the time I reach the hosta, they all rest comfortably in plastic pots.

"Man, he's fast."

A pickup engine sputters, and I run toward the truck. George gets out and counts some plants.

"Three lilies short." He slaps the outside of the truck. "Even shorter on time. I'll run out and grab us some lunch. Chop those trees off near the ground. Drag 'em up by the hosta."

"Okay." I look toward the open garage, and back at George. "Is this all we do? Dig stuff up? Chop it down?"

He guns the engine. "You're a gardener now. Everything dies before it lives. Be right back."

I can't hold it any longer. "Wait. Yesterday, you said we'd see—"

Tires squeal, and the truck vanishes. "Naomi."

Nobody is around, and I allow my muscles a twitchy minute. I dash into the garage. I'd failed a kindergarten-level hosta task; I won't fail again.

"Ax, ax. All I need is a stinkin' . . . red Porsche convertible." The car calls to me from the far end of the five-car garage. *Would be unkind to ignore it.*

I step nearer. My fingers dance along its frame, but both of us want more. The car wants me to get in, to stroke it, and caress it. I can tell. It wants me, twitchy me, to move within it.

"No." My arm jerks back. I turn from the car, wipe my brow, and haul myself toward the tool wall. "The man told me to chop." I straighten and grab an ax.

Treads squeal on the driveway.

"Back already? I got nothing done again!" I race the length of the garage toward the open door.

I regrip the ax and leap into the sunlight.

Naomi stands an arm's length in front of me. My eyes widen, and I skid to a stop.

"Hey, Naomi!"

She screams, whacks me over the head with her gym bag, and bolts. I straighten in time to see her front door open and slam shut. I tongue the inside of my cheek, nod, and drop the ax. The metal head falls onto the ground.

"Tree saws, hammers, axes. If I see her again, I'll be packing a chain saw."

I peek at her house. Probably isn't the best time to knock and apologize. I walk away from her home and toward her car, peer through the driver's-side window. I touch my eye. Straightening, I shuffle around to the back. I lean in to the car, rock it—feel it move. And remember how it plowed through a drift.

A tingle warms my cheek, and I glance back at the ax. "Some hero."

chapter fourteen

GEORGE AND I MUNCH WHOPPERS ON THE STEPS.
I want to tell him what happened, to ask him for advice. I
want him to tell me why I keep screwing up with this girl. But
he's old and he's a coot and he doesn't know anything. I peek
at him. Ketchup fills the corners of his mouth, and he belches.
I've known three men in my life. One's dead. One's cruel. And
one belches.

"You're mighty quiet," he says, and wipes his face with his
wrist.

"Thinkin' on something." I exhale and stare at the ax. George
hasn't noticed it. I wish he would. I wish he'd see it and ask
about it and then I could ask him all my questions. But he just
burps again.

"While you were gone . . ." I pause, but he says nothing. "I
had a run-in."

The door behind us creaks and a sliver of face peeks out.
"Get in here, George!"

He turns from Naomi to me. "Whacha do, Jack?"

We both stand. Naomi's finger pokes out, zeroes in on me. "Not you. You stay right there where I can see both your hands."

George shoots me a terrible look. "What did you do to Nae?"

Never seen that face on George. I swallow and my gaze drops. "Charged her with an ax."

"Oh." George's body relaxes, and he nods. "Yep. Had me concerned there." He pats me on the back and disappears into the house.

Five minutes later, the door opens and George and Naomi step out.

"She says you jumped her in the garage. That true?"

I peek at Naomi. Her eyes are hard and I want to run.

"I might have jumped. But I wasn't jumping *her*. That didn't come out right. I wasn't coming after her, I mean, I was going to kill trees, not—I didn't know she was there—"

George holds up his hand and turns to Naomi. "Satisfied?"

Her face softens and she exhales hard. "Yeah I—I didn't think you were like that." She breathes deep. "I've been sort of jumpy lately. Just stuff going on, you know?"

I nod, and she continues. "How are you two doing?" Her smile starts and stops.

"Been well." George rubs his chest.

"Same," I say.

It's quiet for too long, and my arm leaps.

"I think that's our cue." George walks down the steps and

heads to the truck. "We have to be going, Nae. I'd like to wait for Melissa, but I need to be done planting at the retreat house by six."

"Okay. Bye, George," Naomi says.

It's her and me left on the step. We both shuffle our feet.

"I'm sorry for the ax thing. I feel stupid and . . . well, that's what I wanted to say."

"We're all stupid sometimes." Naomi turns and vanishes behind the door.

We don't stay to chop trees. George pitches plants and tools into the truck. "In, Jack."

I obey like a poodle. Back on the road my mind swirls, and my anger rises. He could have helped me explain.

George gulps from his thermos. "So, you attacked Naomi."

"Well, yeah. I mean no . . . no! I didn't. You heard me. She was just there." I run my hand through my hair. "She keeps popping up."

I tell him about the 10K, about Christmas Eve, the Dairy Queen. He's quiet a long while.

George reaches over, grabs a toothpick from the glove compartment. "What do you think of her?"

"She's okay."

George nods. "Real pretty, though."

"Yeah, she's that." I clear my throat. "And Melissa is her mom? And that really is her house? And you really are their gardener?"

"Yeah. That's a—that's all true." George squeezes his forehead between thumb and forefinger and lets the truck drift into the other lane. "Been gardening there near twenty years. Watched Nae grow, change hands four times." He exhales hard. "Melissa's on husband four."

"What else do you know about her?"

George glances over at me, smiles weakly. "Probably too much."

With no response to that, I drift into my own thoughts.

We pull up to a flowered, gated entrance with a sign out front:

JESUIT RETREAT HOUSE—DEMONTREVILLE

"We got three hours to slam one thousand impatiens."

"Translate," I say.

"We have a hell of a lot of flowers to plant. I promised Father McCullough I'd have these in by the time this weekend's retreat started. We're lining the outside of the monastery on the hill."

"A monk place?" My stomach turns. "Never been into God stuff." I grunt and George's eyes twinkle.

"Ain't askin you to go to confession, just plant a damn flower."

We pull into the retreat center, rumble past the chapel, and skirt beautiful Lake Demontreville. The truck turns up between the stables and chicken coops, weaves through woods. The monastery looms before us. Big and brick and fortresslike.

George pulls over and pushes out the door. "Grab a flat and follow me."

I scoop up impatiens and catch up with George, who's already dumped his load in front of a ten-foot statue of Jesus.

"Area around His feet needs to be covered. Don't worry about perfect rows."

I look around. The place makes me queasy.

"How'd you find this job?"

George takes his trowel and scoops up some dirt. He cracks a plastic holder, lifts up the flower, and slams it into the hole. With one deft motion the roots are covered, pressed, and mounded with earth. "Do that one thousand times and we're done." He points at the fortress. "I'll be working along the brick."

"You didn't answer me."

George turns on his haunches and stares into me. "Your dad used to come here. Make silent retreats here. Came every year." He stands up. "That's the connection."

"Why'd he come?"

"It was a God thing. You wouldn't understand it."

So he was a religious nut, too.

I glance at the statue. He stares down at me. "He's never been interested in me before." I point at His face with my trowel.

"Feel free to get acquainted." George spins and walks toward the monastery. "Now slam."

The ground is hard and my progress slow. Late afternoon fades into early evening and the sun dips behind a row of trees. Horseflies and mosquitoes attack.

"Damn bugs." I shoot a glance at the marble face. "Sorry." I don't feel forgiven.

Why am I apologizing to a statue anyway? I stuff another flower into the ground, but my mind fills with words—words I shouldn't say at this statue's feet. I grab another mold and swear.

Not now, Sam!

Curses fly out of me at regular intervals. It's a sickening rhythm. Stab the earth, bust the mold, slam and mound, curse! Stab the earth, bust the mold, slam and mound, curse! There, at the feet of God, I explode and give a full-body twitch.

When my body stills, I jab a trowel toward the statue.

"So You listen to people. Guess I didn't cry loud enough for You to hear, huh?" I whack a bug on my cheek. "If You had anything to do with making me into a monster, You could at least turn the other way."

Jerking arms send dirt airborne—onto my face, into my hair, and I grovel in the garden. Tension fills me, and I work faster and faster.

I hear George's voice, but I can't stop moving, and the words don't register. I whip around to find him gone.

"Fine. Leave me alone with this . . ."

"Statue?" A man, black pants and short-sleeve shirt, stands above my deformed shape. I'm covered with dirt—God is, too. I quickly rise. The man's collar is starched white, and I brush off my shirt.

"George asked me to come and get you. Our retreat has

started, so he had to pull his truck off the grounds." The priest looks at my work. "I'll water them in, son. Thanks."

I nod, pick up my trowel, and gather the plastic cups littered about. With my arms full of stuff, I look pleadingly at this man.

"Leave your garbage, if you like. We'll take care of it."

I shake my head no. I would leave no record of being here.

He smiles. "Walk out the way you came. George is by the gate. He might have told you, the guys don't speak while they're on retreat. Please respect that."

No talking? Dad really was crazy.

A cup tumbles from my grasp, and he leans down to pick it up. "Hope to see you again, Jack."

"Sam."

He stares at my tensing arm and his eyes narrow before he breaks into a broad smile. "I knew your dad. You're Jack Keegan in my book."

I lurch away, bent double with my load. Behind me, all down the hill, I leave a trail of plastic molds. A mosquito buzzes my ear, and I drop everything.

"Oh, dear God!" My words echo across the acres.

I look up.

Fifty men stand stationary, silent, like statues that dot the huge lawn. They stare at me. Unforgiving. I gather my things, get a good hold.

And run. Across the grassy expanses, right by the men. Embarrassment mixes with words inappropriate.

He might have told you, the guys don't speak.

I don't need silence to figure out what God thinks of me. It comes through clearly in the laughter of his perfect ones; his still ones.

I dash out the gate, see the truck, pitch the garbage into the back, and keep running.

chapter fifteen

IT'S DARK AND I'M STILL RUNNING. I'LL RUN UNTIL I fall, and when I do I'll crawl to the side of the road and that's where I'll stay. And when someone finds me and asks where I live, I'll shrug my shoulders and stare at the ground because I don't belong anywhere.

The gravel road crackles behind me and I'm flooded with light. George pulls his beater truck alongside me and slows to my pace.

"You 'bout done?" I try to speed up, but my legs have nothing left.

"Since knowing you, I've been paraded through Pierce, nearly arrested, and laughed at by a priest." I huff and swallow hard.

"Hold on!" The pickup skids to a stop, and I do, too. "Father McCullough laughed at you?"

I look away. "Inside he was. He's probably good at holding it in, listening to all them confessions."

"You self-absorbed whiner. Get in the truck!"

George guns the engine. "Inside he was." He shakes his head and curses and I feel like an idiot.

We have our own silent retreat on the way back to Pierce. Even my muscles, normally active come evening, take a break.

Our truck rumbles down his drive and eases to a stop next to the machine shed. The moon shines bright, and in its light George's face looks haggard.

"Empty the truck. We'll try again tomorrow." He forces a smile, but his voice is tired, I think tired of me. I haven't done one thing right.

He heads into the house, so I grab an armload of tools and stumble into his shed. Hoses catch my feet, and I trip and drop my load with a clank. Shovels and pots litter the concrete, but I leave my mess and slam metal doors behind me.

"Great first day on the job." I sigh, turn, and plod toward my storm cellar. My lower back twinges as I reach down and throw open the doors.

"Dang!"

Eyes stare at me from inside the cellar.

My heart races. "What are ya trying to do? Finish me off? Dang!"

George climbs the steps and pushes by me, an old shoe box in his hands. "Left some stuff by your door. Wanted you to have this, but I can see it ain't the time. Get to sleep. Be rapping early."

He hobbles out of sight. I peek my head into the blackness and then slowly walk down. "He probably loosed a snake."

Inside, I make myself a peanut butter sandwich, plunk onto the couch, and dream about the girl I attacked with an ax.

I crack an eyelid, roll over, and sigh. Drifting back off, I mumble, "I'll apologize for being such a freak."

"Ain't been called a freak before. Crazy yes, but never a freak." George's blurred head comes into focus. "Got tired of bustin' knuckles on the door."

"What—what time—"

"It's late. Truck's loaded. I'll be waitin' in it." George hobbles out. "Bring some heavy clothes. Later today we'll be in the thick. Try to hurry, Jack."

I squint at the clock: 5 A.M. I stand and peel peanut butter sandwich off my shirt.

I change and stagger out of my cellar. The truck's passenger door hangs open.

"You look awful," George says. "All dressed for winter? I said *bring* it, not wear it."

I don't need suggestions from George. I can dress myself, thank you very much. I climb in and slam the door.

"Where we goin' today?"

"Finish up at the Archers', move on to the neighbors."

"Same pla—" My cough catches me unprepared. "Same place as yesterday?" I flatten down my denim shirt, and grimace into the rearview mirror.

Finally, I have advance warning. If Naomi's there, today she'll see the real me in action.

♦ ♦ ♦

The morning had promised sun to Pierce, but changed its mind when it came to Minnetonka. Still, heat was everywhere. Minnesota muggy.

WCCO reports eighty-nine degrees at 8 A.M. with a shot at a hundred. George's pickup has no air-conditioning, and I arrive at Naomi's a stinky-pitted, nappy-haired, foul-breathed sweat ball.

But I'm ready for Naomi. I breathe deep as George pulls up to the fountain, and summon all my Carrier charm.

Still as a statue, bold as a lion. Still as a statue, bold as—

George interrupts my mantra. "Melissa loves color." He points at the side of the garage and the line of potted hosta. "Plain green wasn't working for her." George pushes out of the truck, still talking. I sit for a moment, eyes closed, palms raised.

Just one calm day. It's all I ask.

I exhale hard and join George behind the truck. He hasn't stopped blabbering.

"But that's garbage if you ask me. Naomi's smarter than that."

My shoulder jerks. "Garbage? What's garbage?"

"Nothin's garbage, Jack." He gestures toward the plants in the truck. "We'll plant it all."

"No. I know about the plants. You said something was garbage!"

George looks at me blankly, as if I'm crazy.

You said her name, crazy coot! I throw my hands into the air and kick a tire.

"Calm down. We'll get 'er done." George pats me on the

back and points at the pots by the garage. "All those we—well, I, took out go in here." He slaps the back of the truck. "These here coleus? Slam them in their place." He hands me three plants—white, orange, and burgundy mixed with green. "Get creative. Use all we have in the truck."

I stare at the flowers as he walks away. "How 'bout I plant them in a straight line?"

George attaches a hose to the spigot near the front steps and lifts his hands with a flourish. "Create! You're an artist!"

"An artist. Right." I haul hosta to the truck and carry over their replacements. Sweat pours down, and I stare at the hosta holes with stinging eyes. "So maybe I did dress too warm." I whip off my denim shirt and wipe my face with a sleeve. Sweat refills my eyes.

"Can't even see!" I tie a shirtsleeve around my forehead to stop the flow and wrap the rest of my shirt around my neck. The other sleeve swings down in front of me like a pendulum and knocks petals off the plants I hold. I set them down and stuff my sleeve into the front of my jeans. I pick up the smallest coleus.

"You don't care where I stick you?" It's a polite plant. "Okay, Carrier. Create!" I wave my hands over my head like George had done, but I stink and lower the flower. I look off into the woods.

"Let's leave it to luck." I close my eyes, take a step, and drop the plant. "You will be there!" I say triumphantly, and punctuate with a mighty body twitch. I grab another, close my eyes, step forward, and repeat the process. Grab, grope, drop, twitch. Grab, grope, drop, twitch. A bed takes shape.

Better Homes and Gardens *will call me and ask how I did it.*

I fist a plant, let it fall, and let my body rip. "And I'll tell 'em. Grab, grope—"

I stop, arms extended, eyes closed. My right hand grips a plant, but my left presses against something smooth and firm. I feel the something tense and relax, and I open my eyes.

She stands so close. I feel Naomi looking at me, but I can't take my gaze off the hand that quivers against her tanned skin; because it's my hand that rests on her abdomen, above the Nike shorts and below the cutoff T-shirt.

My arms stretch forward like a flower-bearing Frankenstein, but I don't care and I watch my index finger shift against her body. Yes, it's official—I caressed Naomi. She doesn't seem to notice. Probably because my other four fingers tense and twitch something frightful.

She wraps a hand around the plant and gently takes it. Her fingers touch mine. "Is this for me?"

I nod, and my limp arms fall to my side.

"I have something for you, too. I wanted to return this." Naomi lifts a knife. The shaft resembles one I'd seen George fling into maples.

"Thought it must be yours. You know, saws, axes, knives."

"It's not mine." My gaze flits up to her eyes, before falling to her waist. *There, I touched her there.*

My body jerks, wild and full, not eighteen inches in front of her. There's no hiding, and I brace and raise disgusting eyes to hers.

She cocks her head. "What makes that happen?"

She asked straight out. No chance to impress her now. No chance for anything if I tell her.

I take a deep breath. "Hard to explain."

Naomi smiles, and I shut up.

"Thanks for the plant." She closes her eyes, spins around, and takes two steps.

God, she's beautiful.

Naomi lifts the plant to eye level and drops it. "You will be there!" She turns back toward me. "Leave that one there, okay?"

I nod and she walks toward me, lightly touches the denim sleeve that hangs down over my chest.

I blink hard.

"Better leave you to your work. Be seeing you around." She brushes past me, and the sound of her footsteps vanishes in the distance. I can't turn. I stand—smelly-pitted, nappy-haired, stink-breathed, sleeve-hung-over-my-crotch, knife wielder that I am, and shake my head. I drop the knife, pick up the shovel, and sink Naomi's plant right where she wants it. Rising with a twitch, I stare at my own placements and gaze back at hers.

"Perfect."

chapter sixteen

I SPEND THE REST OF THE DAY BEHIND THAT garage. I plant and sweat and feel my head spin.

"Come on, kid. Take some water." For the second time in a day George's rough hand slaps my face. "Why aren't you drinking?" He yanks at the hose for more slack and holds the spewing end in front of me. Slumped against the garage, I reach for one of the three hoses I see but grasp only air. The world spins again.

"Cripes." George douses me with water, and then aims some into my mouth. I cough and sputter.

"You're a runner," he says, "figured you knew better."

George unwinds my denim scarf. "Young fool." He lays my head gently back against the wall. "Enough for today."

He hoists me up by the waist and throws my limp arm over his shoulder. We stagger back toward the truck. He stops and turns and scans the flower bed I created.

"These are some darn good placements. Except that one there on the end. Don't fit with the others."

Straining back to see Naomi's plant, I roll my eyes. "Tell me about it."

We skip work at the neighbors' and head home. A gallon jug rests on my lap, and every five minutes George gives it a tap.

He talks the whole way about stuff I don't care about and don't want to hear right now. Like gardening. I must've dozed off, because when I wake he yaps about nuns.

"I'm a big believer in wandering." George taps my water jug. It's empty. My arms wrap around the plastic, and I squeeze it as if it's a friend. I turn and stare out the window.

"Bumped into this tiny sister outside of Dublin. I was fresh off one fight and looking for another. Figured them nuns all cut from the same hand-smacking cloth. I'm surprised Catholic school left me any fingers at all." He cracks his knuckles and I wince and press my nose into the glass.

"So I hollered at that little woman—must've let her have it for five minutes." He pauses until I peek his way.

"Know what she said?"

I don't answer.

"That's it. Nothing. So I scream, 'Say something, Sister!' She shakes her head, starts to sob, and buries herself in my chest. Cried right into my heart, and I tell ya, Jack, my heart heard it, and I was scared to death. I staggered into the nearest pub. That's where I met your dad, and it changed my life."

My stomach feels sick. I don't want to vomit into my water jug, but Dad's everywhere, and if I hear much more about him, I'll lose it. I squeeze the jug tighter and close my eyes. My shoulder gives a huge jerk. The twitches are from him, and Old Bill is around 'cause he's not, and the only thing he left me is alone—alone with a coot.

The last embers of sunlight glow as we turn up our drive. I blink, and when I open my eyes, I'm in bed.

My throat burns, and I feel my way into the kitchen for a drink. As I collapse on a chair, my gaze falls on a note resting on the kitchen table. I stretch for the paper, turn it over in my fingers. It's covered with erasures, but the words are legible between smudges.

Don't rehearse your speech. You'll see her, and your mind will blank because she's pretty. But that's fine. What you say don't matter all that much. She doesn't care about the words, though she'll pretend to. Look at all the dopes with wonderful women at their sides.

"Old Bill," I whisper.

Nae cares about this: When she's with you, do you make her feel special? So keep your trap shut, Jack.

I read my name and flounder off the couch. "Jack? So this is why you adopted me. A chance to analyze poor, twitchy

Sam. A little matchmaking, relationship therapy for the charity case who lives down the road."

The world spins as I rise, and I take some water. "No more, Coot. Had enough therapy at school." I glance at the space that once held Dad's picture. "What am I doing here?"

I dress and push out into the night. It's raining, and though my bones ache, I manage to hobble into Pierce. My pace picks up as I walk out the far side of town. Ahead, Old Bill's farmstead looks dark. The Malibu is gone. *Things haven't changed much.*

The back door is open. I slop inside and stand dripping on hardwood.

"Like I never left." I whisper. A hint of heat escapes coals in the fireplace, and I add a log, stoke the flame. I press against the hearth and stare at the popping, crackling tongues.

"Every problem I got is because of Tourette's."

I lower my soaked body and stretch out on the floor.

I wake with a divot in my side where I'd leaned against bricks. The Golden Child wails upstairs. The teakettle whistles. Old Bill's raised voice booms from the back bedroom and there's a strong knock on the front door.

Mom scurries down the stairs carrying The Child. Old Bill stomps out of the bedroom and storms after her. She takes a right into the kitchen and grabs the kettle while Old Bill huffs toward the front door and throws it open.

The house is silent.

"Mornin', Bill." George hints a smile. "I was just wondering if you've seen my hired hand around here."

Old Bill looks back at me, and his eyes narrow. "No. Just a mangy dog that wandered in. I better start lockin' the back door."

I don't see the blow. I do see Old Bill's frame reel and smack the floor.

"Bill!" Mom hurries to his side, kneels beside him, and gently cradles his head. Lane cries and crawls onto Old Bill's chest.

George stands over them and shakes. "Lydia, I—I couldn't—"

"I know." She looks up and tears stream down. "I know."

Mom rocks gently and strokes Old Bill's hair. She glances at me and catches me midtwitch. Pleading eyes hold me for a minute before she turns back toward her husband. I rise, walk over, and pick up little Lane. His tiny body wriggles and pushes against mine, and his cry strengthens to a shriek. I reach him back down to Mom, who squeezes her son to her side.

And it hits. Something about the sight. The three of them together. A family. Complete.

"I'll, um—I'm gonna go now." I step toward the door, turn, and take in the scene one last time.

"Good-bye," I say.

Mom looks up. "I love—"

I slam the screen door on her, but she hollers out the door. "I love you, Jack Keegan!" Her voice rises to a shout. "Don't forget your father's name! You're a Keegan! You hear me? A Keegan!"

I stand motionless on the porch until Mom's hollers give way to sobs. Nothing makes sense. Not Old Bill knocked out on the floor, not Mom finally talking about Dad, not her calling me Jack after all these years. I'm wet and I shiver and I just want someone to tell me who the hell I am. George sits statued on the rocker and stares at the fields across the road.

"Didn't mean to—if I learned anything from James—but him callin' you a dog." He runs his hand across his chin stubble. "Some things a man can't stomach."

So much for my manhood. I've been eatin' stuff like that for years.

George turns to me and brushes off his jeans. "With a start like this, I'd understand if you need space from me today."

I look at him, and want to go wherever he goes. Suddenly this crazy man is the only one I know who makes sense. I stare, and a strange warmth fills my heart.

"Let's go to work."

chapter seventeen

EXCEPT FOR A SHOVEL, GEORGE'S TRUCK SITS
empty in Mom's turnaround. We hop in and rumble out of town.
"Don't we need to pick up flowers or something?"
"Yep."
He takes the right onto Farkel's drive. I haven't risked
this turn in ten years, but not much has changed since the
Dahlgrens' dare sent me quaking into the Butcher's barn.
Zeke Farkel ranked beneath George on the mystery meter,
but light-years beyond on the terror gauge. He'd been known
to flat-out shoot cows who wandered onto his property. But it
was the cat incident that cemented him in our nightmares.
I don't know why Jace started it, why he tied up his cat's
unwanted litter in a burlap sack and pitched the helpless
kittens into Farkel's field. But that's what he did. Jace hid
behind some junipers and watched Farkel, high on the tiller,
grind right up to that bulging, meowing bag. The old guy

stepped down from the tractor, picked up the sack, and shook his head.

And then dropped the sack and made cat-burgers. Jace saw it plain as plain. Farkel became the Butcher.

"Why are we turning here?" A fluttering fills my gut.

"Need to see Zeke."

"Farkel's your friend? Don't you know what he's like? Animal-hating butcher who'd mulch innocent—"

We slow at the shelterbelt and my mouth gapes.

"Cats."

Everywhere. Cats large and small own the drive. Must be a hundred of them.

"Come on." George parks near the decrepit farmhouse. "'Bout time you meet Zeke."

I quietly exit and follow George to the door. "Zeke! Got a kid here wants to see the animal butcher."

"Ho, George!" a voice echoes out. "Sharpening my cleavers. Send him in."

I take a deep breath and push through the screen door. Farkel sits at the kitchen table. Dressed in oily dungarees and an old railroad cap, he looks straight off the lines. He pushes back from the table, stands, and stares into me. I expect to see the eyes of a monster, but he looks like a twinkly, old man. Stubble-chinned like George and wrinkled deep, he seems harmless. So much for Jace's Kitty Killer story.

Twitches overtake my shoulder, and I stare at my boots.

"So this is the man," Zeke says. "These parts is ready for another Keegan."

I force my gaze to his and stretch out my hand. "Sam, Sam Carrier. Nice to meet you."

"Boy suffers from name confusion." George wanders around the kitchen. "Wanted you to know him by face so you don't shoot him when he enters."

I wriggle free from Farkel's grip. "Shoot him? Me? What am I entering?"

George ignores me and stares at the kitchen counter. "What kind of crazy contraption is that?"

The farmer lumbers over to the counter. "That durned Trixie. Stupid cat jumps up on my counter and licks my butter. I'm tired of cats lickin' my butter."

I walk over behind them and peer over their shoulders. The sink is full of dishes, but the countertop's scraped clean, except for two car batteries—their terminal wires plunged into opposite sides of a butter stick.

George stares at Zeke. "You *are* trying to kill 'em."

"No, no, just give 'em a jolt, remind 'em who's boss—and to keep their tongue off my butter!"

My brows raise. "Think it'll work?"

Zeke raises a finger and points back over his shoulder into the living room.

What the—

At the top of a thick yellow curtain hangs a cat. His paws grip the curtain rod, while the rest of him hangs down stiff and spread-eagled with hair on end. He's twitchy, too, but I don't reckon it's Tourette's.

"Zeke!" George jogs toward the cat. "Is it alive?"

"Reckon so. She's still quivering. Never seen a cat bolt so quick."

I walk over toward the poor creature and stare. When I turn, George and Zeke are gone. I hear their gravelly voices outside, and I join them behind the truck. Zeke faces me with a somber nod.

"Okay, Jack. Sounds like George done given you the keys, so feel free to head in anytime. Don't have to tell me. Just drive slow. I got lots of cats."

"Keys to what?"

"Hop in, Jack." George starts the truck.

We pull past Zeke's house, past the first two pole barns, and head straight for the third. We don't slow.

"Uh, George?"

He reaches into his pocket, pulls out a garage-door opener, and clicks. The whole barn front raises and we hurtle inside. The barn is long and spotless and well lit. Gardening tools and bags of wood chips line each side. George clicks again and a smaller rear door opens as the front shuts behind us. We cruise onto an ascending tarred path that winds through Zeke's shin-high corn. The truck slows near the top of the ridge. George stops, and I swear.

"It's my garden. I may need you to yank a plant from here someday. Zeke's good about keeping this here front door locked, but we can't keep out every kid who runs away from his graduation and ignores my trespassing signs." He points at one posted twenty paces off, looks at me, and smiles. "Serendipity, I guess."

I peer down into the bowl—green and wild with bark-chip paths that lead to the center like spokes on a wheel. And in the center, that windmill. It's not the tall spindly kind. The base is thick and strong and looks like it jumped off my potato-chip bag.

"Do you like the mill?"

I squint. "Hard to tell from here. It's a long way off."

"James built it."

George guns the engine, and we wind down into the beautiful bowl.

"Stay here." George brakes and gets out. "I'll be a minute." He vanishes down a bark-chip path.

It's quiet. Not spooky quiet, but heavy quiet. I don't want to move quickly or breathe hard or disturb anything. Inside the truck, my muscles are at peace. The place feels safe.

George reappears carrying two leafy somethings. He says nothing, which feels like the perfect thing to say. We creep up the side of the bowl, chug through the barn and out Farkel's drive, and speed down the highway. I look over at this man— the one who slugged my stepdad, who hides beautiful things behind cellar doors and Farkel's barns—who calls me Jack.

"Your dad helped me plant that garden twenty years ago," George says.

The graduation card, the pictures under my couch, the windmill, the garden. The dad this strange man has shown me doesn't match the man I know from Old Bill's stories.

I stare and twitch and ignore the pit in my stomach.

"All right. Tell me about him."

chapter eighteen

WE DRIVE TO PRINCETON ANCHOR STONE AND
Gravel in silence. George winces, scratches his chin like he
does when he's stuck in a thought. The more I think about my
question, the less I'm sure I want to know. We pull into the
gigantic storehouse of decorative rock. George stops scratch-
ing and maybe he forgot it. Probably for the best.

We carry the two plants around to the back of the
warehouse.

"Why do you want to know him?" George finally asks.

I stop. He stops. I start to walk. So does he.

"What I know isn't making sense, is all. Besides, he's sort
of—he's my dad. Right?" I frown.

George nods. "Yep. But he was your dad last week, and you
didn't care then."

I turn and my arms jerk so fiercely, I almost lose hold of the
plant. "Not asking ain't not caring."

"Nope, you got that right." George scratches and shuffles to a small bed of flowers. Hidden behind the showroom and surrounded by a vast ocean of tar, the four-square-foot bed of dirt looks more like a bad miss by Bill's Bituminous than a planned plot.

"You're gonna stick these here? No one will see 'em."

George looks around, pats his jeans and breast pockets. "Shoot. My shovel. Must've been your question that threw me." He wrinkles his nose at the plants. "Ah, these ain't going deep." He plunges his fingers into the black dirt. "Shelly, who owns this place, loves to smoke, and she loves flowers." George walks over to the spigot and fills the five-gallon pail that rests beside it. Sloshing back to the tiny garden, he fills the hole with water and slams the plant into mud.

"So on smoke breaks, she wants something to look at."

George nods toward the earth and soon my fingernails are dirty. I feel his stare as I get the water, slam the plant, and mound it and water again.

"How'd I do?" I ask.

George stares down at the plant and winces again. I wince back at him. I'm sick of waiting.

"So you knew my old man pretty well?" I grab the bucket, flip it over, and plunk myself down. George leans over and sinks my gaze.

"Walk with me." George straightens and ambles away.

I cross my arms. "I'm not movin' till I get at least this one answer."

"Sure you will."

"George!" I hurry after him.

He stops and exhales. "Knew him well." He nods, and I twitch. "James had the jumps worse than you."

"Worse?"

"Well, let me see." George closes his eyes, reopens them. "Yep. Come to think of it, he was in near-constant motion, exceptin' when he was building."

"'Come to think of it?' How can you forget that?"

"Doesn't stick out, is all."

We reach the truck.

"Then you couldn't have known him like you say. So why did he give you that letter?"

"James was my best friend." He climbs into the bed, stretches out his legs with a grimace, and eases against the cab. With a sigh, George swings his head toward me. "What do you know already?"

"Too much." I jump aboard, scoot toward the wheel well, and throw my arm over. "Where to start. Dug ditches. Dumb and lazy. Ran off with some woman and wrapped his car around a telephone pole. Old Bill's told me more, but those are the lowlights." I stare at George. "He wasn't anything like you. Why'd you hang out with him?"

George is silent and stares at the bottom of the truck.

"You okay?" I ask.

"That's what Bill said?" he says quietly.

"That's what I know."

"Lydia, Lydia." His eyes roll, and focus on me. "No wonder you're such a mess. Knowin' where you come from just ain't optional, kid." He picks dirt off the shovel and sighs.

"You got a different story?" I ask.

George rubs his face. He moves his hands and looks ten years older.

"So, yep, James dug a lot of holes. Wells, not ditches. Hired me to help. Your dad loved water, always did. Loved bringing it up. Loved building those mills to do it. It used to drive me crazy." George smiles. "Him coming over in the wee hours to build them towers. Your mom and him didn't have room in town."

I raise my hand. "He built windmills for a living?"

"The towers, anyway. Usually ordered the machinery, but he pieced together a few—all those are probably still working. He looked at a machine, and his fingers knew what to do. It was in his blood."

Whatever was in his blood would be in mine.

"Can't unravel all Bill's words today." George lifts his eyebrows. "But your dad never dug a ditch, and he worked so hard it put me to shame."

His eyes glaze over, and we sit in silence. In time, George shifts. "Maybe enough for now—"

My hand shoots out and squeezes his forearm. "Where did you meet?"

We both stare at my limb, and I sheepishly pull it back. George smiles.

"I told you. In a pub. He grew up in the States, but went to Ireland after graduation." George rubs his arm, squeezes his hand.

I don't say anything, and he continues.

"I was drunk the day of the brawl. Bunch of Aussies off the

docks set to haggling two young women seated at a table near the bar. Pretty young gals. Haggling became roughing and roughing became groping, and soon those gals are screaming. Bleary-eyed me barely lifted his head, but when I did, I saw this tall fellow next to those women. And James says, 'There'll be no more of this here.'"

George shakes his head and looks off into the distance. "Right then I knew your dad would die."

I blink hard. "Keep going!"

"Easy, Jack. Getting to it now. James turns toward those frightened women, takes their hands, and"—George spits over the side of the truck—"he leads 'em right out of the circle."

"Like pushed through, kinda?"

"Nope." George scratches his stubble. "He walks through and pops out on the outside." He shrugs. "Probably the drink. The girls ran out—James could have, too—"

"But?" I lean forward, eyes wide.

"One of them brutes says, 'Hey, mate, what's with the jump?' James spins and catches a fist to the jaw. Didn't seem fair. Those guys were huge and your dad was only nineteen."

I lean back and exhale slow. *Great, Dad gets pummeled.*

George bumps my boot with his shoe, and I glance up at his twinkling eyes. "But he didn't go down. His head snapped back and he rubbed his chin and stared at the red-faced bloke. James was upright and that made the lug look bad and his friends let him know it."

"'Fool!' one says. Another smack, still your dad stood."

"James says, 'Go on home.' He didn't talk like a kid. The

next blows were to his waist and his face, and I don't know what kept him up. Well, I could take no more. I staggered from the bar along with a few others and soon chairs flew and men crashed to the ground. Including me. I woke up in the apartment of James Keegan, my best friend ever since."

"Dad fought you out?" I felt a twinge and straightened.

"Doubt he ever threw a punch, being a Mennonite and all."

A strange look must've crossed my face. George smiles and stands with a grunt.

"James was raised a pacifist. Real conservative. No drinking, dancing, or cardplaying. Still don't know why a person with religion was in an Irish pub. James said he just knew he was supposed to be there. Enough for me."

We look out at mounds of rock. George climbs over the side of the truck, leans back over the edge. "I come back with him. He marries. I marry."

"You were married?"

"Don't look so surprised. I wash up pretty good. But my ex and I were two ticks without a dog. Sucked the life right out of each other. Now I ain't saying the divorce was wrong. I ain't saying it was right. I'm just saying we started wrong and couldn't make it right." He puffs out air.

I'm eager to leave my father for a while—too much at one time—and I push.

"Kids?"

He's silent.

"Grandkids?"

"Couple boys and a girl."

"Get to see 'em much?"

He pauses. "No." George's voice is tired. "I don't. Just my granddaughter, on occasion."

The sun is high in the sky. "No more working today," he says. "I'm beat."

We drive back to Farkel's and spend the remainder of the day in George's garden, our feet propped up against the mill. He jokes and I laugh and wish this afternoon would stretch into tomorrow. But mosquitoes come out and George slaps and stretches and slowly stands. He quiets, reaches out, and strokes a blade.

"What do you think, Jimmy? Reckon he's ready?" George peeks at me, winks, and again faces the mill. "Yep. Me, too."

I stand. "You're talking to a windmill blade."

"Guess I am. Try it sometime." He smiles. "When the accident took your dad, I couldn't dig holes no more, least not as deep—not unless something living was gonna come out of them." He tousles my hair. "Come on, kid. Got something for you back at the house."

"A goat?"

"Nope."

"One of those white tuxedos."

"Nope."

I've been guessing since we left the garden and I'm out of ideas. George yawns and brakes and we putter through Pierce.

"You are the worst damn guesser I've ever met in my life." He leans forward and peeks at Old Bill's place as we pass.

"You could end your agony. Why don't you just—"

"Why don't you just shut up until we get home?"

I chuckle and whistle a tune I can't name. Minutes later we turn in to his drive.

"Be right up." I shove open the door before we come to a stop and leap out.

"Don't take too long down there." George slams his door, opens it, slams it again. "I'm going to bed."

I throw open the storm cellar and burst into my home. Flopping onto the floor, I stretch beneath the couch until I feel the pictures I stuffed. More than my present, I want to look at him. I want to see the guy who stood up to those dock-workers. I grasp a frame, close my eyes, and yank.

George raps hard on the ceiling.

Look once and get up there.

Another rap.

But what if Old Bill is right? If I see his face, if he holds me and laughs at me, maybe pretends to drop me . . . My stomach flutters. I can't take the laughter in his eyes.

I jam the picture beneath the couch and jump up. "You helped out some women. But that was before me. Might not mean anything."

A shuffling upstairs. "Besides, I got a gift waiting."

It dawns on me I've never been on George's level. I climb the steps, knock on the ceiling door, and push it open. I peek above George's floorboards.

Seated with his back to me, George rocks in his rocker.

"Hey." I clamor up and walk over beside him. "I figured it out. It's a new shovel."

His body slumps suddenly. I lurch at his frame, haul it upright, and kneel before the chair, my hands pressing against his shoulders.

"George, are you okay?"

He looks through me.

"Listen, George, what do you want me to do? I'll work harder. Just tell me how to—no! You're not leaving me!" I move closer, whisper, "Not you, too."

His eyes refocus, and his face softens.

I swallow hard. "God, no."

He slowly raises a hand, strokes my cheek, and blinks hard as his purpling lips part.

"God. Yes."

chapter nineteen

SOME THINGS HAPPEN ALL BY THEMSELVES. LIKE George's funeral. I glance around my apartment and refocus on the obits. George, my friend, is going to be buried in two days. They'll dig a hole, slam him into the earth, mound over him, and that will be that.

I stare at the table. "You'll probably like being planted. 'Everything dies before it lives' and all those things you said." The newspaper blurs, and I wipe my eyes. "But I don't see a bloom.

"Who plans funerals, anyway?"

Maybe his boy, or one of those grandkids—certainly wasn't my doing. Since releasing his shoulders and letting his stiffened body fall into my twitchy one, I'd made one phone call—to 911. Officer Biscuit—technically Officer Biscus—arrived first.

"I didn't know you were related to Old Coot," he said.

"Wasn't. He was . . . my best friend."

As more uniforms arrived, I faded into the backdrop, faded down the stairs and onto a couch, where I hugged a shoe box I stole from the upstairs kitchen table. Seemed an okay thing to do. It wasn't evidence from a crime scene. And George had tried to give it to me. It was as close to a gift as I could get and it belonged with me, he belonged with me. Crazy that a coot could become my closest friend in a matter of days, or that something from him mattered so much, but it did, and my gut ached.

It still aches now, days later. The unopened box rests on the couch. It's the last surprise from George, and the moment I open it, he'll be gone forever.

I scan the newspaper print. Three other people will soon be slammed into the earth. From their bios, each sounds as if they deserve a Nobel Prize.

Faithful, Glowing, Helping, Just, Loving, Mending . . .

To describe Eloise Kratchkin as a mending person is a stretch, but Clovis at the *Mitrista Country Times* has a limited vocabulary and a mighty thin thesaurus. And then there's my friend.

George Rankin, age 61,
Outdoor Service Tuesday, June 29 at his home
Burial to follow

"Outdoor. He'd like that. But, Clovis, where's his alphabetized list?" I blink and reread. "At his home? That's my home, I think."

I set the paper down on the table and look at all the windmills on the walls. "Looks like junk on the outside, but someone will buy the place, or it'll end up owned by a bank or whoever takes over dead folks' stuff." I scratch the top of the old box, fingernail the Scotch tape.

Either way I need a home. I walk to the center of the room, lie down on the floor, and cry.

Three hard raps. I rub my eyes, shuffle toward the sound, and open the door. An old guy in a fancy suit smiles at me from inside the cellar.

"Not interested in what you're selling." I try to shut him out, but the geezer is quick, and doorstops with his toe.

"Let me in, Jack." He knows who I am, and I step back from the door and let the stranger hobble right into George's house. The man is old—Mildred Moury old.

This guy should be the one in the obits instead of George.

He plunks his briefcase down on the table, eases off his suit coat, and seats himself. Two clicks later, papers litter my table. I look at them over his shoulder, and my leg bounces hard.

"Are you the new owner?" I ask.

"You are. Sit down."

I plunk into a chair and stare at him across the table.

"How do you know me?"

The old guy digs in his vest pocket and pulls out a dog-eared Polaroid of *The Thinker*. He squints and peers from me to the picture. "It's you, all right."

He hands me the photo George took, leans forward over

the table, and removes his spectacles. A gentle man, I know
it.

"I'm Michael Malley. I handle George's legal affairs."

I twitch hard.

"You look like your father," he says.

"It's the twitch."

Mr. Malley waggles his head. "It's the eyes. And the square
jaw. Your father was a handsome fellow."

I don't know what to say to that.

"Well, young man. I had hoped I would not live to see
this day—hoped George would take care of this himself."
He stops and lowers his spectacles. His chin quivers, and he
smiles weakly.

"Let's get started. George left you some land. The plot we're
on, of course. I won't go into its legal description. I assume
you know the boundaries. And then another parcel between
Pierce and Mitrista, identified as the north-by-northwest
quarter . . ." He continues but I can't make sense of the words.
George left *me* his farm? I blink hard. Mr. Malley's voice gets
louder.

"A piece henceforth and herein referred to as the Garden
Bowl."

"Crap," I whisper.

Mr. Malley adjusts his glasses.

"I'm—I'm sorry," I say.

He talks, and I sign papers for a good hour. I stare at the
pages, my hand twitches, and the pen flies free of my hand.

"Hold on," I say, and reach down to retrieve his pen from

the floor. "I'll take care of the place for him. You know, fix it up? But I can't afford this much property." I dig in my pockets and slap a twenty on the table. "I only have enough money for a week's worth of meals. Not taxes, not the electric."

The lawyer glances at a document. "George has indicated that all expenses be automatically drawn from his individual account. That will continue, unless you wish to make a change. Those monies are yours as well."

I grunt, and he continues.

"Based on your account balance, you should be able to live here for the next"—he punches on a calculator—"five hundred years or so." He smiles. "Don't worry, Jack." Mr. Malley gathers his papers. "Now, here are the keys for the farmhouse and outbuildings." He slides them across the table and points. "That one looks like a truck key, and here's his garage opener. It is marked."

I pick it up. *Zeke's entry.* I stare up at Mr. Malley. "This is the entrance to his garden."

"Your garden, son."

"So, I live here?"

"If you want to."

"And he set up all this for me?"

"Last Wednesday. Of course, we discussed matters years ago."

He winks, rises from the table, and walks to my door. I follow, but Mr. Malley pauses and spins around. "To think I nearly forgot." He reaches into his breast pocket and pulls out an envelope. "George asked me to give you this. He made me swear to place this in your hands. He said you'd know what to do."

I grab the letter and close my eyes. It's all I wanted. Words from him to me. Words he wrote that I can read tonight and tomorrow and every day until this pain goes away. The money, the farm—they remind me of him, but the letter *is* him, and a smile crosses my face.

"Thank you, Mr. Malley." I open my eyes and slide my finger under the fold. "Thank you so much!"

Scrawling on the outside stops me mid-rip.

"My number is on the card clipped to your copies. Call if you have questions." Mr. Malley moves to let himself out, pauses in the doorway. "Do you have any clue as to what's just been given you?"

I tremble and shake my head and reread the words on the envelope.

"Was that a twitch or an answer?" He grins.

"Both," I whisper.

Mr. Malley looks around. "This place could not be in better hands." He pats my back. "I'm sorry for our loss, Mr. Keegan."

Minutes later, I stand alone at the doorway and my eyes hold tears. Inside, I boil, because it's not fair, and it can't be true. I fling the letter, but it flutters to the ground at my feet.

"Why didn't you tell me?"

I listen and hear nothing. But I feel his cold hand on my cheek and see his last smile. I exhale long and slow.

"Okay, George. I'll deliver it for you."

I reach down, pluck it up, and feel incredibly stupid.

To Naomi, my precious granddaughter . . .

✦ ✦ ✦

I go for a run—there's nothing else to do. My feet pound and my mind blanks because it doesn't make sense that I have everything I need, but can't bring back the only thing I want.

I miss him so much. My legs lose their will and head back to the farm.

I do have my shoe box. Something personal could be in there. I accelerate, fly up the drive, duck into my cellar, push through my door, and beeline toward the battered box. I rip off the top and blink at its underside:

GO, JACK!

I claw my hands and bend the lid in two. "Go where?"

The box is nearly empty. Squashed into the bottom rests one crumpled U.S. map.

"Junk." I sigh, and my shoulders twitch and slump. "Typical. Think I'd rather have a goat." I flatten the map out on the table. *Looks like you were a doodler. No surprise what you liked to draw.*

"Tall windmill, fat windmill, colorful windmill, garden-bowl windmill," I say, and dot-to-dot my way from the first sketched mill on the map to the last.

"And finally, windmill in water." I frown. My finger is in California. Jerk, California. "My kind of town." I squint at addresses written beside each drawing, dates beside each address. Next to each, more red marker: STAY HERE.

"Whoa. You want *me* to go to California?" I double-check the dates. "That's next week, you idiot."

George's answer stretches from coast to coast across the bottom and covers all of northern Mexico.

GO, JACK. IT'S TIME.

"Yeah, heard you on the cover. But I've never been anywhere."

I plop into a chair, sigh, and lean back. "'Go, Jack. It's time.' You couldn't write anything more personal than that?"

chapter twenty

IT'S SUPPERTIME WHEN I REACH THE ARCHERS'
neighborhood.

"Go, Jack, it's time?" Seems like a stupid time. I bite my lip
hard. *He gives me all that crap and then wants me to hop in his
truck and take off? We could have gone together if—*

"No!"

The flowers and plants are dying.

I leap from the truck and race to the spigot. I grab hoses
and tear around the house.

I'd have given those plants CPR if our breathers were com-
patible. My spray rips wilted leaves from what's left of stems.
Everywhere I turn, George dies again, and I can't do a thing. I
reach the garage and drop my hose.

"What in the—"

The coleus I planted thrive, except for one on the end.

"Naomi." I rewrap the hoses, and check myself over.

"Every time I see her, I look alien." I tuck in my shirt, tousle my hair, and walk over to the truck mirror to check my teeth. I grab the envelope from the passenger seat and slowly approach the house.

My gut lurches, and I start to sweat. I don't want to see her right now. I want to set the letter on the mat, play ding-dong ditch, and take off. Because the more she sees me, the less she'll like me, and at least this way I can dream.

I shuffle up steps toward the massive door; only the letter in my hand keeps me moving. That and my mittens that hang from an upstairs window.

The door opens, and Naomi grins. Every atom that floats around us speeds up and crashes together. She makes electricity, and my skin tingles. I stand gape-jawed in my soaked T-shirt and jeans and stare at her, also in a soaked T-shirt and jeans.

"Just about gave up on you two. It looks like the plants already did." Naomi shivers. "I was just going to lay these things outside to dry." She runs her hand across her midriff.

Words don't come, so I nod.

"Wait, your mittens. I hung them so I'd remember. I bet you want them back. Take off your boots and come in."

Knees lock, and I stand frozen.

"Really, it's okay. You're unarmed." She reaches out her hand, takes mine, and pulls me into her house. Fancy statues fill the home, but I can't concentrate. I'm busy holding a hand.

She leads me deeper inside. We pause at the base of the stairs, and my body tenses. Movements scream at me. They want out.

Still. Easy now.

I funnel anxiety into the shoulder opposite Naomi and let it jump. Naomi turns too quickly.

"Never met anyone like you," she says.

I release her hand, and my gaze falls. I tense and brace for the other shoe. Jerky, Twitchy, Retard.

Please just say it and let me go home!

"Why'd you give me your mittens and your coat?"

"Huh?" I risk a glance.

"When you found me. You could have frozen."

I twitch hard, look down. "Didn't have nothin' else to give. Not like Jace—"

"Jace? Oh, your friend. Yeah, he wanted to give me a ride." Naomi puffs out air and her eyes glaze. "But he didn't really care."

"Care or not, he offered to take you someplace warm."

Her eyes narrow, and soften. "They all do, Sam."

Minutes later, I hold mittens, and we walk back down the stairs. Naomi chats about some party like the incessant bird outside George's window. And like bird talk, it makes little sense. I'm lost in replays. Never met anyone like you? They all do?

"They" being guys, which I guess to you I'm not. It hits. Sure. Safe-creature Sam. You talk to him like one of your girlfriends. Like a freakin' eunuch.

Explains all the handholding, cheek kissing, house inviting—a nonguy like me would never want to take you someplace warm.

" . . . Heather's still upset about the Mitrista move, but here's the thing. Her dad, her first and only dad, I might add, wanted to spend more time with the family. He quit his job and started working from home out there. Heather's an idiot 'cause that's cool. There's an adventure, you know? I mean, just packing up and leaving because of love? What a romantic."

When had Heather shown up?

"My mom, Ms. Practical, would never do that. Her idea of love is buying my way into Harvard so she can brag to her friends." Naomi turns and stares out a window. "Not that the university is horrible. It's just next year would be a bad year to start." Her voice is barely a whisper. "A really bad year. I was thinking of traveling. I have two brothers in Ireland, and I'd love to see Europe." Naomi tosses back her hair, and looks at me over her shoulder. "Not everyone goes to college just out of high school, right?"

"I'm not."

"See?" She steps toward me and pauses. "But if I did, Mom'd be happy for the first time . . . ever."

She quiets and squirms and for an instant I feel comfortable.

"So where's George?" Her bounce returns, and Naomi looks at me as if we both love this chat.

I freeze at the door, my face prickly and hot. I twitch big and ugly, and Naomi blinks.

"There." I raise my palms. "That's me. That's what I do from when I wake up until I sleep." Suddenly I'm furious. "Don't have choices. No Ivy League, no Europe. And Jace ain't my friend. Think a lot of people want to hang with this?" I pick up my boots, throw open the door, and whip them toward the truck.

"Well, one person did—George. Here!" I reach out the letter, shake it before her wide eyes.

She licks her lips, slowly takes it, and sets it on the table beside her. "What'd I say?"

"Nothing. I mean, everything! George is a lot more important than one of your stupid parties."

I turn and storm sock-footed to the truck. I scoop up my boots, hop in, and slam the door. My skin tingles as truck tires screech. By the time I calm down, I'm almost home.

"Ah!" I pound the wheel. "She didn't deserve that! I'm sorry, George. You leave that for me to deliver, and I yell at your granddaughter. Stupid, Sam!"

I turn in to my drive. *What is going on?*

Two motorcycles, a beat-up Mercury, and three small tents dot my property. Near the shed, four men sit around a fire. I ease to a stop and peer out my window. Riffraff. Even by Pierce's standards. Outcasts of society camp on my land.

"Can I help you guys?" I step out of the truck, and three of them rise and move toward me.

"You Jack, right?" says a graying black man with a voice deep as I've heard.

"Well, Sam. But yeah, I guess."

"Knew it. Being in his truck and all."

The guys touch the truckbed, turn to one another, and nod.

I clear my throat. "You here for George?"

Deep Voice shifts his weight and winces. "Mind us campin' till the funeral? Couple of us come a long way."

"Uh. No, that's okay."

Two younger men with backpacks come up from behind, pat my back. "Nice to meet you, Jack."

Why does everyone call me that?

They turn and slump back to the campfire. From the truck, I listen to the crackle of flame and the sound of muted voices. *Couple guys sleeping outside can't hurt.*

All the next day they come. The lost and the least. By evening, near thirty men litter my farmstead. Inside comfortable quarters, I feel guilty—but also safe.

Outside, there's laughter. I crack a window and jam my ear to the opening. Doesn't sound too sinister.

I breathe deep and venture outside.

"Get over here, Jack. Waitin' on you to come out," says Deep Voice.

The ring of men parts to make room for me by the bonfire.

"How did all of you know him?" I ask.

"Same way's you." Deep Voice looks around. "This used to be home. Feels like it still is."

Men murmur, nod. I ease down on top of a rusty paint can.

"And me? How'd you know me?"

A voice from the other side of the fire fights through the smoke. "If George wasn't talking about James, he was talking about James's boy. Good to meet you, kid."

That's enough to launch them into a new round of Crazy George stories, and soon everyone's laughing. I'm laughing. It does feel like home. I twitch, but nobody watches. Surrounded as I am by the one-eyed, the limping, the trembling, my twitches don't seem to matter.

Late that night, I enter my apartment and stand in the darkness. It feels emptier. Just me doesn't feel enough anymore.

I flick on the light and walk to the table where the map rests. I pick it up and feel a flutter inside.

What do you want from me, George?

"This trip would be crazy. You know that, don't you?"

George doesn't answer. The quiet feels heavy.

"Of course you were crazy, too."

I lay the map back out on the table.

Outside a loud laugh interrupts the crickets' rhythmic chirp.

I smile. "Crazy."

chapter twenty–one

"TIME TO GO."

George's words! His death must've been a bad dream, but now that I'm awake everything's okay. I roll onto my back and force open my eyelids.

"Hurry on, now."

I rub my eyes and squint. The face comes clear and sinks my heart. Deep Voice stares, his face twelve inches from mine. Chew juice dribbles down his chin.

I dress and don't say anything to the stranger who invaded my house and waits at the kitchen table. Don't care why he's there—I just know he's not George and nothing's right and I might as well follow him as anybody. I tuck in my shirt and follow the old man out.

Outside, men have pulled up camp.

They stretch single file down the lane. Wind rustles the leaves and creaks the windmill, but the men stand silent. Waiting.

"They wait on ya." Deep Voice looks up at me. "Mind if I hitch a ride? This leg would slow us down."

"No, that's fine." I say it confident, as if I know where I'm going.

We push through the line and someone pats my back. I don't stop. Deep Voice and I reach the truck, and I climb in.

"Got the key?" he asks.

"Key?" I jingle the key to the pickup, but he shakes his head.

"To the cemetery."

"Why would I have a key to a cemetery?"

"His garden, Jack. Ain't gonna lay him anywhere else."

"One minute!"

I dash into my cellar, comb my hair, and grab the shoe box that now holds all my George stuff.

Back outside, I jog to the truck and open the door.

"You lead." Deep Voice lays his head against the passenger window. His two words don't sound right. I've never led anything, and my fists tighten on the wheel. What if I screw up his funeral?

I start the engine and creep past the line of men—most backpacked and on foot, some on bikes, a few in cars. They look at me, purse their lips, and give a quick nod. What a procession. I reach the front of the line.

"Wait." Deep Voice grabs my forearm. "Wait a minute." He turns toward the windmill. I lean forward, follow his gaze, and almost vomit.

George lies in a roughly hewn box between the mill and the

machine shed. His tanned, leathery skin is unnatural gray. My stomach feels like lead. Six men hoist the open casket onto their shoulders and walk toward my truck. I don't watch—can't. But I hear the truckbed latch, feel a large weight in the back. The truck purrs, as if it knows George's inside, and can be happy again. I stare straight ahead and bite my lip so hard it bleeds.

"You loved him." The man beside me smiles weakly. What business is it of his how I feel? Don't matter now anyway.

Knuckles rap my window, and I lower the glass.

"All set in back." The man outside reaches in and squeezes my shoulder. "Take him home."

Seems all of Pierce lines Highway 23. Jace points and laughs, but Andy and Lars watch quietly as I twitch the truck forward with erratic jerks.

But the farther I idle down the shoulder, the less I care that I lead a line of losers. 'Cause I'm close to George Rankin, and even though I can't stand to look at him dead and all, there's no place I'd rather be.

I pass my old house. Mom pushes out the screen door with Lane in her arms. I roll down my window, but I have nothing to say to the woman, and I wave weakly. Mom walks onto the street, follows alongside the bed, and stares down at George. I hear her cry and sniff and it might all be for show. She quickens her steps and appears at my side. Her face holds a look I've not seen before.

"I'm so proud of you, Jack."

She spins on her heels; I shake my head.

"Met George two weeks ago, and now I ain't sure of anything."

Deep Voice nods. "Give it time. Maybe your trip will help sort it out."

"How do you know about that?"

He points to the open box set between us. "This here lid gives you clear orders, and you have a map. Any man with orders and a map likely heading somewhere." He removes it from the box, flattens it over the dash. "See, you have it all planned out." He scratches his stubble. "Odd way to get to California."

"I don't know what that is. George left it for me."

It's silent for a long time.

"If George left that to you, would you go?" I ask.

My passenger turns and looks at the body in my truck. "Hell, I'd sell all I owned. I'd sell stuff I didn't own. But—"

"But what?"

His voice softens. "If George is sendin' you, won't be no pleasure trip."

Hanging around Pierce ain't no pleasure trip either.

By the time I turn in to Farkel's drive, my mind's settled.

I never finished a single job you gave me. I'm not screwing up this last request. I'll make it to California, George. I promise.

We bury George in the middle of his garden. Afterward, we back down the path, gather red metal chairs into a circle, and wait as each man says a private good-bye. It takes all day. I don't say any farewells. George'll be with me a while longer.

Finally, I drive through the barn and close the garage doors. The men are gone, trickled back to wherever they came from. All I see are cats.

A light flickers on the farmhouse porch. Farkel steps out and gestures to me from the front steps. "Had supper?"

I follow him inside. We both sit down at the kitchen table. For half an hour neither of us speaks.

"What now?" Farkel thumbs his overalls, reaches down, scoops up and strokes a cat.

"I'm thinkin' on taking a trip."

In the distance, car treads squeal onto Farkel's drive. Farkel and I exchange glances, stand, and walk outside. Cats scatter before two oncoming beams. A red roadster skids to a halt in a cloud of dust. The driver pushes out into the night and scans the farm, before seeing us and slamming the door. Dressed as she is in a black top and skirt, I can't see much of her, but from the way she races toward us, it's Naomi.

"I've spent three hours sitting on that hood in your drive-way." Naomi points to her car and then pokes her finger into my chest. "Know why? Sure you do. Everyone but me knew. I was waiting to see my grandpa." She takes a breath. "Who my mom, uncaring wench, lied about for eighteen years! Who I watched slave outside every summer without a clue that he's my—and you!" Another hard poke to my rib cage. "The paper says George's home. George's *home*! You didn't even tell me where the funeral was!" She breathes. "So now I'm wearing black, in the middle of summer, and it's practically night, and I never got to see him. Never got to see my—" She breaks into tears.

"Zeke, like you to meet Naomi."

Farkel smiles, walks over to her, and gently leads her into the farmhouse. "Oh, the damage we do."

He eases her onto the couch, cups her cheek in his big paw, and glances into the dining room, where I work off excess twitches.

"Let me scrounge some dinner." He leaves Naomi quivering and lumbers toward me.

"Go to her." Farkel whispers as he passes.

I step quietly into the center of the living room. Naomi looks small with her face buried in her hands. I should sit beside her because she hurts and that's what normal people do. Stuffing my hands deep into my pockets, I shuffle forward and stop. She looks at me and wipes tears away with the heels of her hand. She wants me to sit beside her, I think. Or she wants to make sure I don't.

I plop down into the La-Z-Boy across the room and watch her cry from a distance. It's the wrong place to sit, I know.

Dinner with Farkel consists of butter, bread, more butter, baked beans, and apple pie for dessert, with a dollop of butter.

"What's the matter? Food don't suit?" Farkel asks.

"No"—Naomi forces a smile—"it's good. It's just that I'm training for my first marathon. Andrew—Coach Zimmerman—laid out my diet."

"Two runners. And looky what I'm servin'. Let me see if I got healthy eats in the pantry." Zeke disappears, and his muffled voice floats up from the basement. "Hey, found some butter cookies! That fit your diet?"

"Afraid not," Naomi calls. She looks at me and smiles.

I scrape butter off my pie and take a bite. "I ain't much of a runner. Sure don't have my own coach."

"He's not my own. Andrew coaches at the high school. He's helping me out through the summer."

"That's good." I poke at the pie and force my eyes to her face. "I'm sorry. For the whole letter thing. I didn't think to mention about today. Didn't know what the plan was myself—stuff's been happening pretty fast."

"Like?"

I think what to share, what to hold. I look at her face and wish I had another chance to sit with her on that couch.

"Well, like your grandpa is sending me to California."

chapter twenty-two

IT'S FRIDAY—ADVENTURE EVE.

I sit and stare at the mound of clothes in front of my couch. The empty suitcase waits on the table. Been staring at this pile for half an hour. I throw up my hands, reach down, and wrap them around an armload of clothes. I stumble across the room and fall forward onto the suitcase. Clothes spill over the edges. I straighten, tuck everything in, and slam the case shut.

"That's the easy part." I glance over the list of George's customers.

Visits to his clients keep my mind busy that afternoon. I rehearse gentle ways to share the news, but always it spills out the same.

"Uh, George died."

Women start to cry and look at me like it's my fault. I stare at my shoes, because what they think might be true. Maybe I did kill him. A better helper would take the strain off his big heart and it might still tick. I hate women's tears. Mom's, strangers', all of them. I can't bear to tell the last two clients, so I play the wimp and slip notes under their doors.

It's late when I reach the farmhouse, but I'm not tired. I pace my apartment and wonder why I'm leaving the only place that's ever felt like home.

I stop and stare at each windmill that hangs on my wall.

"With George gone ..." I glance at the map on the table. "Place won't feel like home for long."

You're right. It's time to go.

Saturday comes and a glow lights up the eastern horizon. My stomach drops.

It's leaving day.

I place my shoe box on the front seat. A barn cat leaps onto the hood and cocks its head.

"No reason to do this. None. It's not like George gives a rip anymore."

I kick truck tires and run my hands through my hair. "What do you think, cat? Crazy is one thing. Stupid's another." I shuffle up the steps of the farmhouse. Haven't been inside George's part since The Night. Don't want to be here now, but I need to unplug stuff.

"Nothing's changed," I whisper. But everything's changed. I walk over to his rocker, and sit down beside it.

"Why'd you leave me?" I say, and close my eyes. Inside, I panic. I feel the sudden urge to catch George. I open my eyes and lunge for the empty chair, but he's not there. I rest my head on the seat, push back and forth.

I don't hear him, only the creak of where he was and will never be again. I lift my head. "Crazy Old Coot." I slap the seat and stand up. "Changed my mind. You left me alone? Well, I'm leaving this trip alone, too. Like I want to wander around California."

Goin' back to bed. I walk toward the door and pause at the bookshelf.

His books are huge. Thicker than the *A* and the *M* encyclopedia combined. "Bet you weigh a ton." I grab a massive book; heft it up and down before replacing it on the shelf. I scan the titles, and step back to see the lowest row. Photo albums.

I kneel down and flip through a series of black-and-whites. *Young George. These should pass some time.*

I stack ten dusty albums, rise, and lug my load toward the front door. I push out, squint and blink in someone's high beams.

"Hello?" I say.

"I made it!" Lights speak with Naomi's voice. "Are you packing?" She eases out of the car and leans forward on the open car door. I blink sunspots out of my eyes. She looks like a car ad from a magazine.

"Yeah. But I decided I shouldn't." I make no sense, so I quit.

My feet stick to the steps like they had all week, only this time there's no crying woman. It's worse. It's silent and Naomi watches me, my arms full, shoulders and face twitching. She stands there all pleasant like, and there's no figuring what she thinks.

"Are you taking the truck?" She nods toward her grandpa's rustbucket.

"Thought I would, but I'm not sure it's such a good idea."

She slams her door and the barn cat scrambles inside the cab. Naomi wanders toward the truck, leans over, and caresses the lettering on the side. "'By George.' This old thing has been parked at our place ever since I can remember—I bet the truck'll make it."

She straightens, bites her lip, and throws back her hair. "I bet it could even carry two."

I hadn't planned on taking the cat. "Suppose it could."

Her face brightens. She bounces up to me, stops way too close. I try to look down but my arms are full.

"Well, then, Sam Carrier." She reaches her hand behind my neck and strokes with her fingers.

I drop all the albums right there at her feet. I want them back—they make a nice wall.

"I'll pick these up and put them in the truck." Naomi smiles. "I'll throw my stuff into the back." She kneels and gathers albums and loose pictures. "Do you need anything else from inside? We should probably get going, right?"

She said "we."

She glances up and dawn breaks.

Naomi wants to go with me. I mouth the phrase, but it doesn't take.

Naomi goes on gathering. Her windbreaker lies open. I tingle and twitch.

"But—"

She pauses and stares into me.

"I'll go lock up," I say.

I pound into the cellar. "No one. No one has the right to look like that. I'm going to California with *her?*" I pace and twitch and curse. "George, you asshole!"

She walks forward, and what should Sammy do? She touches my neck, and what should Sammy think? I kick a wall, and a framed windmill photo crashes to the ground. I exhale, bend over, and pick up shards of glass.

"Could have used you here right now. Could use a dad." I place the glass in the garbage, slow, and stare at the windmill photo. "Think you'd like this girl." My hand claws and creases the picture. "So why she's hitchin' herself to my twitchy tower I don't know. I can't speak when she's around."

Outside, an engine roars to life.

I take a deep breath. "But it's what I've dreamed of, right?"

I glance around my apartment and step into the cellar.

When I reach the front drive, Naomi's car is gone. She's in my truck.

"I squeezed the car into the shed," she calls out her window. "Mom won't know I'm gone for days and this way—"

"Whoa." I stop feet from the truck. "You didn't tell her you're goin' with me?"

"And the reason I should?"

"Figure your mom would like to know, is all."

She turns to face the dash, and then whips back around. "I would have liked to have known that the man I watched all these years was my grandpa!"

I have no answer for that.

Our gazes meet and her face changes. I know her expression well. It's the one Old Bill wears when he says he'll be home early, and the one he uses when he finally strolls in the next morning. It's rage and pride and are-you-believing-this-crap fear all rolled into one.

Naomi gently tongues her cheek.

"There's stuff with my mom you don't understand." Her voice softens. "If you knew, you might get it."

I walk around toward the driver's side. "Hey, it doesn't matter—you don't owe an explanation. Home can hurt most of all."

Naomi gives me a hesitant smile. "Yeah, it can."

I slide in. "You mind grabbing that stray?"

"Is it declawed?"

"'Course not."

She grimaces. It's the first nonadorable look I've seen her make.

"Does it bite?"

"Naw." I lift the hissing cat out of the cab.

Her eyes plead. "Can you promise I'll never have to touch animals on this trip?"

I scratch my head. "Can't even promise I know where I'm taking you."

Her eyes sparkle, and her face gleams. She breathes deep and smiles. "Where have you been all my life?"

She shuts her door, I start the engine, and together we chug toward the highway. Naomi Archer and me.

part two
jack

chapter twenty-three

OLD BILL TOOK ME ON ONE ROAD TRIP.

We pushed east and crossed the Wisconsin border. Wisconsin Dells wasn't Disneyland, but at five it felt close.

But that wasn't west. West has its own feeling. Wild and movielike. The thought of West fills me with butterflies. So does the girl seated to my right.

"I love how it feels when you start a road trip," she says. I glance at her—at her limp, unlatched seat belt. Naomi sits cross-legged on the front seat and leans back against the passenger door. She'll see every move I make.

"Never been anywhere." My arms give a solid jerk. Thank goodness there's plenty of play in the wheel. "You've taken a lot of these?"

She starts to speak, pauses, and smiles. "I've never taken a road trip in a truck. And I've never gone with just one guy."

My stomach rolls; I feel dumb. I know she's only with me

because she's mad at her mom, and her mom's a jerk, and I am, too. Naomi's too smart to hop in a truck with a guy who might try something. Forget the her-and-me stuff. To Naomi, I'm Safe Sam.

I slump in my seat. Dreams, even crazy, impossible ones starring Naomi and me, die hard. I pump out air and breathe in another idea. Crazier, safer, truer.

Feels more like a family vacation. I peek to my right. She's still there. *We'll be like a couple on a family vacation. Yep. We belong together, at least for a week or two.*

I smile at the ridiculous thought and straighten.

Go ahead. Fake-flirt all you want. Fits my new fantasy just fine.

"What are you grinning about?" Naomi asks.

Words come easy now. "You. Me. Here."

"Yeah." She nods, and shifts in her seat. "Here."

She looks at me for three hours straight. There's no hiding in this truck, and as we roll into Iowa, she pops the question.

"Tell me about the moving."

"See that sign? We're in Iowa. Ever been here before?"

I glance at her beautiful browns. She waits.

I sigh. "The jerking—it's called Tourette's."

"Why do you do it?"

"Why do you breathe?"

Naomi turns and faces the front. "You can't, like, stop it at all?"

"For a little while. Minutes. When I really think about it."

She makes a gentle thinking noise, but her face shows nothing. I don't want sympathy, but I want something. A nod. A smile. All I get is a perfect face that doesn't move a muscle. I'm an idiot for sharing. Why should a perfect person understand? Outside of the twitchy club, few do. And I hate talking to anyone who has it—hate the me I see in them.

Eyelids grow heavy. The truck drifts. My bed in Pierce would feel mighty good.

"Where are we going?" Naomi asks.

It's been a quiet few hours; her voice jars me from my semiconscious state. I straighten and ease the truck off the shoulder of the Nebraska highway.

"Henderson, Nebraska," I say. "Should be almost there. According to the map, we stay two nights."

"Two? We'd be in California if we kept going. We're not really staying that long in Nowhere, Nebraska?"

I shrug. "I'm following George's route. Don't know why, but it must've been important."

"You two really hit it off." Naomi forces a smile. "I'm jealous."

"Of me? Now, that's the first time I've heard—there. Henderson." I nod at an exit sign.

Naomi perks up and scans rows of corn. "You're kidding, right?"

We exit the interstate and follow more signs. We don't see a town. Don't see a building. The first structure we come to is a mailbox:

FA T

I stop and stare at the cockeyed letters on the side.

"We're lookin' for a family named Fast." I reach the map to Naomi. "Think this is it?"

She doesn't look, doesn't speak either. Naomi scans the fields that surround us and slowly rubs her thighs. "They're waiting for us, right?"

Again, I shrug and set the map on the dash.

We crunch up the narrow drive between rows of corn. Gravel plinks off the truck's underbelly until we wheeze to a halt in the center of the farmyard.

We sit quietly. The world rustles around us. Tens of thousands of stalks rub against one another and drown out every other sound. I don't want to move. I don't want to meet whoever lives here. I want to sit and listen, hypnotized by the everywhere rustling.

I smile at Naomi. Her gaze flits from one outbuilding to another. Her knee bounces as if she's about to explode.

"Are you okay?" I ask. Naomi tugs on my sleeve, but doesn't answer. I shrug and scan the farm and my gaze snags on the tallest windmill tower I've ever seen. I stretch out the window and look up. "Dang. You see that mill?"

I jerk back into the truck, grab for the map, and flatten it against the dash. I peer from paper to tower. "That's it. See the sketch? That mill's on my map!"

"'Bout time you show up!" A woman bursts from the house, wipes her hands, and whips off her apron. She sees me, stops, and breaks into a lovely I-was-expecting-you smile. I step out, nod in return.

"Jack Keegan." She folds her arms. "It's been what? Sixteen years?" She walks up to me. "You were in diapers then."

I wince and glance toward Naomi, who exits the truck. I don't think she heard.

"Do you know me?" I ask.

"Gracious, Jack. Surely Lydia's mentioned her dearest friends."

My face blanks, and her smile vanishes.

The woman hugs me hard and long—too long, and my arm jerks inside her squeeze. "Your mom sends letters. We'd try to call, but that man of hers—" She pushes back. "But now you're here. Let me have a look at you. When George told me you'd be coming, I could hardly believe it!"

"Hi, I'm Naomi Archer." Naomi steps around to my side of the truck.

The welcoming smile leaves the woman's face. She looks to me, to Naomi, and back to me, where she lightens. "George didn't tell me. Oh, Jack, she's pretty. Donald will be shocked—Donald!" she calls across the yard, and turns back to me. "You'll miss him if you don't hurry." She shoves me toward the barn. "Irrigation pump broke again. Come on, Naomi, tell me all about yourself. How long have you and Jack been together?"

Naomi peeks at me. "Actually, we're just friends."

Suddenly I can't hear the corn. The world feels empty, the truth stinks, and I don't know why I left home.

"Friends." Our hostess tongues the inside of her cheek. "Traveling together. My Donald's a bit old-fashioned about these things. He *will* be shocked."

She reaches around Naomi's waist and pulls her toward the farmhouse. Naomi throws a helpless look back over her shoulder, but I don't feel friendly right now and turn my back.

I shuffle up to the barn's side door. Rusted hinges squeak something fierce, and I peek inside at a collection of five Model Ts.

"Damn."

"That the kind of language I can expect, son?"

"No, sir." I straighten, as does the man bent over one of the antiques. Tall and powerful, and his muscles bulge beneath faded overalls. He stares hard for a moment, and breaks into laughter. He tosses down his wrench with a clink, walks up, and bear-hugs me.

"Ain't heard words like that 'round here since your daddy came to call. How are you, Jack?"

"I'm okay. But I go by 'Sam' now."

He wrinkles his forehead, throws open the garage door, and whistles. "Sam! Here, boy!" A great German shepherd bounds into the barn and slobbers on my legs.

"Let's get names straight. That's Sam. I'm Don. And you're Keegan's boy?"

"Guess so."

"I don't think I could stomach calling you anything but what James named you. You'll have to deal with 'Jack.'" Don smiles and I shrug. "Let's go for a drive. Hoped you'd make it before nightfall. Don't figure you've ever ridden in one of these."

Don grunts and leans in to the barn doors, returns, and cranks the Model T to life. We climb in, and with a squeeze of the horn, the car putters out of the farmyard and onto the road.

"What am I doing here?" I whisper.

I don't get an answer. Don't expect to, what with the wind and the crackle of tires in my ears. I don't know where I am or what I'm supposed to do for two days, but I ain't in Pierce, Don's nice, and Naomi is in the farmhouse. It strikes me that I'm pretty near happy.

"Where ya livin' these days?" Don lifts his pointer off the wheel to greet an oncoming driver.

"George's old place."

He nods slow, lifts another finger. "Kate and me still havin' a tough time swallowing the fact. They think it was his heart?"

"Looked like it to me, I guess."

Don faces me square. "You were with him?"

"Yeah."

"Ain't that the irony." Don's brows furrow and his lips purse.

"What?" I ask.

Don chugs into a cleared field. He shakes his head. "You were with him."

"Why does that matter?"

He smiles, jumps out, and tinkers with a pump that extends its pipe arm into a small pond.

Two minutes later, he climbs back in the classic.

"A job for Dirk."

"Who's Dork?"

His jolly face disappears. "I said *Dirk*. He's my son."

chapter twenty-four

WE PUTT INTO THE FARMYARD, PARK, AND WALK toward the warm glow of the farmhouse.

Don throws open the screen door, glances at me, and winks. "Here's the best part."

"Home!"

Two girls dash up and give Don a squeeze. Don catches them up, hoists them beard level. "Oh, my sweeties." Kiss to the left, kiss to the right. He sets them down and turns to me. "This here is Jack. He'll be staying a couple nights."

"Hi, Jack," they answer, and tug on Don's hands. "She's so pretty, Daddy. She came with Jack and her name's Naomi, but we can call her Nae. She doesn't know how to do dishes or milk cows or anything."

The thought of Naomi straddling a milking stool makes me chuckle.

"But she's so nice. Can she sleep in our room? We'll teach her everything!"

"I'm sure you will." Don tousles my hair. "You brought a girl?"

An older boy pounds down steps and barges into the room, pretty crowded by now.

"You're Mr. Keegan's son? Oh, wow. I'm Stu." He sticks out a callused hand. The kid looks thirteen. But when he moves his worked body, he adds three years.

We shake, and he turns toward Don.

"Let me do the pump, Dad, this one time." Stu's leg bounces. He's eager as a puppy.

Don exhales, nods toward the door.

Stu's gone.

"Boy loves machines." Don smiles and waggles his head. "Now, where's this pretty girl I'm hearing about?" He frowns at my hands. They're obviously pretty conservative and I can guess what he's wondering—a guy and a girl traveling the country alone together . . .

"We ain't married or nothing," I say.

"Girls, to your room."

"But, Dad!"

One look from Don sends them scurrying. He turns to me. "Lord knows times have changed, and young'uns around here are making the same kinds of trips. But this is still my home. Makes me responsible for what happens under this roof. And no one"—he pauses and steps nearer— "no one—"

"Yes, sir," I say.

Don throws his arm around me, and I flinch and jerk mightily. He escorts me through the kitchen. From deep in the house, Naomi laughs. It's light and free and I haven't yet heard it on our "family" trip. Nice to hear it now.

I enter the parlor, a fat, goofy smile plastered on my dumb face.

Naomi sits on the couch as she had in the truck, cross-legged and sideways, and gushes over some huge, husky guy. Reckon him about my age. He stares straight ahead and peeks at Nae only to offer "yes, ma'ams" and "no, ma'ams." The guy is flustered—Naomi does that—and his hands fidget in his lap. Grimy overalls, gentle smile. Had Naomi not been drooling over him, I think we'd have gotten along. But she is, so I hate him.

Don gazes from his son to Naomi. "Finish up outside, Dirk." The young man rises, walks toward me, and extends his hand. "Name's Dirk. Pleased to meet you."

"Nice to meet you, too." We grip hands and squeeze, hard. To the observer, a greeting. To our whitening knuckles, a sizing up.

"'Fore ya go, seein' you two together, I think tomorrow'd be a good time to put up my pasture fence." Don licks his lips, nods. "Start in tomorrow morning. Stu will cover in the fields."

"Yes, sir," Dirk says.

"Will this be a cute white picket fence? I love how they look."

Everyone turns and stares at Naomi.

"No." Don finally speaks. "Just sturdy posts. Don't think you'd find a white fence within a hundred miles of Henderson." He turns to Dirk. "Get going, son."

Yeah, get going. Dirk isn't in any of my family-vacation mental photographs. I want him cropped out.

"Won't you sit down, Jack?" Mrs. Fast motions toward the couch, but that's where *he* had sat. His rear imprint's on the cushion. I plop down on a rocker and face the floor, but not before I catch a confused look from Naomi.

The Fasts take seats, and for a minute no one speaks.

"Where do you go to church, Jack?" Don breaks silence.

"Nowhere."

"Lydia doesn't take you?" Don looks to his wife, who mouths the word *Bill*. Don grunts and nods. "There's no Mennonite church near you anyway." He works a toothpick inside his mouth.

"Mennonites? Don't they, like, well, I saw this movie and they were in buggies and the narrator said something about relatives marrying. That's not you two," Naomi says.

"Kate. You been holdin' out on me? Are we cousins?" Don smiles.

"You know I couldn't resist. That buggy of yours was so handsome."

Our hosts laugh, and I shoot a glance at Naomi, who blushes.

"A few ride in buggies and live simply," Kate says. "I think we look normal. I'm surprised Jack and George didn't explain more to you."

"Mom didn't let Grandpa tell me anything," Naomi explains. "I didn't even know George was my grandpa until after he died."

Don leans forward. "This is George's Naomi?" He looks to Kate, who smiles in return. "James's son and George's granddaughter. In my house. How did you two meet?"

I listen to Mrs. Fast retell the race through the rain. She leaves out my flop into the mud.

Don leans back in the love seat and puts his arm around Kate. "Small world. Two runners. Little town." He faces Naomi. "We Mennonites just try to serve folk and serve God."

He looks at me. "And you. Being James's son, don't seem right you don't meet up with God somewhere on Sundays."

"I don't think God visits Pierce. Least He doesn't visit me."

It's quiet.

A hot feeling bubbles from my gut to my mouth. Whatever I say will be ugly.

"I ain't my dad. I've only been to church twice. Once some church guy tried to cast out the 'jerky demon,' and once the preacher booted me out of the building 'cause I barked too loud." My gaze rises, rests on Naomi, who bites her lip. Not the cute bite she showed Dirk.

I rise. No one moves.

"There you have it. I'm not James. So maybe you don't want me here. Let me know and"—I look at Naomi—"I can be movin' on. Promised George I'd make it to California, and that's what I'm going to do." I grunt hard. "I need a run." Turning in to the kitchen, I hear Don clear his throat behind me.

As if I belong here or with Naomi or anywhere.

I jog to the truck and check my duffel. It's been moved inside.

I'll come back, get my things, and go. In the distance a large shadow exits the barn. "Dirk. Glad I could introduce you and Naomi. I'm sure you two will get along famously."

chapter twenty-five

MY HARD TWO-HOUR RUN ENDS. CRICKETS AND fireflies and bright stars remind me of home, but there are no trees, no landmarks, and I'm lost—lost and out of fuel. Legs cramp, and I plop onto the ground for a painful stretch. I feel exceptionally dumb.

"Still running." I wince, lie on my back, and stare. Stars visible only when a guy is nowhere shine clear down to the horizon, and I make a gravel angel for no reason. "Alone in this world."

A light flickers through cornstalks, then strengthens and becomes two lights. The beams turn on to my road and approach. I stand, brush myself off, and step into the ditch. But it's too late and a squad car slows and stops. I shield my eyes as a door slams.

"You Jack Keegan?"

"To some people."

"Don Fast put in a call. He thought you might be lost. You Jack or not?"

"Sure. Why not?" I don't mean disrespect. I just don't care.

"Hop in, son." The officer smiles and motions me into the backseat.

Minutes later I stand before the Fasts' farmhouse door. I walk the length of the porch and peek into the kitchen, where a lone bulb flickers above the sink. I don't have anything in common with them, but my legs are too tired to run anymore. I light-foot my way into the kitchen. A note rests on the table.

Jack. Please stay. Guest room off the parlor is all made up. We're glad you're here.

I crumple the paper and enter the parlor.

"Naomi," I whisper.

She half reclines on the couch, and a small lamp burns by her head. Doesn't look like she's moved from when I left.

I've not seen a perfect human sleep before. No saliva pools, no snores, only gentle breathing. I step toward her, and she shifts. Her eyes open lazily before popping wide.

Upright in an instant, she rubs her face, looks up at me, and exhales loudly.

"Sam Carrier. Don't you ever do that to me again!"

"Do what? I went for a run, is all."

"You don't get it. You really don't." She pushes by me, pauses, and turns at the base of the stairs. "Do you know how tiring it is to pretend? I need you."

She disappears up the steps.

Collapsing onto the couch, I lift heavy legs horizontal. "You're up, you're down. What am I missing, Nae?"

Morning fills with sounds of kitchen bustle. Dirk pounds around in search of food to feed his beefy body. I rise slowly and stretch. All I want is a bathroom. Dirk spots me and waves me into the kitchen.

"You run that late every night?" he asks. I straighten because at least the guy's dumb.

"No. Last night was a special case."

"How far did you go?" he asks.

"Don't know. Couple hours."

Dirk pulls up a chair, plunks down, and motions me to another. "That'd be quite a workout. Coach never makes us run like that."

I sit and get ready to vomit if he answers yes. "S'pose you're a runner, too?"

Dirk smiles. "No, sir. Tight end. University of Nebraska."

"The Cornhuskers? You play football for the Cornhuskers?" As far as I'm concerned, that team is the only thing worth knowing about Nebraska.

"Yes, sir." He jams his face full of bread and downs a glass of milk. "Had plans to leave this state, but Presidential Scholarships are hard to pass up."

"So much for dumb," I mutter, and twitch hard.

"What was that?" Dirk tosses me the bread loaf.

"So much to be done." I bite my lip hard, and exhale when he stands.

"You need to do anything before we head out?" Dirk asks.
"Likely diggin' most the day."

I remember the fence. They take days to raise.

"Maybe I should let Naomi know we'll be out there."

"I already talked with her about today's plan. But feel free.
She's upstairs."

My tongue pushes out my cheek, and my face gets hot.
Muscling in on my Naomi? This is my trip, not yours—we'll
see who can put in a day's work.

I down some water. No time for the restroom. "Let's go."

The sun sets the sky on fire as we walk to the barn. The
door opens with a creak. I step in, jump back.

"Mornin', boys." Don looks up from his milking seat. "We'll
give Naomi another crack at this tonight. Her hands chafed
something fierce her first go-round." He strains his neck to catch
a glimpse of the sky. "You're getting a late start, Dirk. Have a
tough time sleeping?" Don throws a sly smile at him and scoots
up to the Hereford. "Someone on your mind?"

Dirk reddens. "We'll catch up by noon."

He leads me past his father and out the other end of the
barn to a small shed. We grab some post diggers, sling them
over our shoulders, and traipse into an open field. Dirk pauses
and peeks at the second story, at a silhouette in the corner
bedroom. I join him and we stare at the smooth movements
behind the curtain.

So beautiful.

The curtain flies open. Naomi throws back her hair and
smiles down at us.

"Shoot!" Dirk spins. I don't have tight-end reflexes and stand gape-mouthed, caught in the act. Naomi looks beyond me to Dirk in full stride away from the house.

"Figures." I sigh.

Her gaze falls to me. She lifts her hand and presses it onto the glass, leaves it there. I feebly raise my hand. I spin and catch up to my competition.

"Think she saw me?" His foot bounces, he can't keep still.

"She sees everything."

He nods and jams his post digger into the earth. "Doesn't she make you—"

"Feel like you're walkin' around buck naked? All the time." I toss my digger onto the ground. "Where do we start?"

Dirk exhales and shakes his head violently.

So that's what I look like.

He points out the boundaries of the horse pasture. "Tore down the old fence day before you arrived. If you're leavin' tomorrow, Dad'll keep us busy until sundown. You ever done farmwork? If you're not up for it—"

I watch my shoulders and biceps tense and relax. Probably the most worked-out muscles on the planet. "Walk the boundary."

We mark the location of each hole with a stake from the pile near the clothes line and start to dig.

Plunge the digger. Pull up dirt. Check Naomi's window. Keep up with Dirk.

The pattern normalizes, and after a few hours we each have twenty holes dug.

Plunge the digger. Pull up dirt. Check Naomi—

Her face beams, and my pace quickens. So does Dirk's, who works the opposite side of the fence line. Plunge. Check. Plunge. Check. Dirt flies, shoulders twitch, mouth curses— I'm a twisted, gnarled, feverish-looking creature.

"Huh. Huh." Dirk's grunts echo across the pasture as we chase each other around the perimeter. Forty-one. Forty-two. A quick check. She's gone, and I collapse by a hole, grab my stomach, and moan.

"Might as well . . . be digging . . . my own burial plot . . ." I gasp up at blue sky. "Dirk wins. He wins. I can't keep up."

Rolling onto my side, I glance at the victor. Dirk doubles over and vomits all that hulk food onto the field.

"Well, now." I wince and rise. I walk to the next stake. Plunge. Plunge. Plunge. It takes three times as long, but I dig it.

"Hey!" Dirk's voice reaches me, and I glance in time to see another good heave.

Where's Naomi when the show gets good?

"Noon," is all he can say. He motions for me, and I jog over to him.

"You want me to carry that?" I point at his digger.

"No, sir." He straightens, his pale face level with mine. "You can sure go. Ever play football?"

I smile and waggle my head. Together we stagger toward the back door.

Dirk goes inside to take the first shower. I pace near the entrance.

After all that work, my muscles are still. Why can't she see me now?

Don strides around the corner of the house, stops, and stares at me from frothy face to mud-caked shoes. "Ain't supposed to eat dirt, Jack, just dig it out. Where's Dirk?"

"Upstairs."

"Hose down outside. Towels by the door." He points to a green one heaped on the step. "Hurry up. We're all at table."

I wait to move until he steps inside and the screen door slams behind him.

I find the outside spigot and strip to my boxers. Once clean, I drape the towel around my waist and enter the mudroom.

"Naomi."

"There you are." She looks at me a long time.

"I was just—"

She smiles, spins, and walks into the parlor.

"Dirk!" she says, and disappears into the kitchen.

"Go, go." I whisper directions to my legs, but they don't move. "Get in there, Carrier." I tiptoe forward and peek into the kitchen. Naomi's back is to me, and barf-boy sits beside her.

That's my spot!

Legs spring free. I leap into my room, dress in seconds, and pound into the hushed kitchen.

"I'm here!"

"And so we thank You, dear Lord, for all these blessings." Don cracks an eyelid and winks at me. "Including Jack, who is now here. Amen."

chapter twenty–six

"I'VE NEVER SEEN HOLES DUG AS FAST AS YOU TWO dug 'em."

Don's mealtime comment hangs with me as Dirk and I haul back to the pasture. We don't talk, which is good because the morning wasn't fair. Dirk sneaks upstairs, changes, and comes down clean. I stagger half nude into the mudroom. This Cornhusker snatched my victory. It's nothing new, just something I thought I'd left in Minnesota.

We finish the remaining ten holes and firm in the posts. It's a two-man job—there would be no more competition as we'd work side by side. Words come slow.

"So you two aren't serious?" Dirk finally asks.

I don't like the question, but he's the nicest guy I've ever hated and deserves the truth.

"Not even close." I pound a post deeper, stop, wipe sweat from my brow. "Just two people heading west in the same truck."

"Where west?"

"Jerk, California." Another swing. "Heard of it?"

He shakes his head. "Me neither," I say. "A friend of mine left me the address when he died."

Dirk chuckles. "George got us laughing like no one else. Loved it when he passed through."

My sledgehammer falls to the ground.

He continues: "Oh yeah, I knew George. He'd stop in, or we'd head north to see him and your dad."

"You saw my dad?"

"That's what I'm told, but I was too young to remember." Dirk takes a swig of water and reaches me the bottle. "We were up when his accident happened."

I freeze mid-drink, and water gushes down my cheeks.

"Had to be hard losing him so young." Dirk takes the bottle from my hands. "You okay?"

I twitch and sit. "Didn't know you folks knew him like that."

"You're kidding. Dad's full of stories, ask him."

He whistles and gets to work. I stand, lift my hammer, and pound. But I'm tired and weak and finishing this job doesn't matter anymore.

Dirk blabbers—his sentences sprinkled with "Naomi" like Old Bill sprinkles pepper on tomatoes. That's fine by me, but though it aches my gut, I want more about Dad.

In the distance, Stu pops out of the fields and crosses the pasture. He stares at the hundred or so wooden fingers poking straight and true out of the ground. Stu scratches his head. "All today? What got into you two?"

Dirk elbows me and smiles. "More like a *who*, right?"

For once, the thought of Naomi brings no joy.

Laughter floats from the front of the farmhouse, and while the Fast brothers head inside to clean up, I wander toward the sound that comes from the cattle barn. I peek inside. Naomi sits with jaws clenched in front of a full cow and an empty bucket.

"I'll milk you if it's the last thing I do," Naomi says, and throws back her hair.

"Will be if you keep squeezing like that." Lizbeth laughs along with Mary. The girls part as I walk in from behind.

"They give you any pointers?" I ask.

Naomi whips around. "They just yank on this thing and milk comes out." She scowls at Mary. "But now they're content giggling at me, aren't you?"

The two break into more laughter.

"Scoot up," I say.

I ease down behind Naomi on the stool, and my legs straddle her body. I catch a whiff of myself, wince, and try to keep space. "Lean over so I can reach." She moves forward, and I wrap my arms around her and grab the udder. My mouth fills with sweet-smelling hair.

"I'm sorry." I start to stand. "I haven't showered yet. I must—"

"Stay." Naomi grabs my forearm, pulls me against her, and whispers, "Show me."

My arm jerks and twitches within her grasp, and half of me

wants to run, but I force myself to sit. "It's in the wrist and fingers. Squeeze from the the top." A shot of milk hits the pail.

"Let me try."

Naomi fights that cow.

"Too much pull." I wrap my hand around hers, my body around hers. "Like this, and this."

After a few squirts, she turns her head and smiles. I feel her breath on the side of my cheek, and I tense and stare straight ahead.

"It's about relaxing, isn't it?" she asks.

I let go of her hand and sit back. "Yeah. Relaxing."

She pats that cow, and soon milks with ease.

"I did it. I did it!"

I stand and back up. "Yeah. You did it. Lizbeth, you could have given her a lesson."

I turn and stare at the faces of Don and Kate. Mr. Fast's hard stare travels from Naomi to me and back to her. But Mrs. Fast smiles and speaks softly. "Supper time."

My chest tingles all through my shower.

"What was I doing, George? I lost my head. Like I have a right to saddle up to your granddaughter and bear-hug her from behind. What do I say to her now?"

I step out of the shower and peek out the window. The Fasts circle out front for a pre–barbecue blessing.

I'm sure there will be plenty of good stories told tonight, but I got something to do. I walk into my room, close the door behind me, and fall back against it.

What a fool. Like anyone wants to be that close to me. I wrapped my arms right around her.

I walk over to the desk, where I grab pen and paper.

Dear,

I ball up the sheet and toss it back over my shoulder.

Naomi,
I messed up. I should never have

"I can't even write it!" I grind my teeth, exhale hard, and face my pad.

Hey, I shouldn't have assumed I could reach around you like that. I understand if you don't want to be near me anymore. Dirk's a good guy. So maybe we need to talk about the rest of the trip. Anyway, Sorry.
Sam

I walk my note up to her bedroom and freeze. I know the soft sound coming from inside her room, the sounds Mom made late into the night. Naomi's gentle cry grabs my gut and squeezes.

What is going on?

I stare down at my note. It's clear I don't know Naomi at all, don't know what aches her when she's alone, and that makes what I did worse. I quickly slip the paper beneath the door, and jog down to my room. Minutes later there's a knock. I don't make a move to get it.

I don't see Naomi that evening, and she's not at breakfast. I feel too stupid to ask. I poke at eggs and trudge back out to finish hanging the rails.

Dirk's in fine form.

"Let's get these hung." He reaches down and lifts a rail into position against the post. "I'd like to go to the city this afternoon before you go." Dirk whistles and tosses his hammer into the air, catches it.

"What city?"

"I'm thinking I'll go to Lincoln with Naomi. Say, you don't mind me showing her around, do ya?"

Oh, hell, no. Makes me all cuddly inside.

I hoist the other end of the rail, place the nail, and pound my thumb.

"Ah! Dammit." I drop the plank and shake my hand. "Go ahead. I don't care what you do."

"Great!"

He whistles and chuckles and waits patiently for me to hang my end of the rail. I move to the next post and hate him. Then the idea comes.

"Let me follow you around the perimeter," I say, and we switch places. Together we lift the plank, pound in our ends with three nails, and move to the next post.

While Dirk pounds, I dig out two of his nails and pound in only one myself. When he turns to move on, I give the whole

rail a whack, and it hangs a-kilter. All afternoon we work—
Dirk in his happy place and me sabotaging the fence. We reach
the last rail just as Kate rings the lunch bell.

"Hey! Great timing!" Dirk runs his hand through his hair
and straightens.

"Um, Dirk? Looking at the fence, it seems a little . . .
crooked."

"What do you mean?" He squints at the rails and drops
his hammer. "No. No. He runs to the last post. "What's
happening?"

"Bunch of your nails were loose when I came to 'em." I
shake my head. "I had trouble, too. Oh well, we almost got 'er
done." I walk cheerily toward the house and listen to Dirk's
frantic pounding.

"Need you inside, Dirk," Mr. Fast booms from the
farmhouse.

"But I was going to take Naomi—"

Mr. Fast stares and Dirk kicks at the ground and hollers,
"Fine!"

Don closes the back door, and Dirk loses it.

I wash and duck into my room to change.

Naomi sits on my bed, her skin glistening. I stop inside the
doorway and think about my hands on that skin. She looks
better than ever in that halter-top thing and those shorts.

"Dirk won't be able to take you into the city."

She stands and stares and my mouth quits working. It's a
new stare and reminds me of a cat before it pounces. I can't

look down. She approaches and reaches out her arms and lays them on jumpy shoulders. Her hand slides into my hair and pulls down my head. I feel her cheek against mine, her body against mine.

"I got your note," she whispers, and her lips brush against my face. "Consider this permission." Naomi presses into me, stays a moment, and glides out the door as the letter I wrote flutters to my feet.

George, she's as tough to figure out as you were.

The bell sounds again and I straighten, but it's too warm to eat.

Naomi sits by Dirk at the table. I stare at my bread.

"You put in a full day. Aren't you hungry, Jack?" Don says.

"I was, but now I'm not."

I try not to peek at Naomi, but I can't help it. Her eyes are magnets.

"Hungry," I stammer.

Naomi's eyes sparkle.

After lunch, I head into my room to pack.

"George, your granddaughter is . . . distracting." I jam shirts into my duffel. "She keeps doing stuff. I apologize and she hugs me. Or did I hug her? Oh crap, probably screwed up again."

My gut turns. I'm anxious to be on the road, anxious to get Naomi away from Dirk. I'm anxious to get somewhere where I'm not so confused about Dad. I glance over the map.

Next stop another two-nighter? Don't know if I can handle this.

chapter twenty-seven

NAOMI'S FOOTSTEPS CREAK THE HARDWOOD floors above me. Must be packing. I walk my things out to the truck and glance toward the shed. Don sits in a lawn chair and watches me. There's an empty chair next to his, and I know he wants me in it. But he doesn't wave me over, so I quickly turn back toward the farmhouse.

"Your dad built that."

I stop. "What?"

"Windmill."

I stare way up at fins spinning free.

"I heard he built those. Sort of wondered if he did this one."
I take another step toward the house.

"Three days is all it took. Lydia stayed with us while he worked."

I turn toward Don. "Mom's been here?"

"Of course. Your folks slept in the same bed you did."

I squirm and run fingers through my hair.

"And you slept in Dirk's crib right beside 'em."

My feet move toward the empty chair. I don't want to sit down, but I can't shake my question.

"Did they look happy?"

"They *were* happy."

"'Cause there's this problem," I say. "I saw them in a picture lookin' all happy, but I know they weren't 'cause Old Bill's told me stuff. And why would he ditch Mom and me if they were happy?"

"Oh," Don whispers. His knuckles whiten on his chair. I said something and he's pissed, and I'm scared.

Footsteps approach from behind, and we turn our heads. Kate walks up and stands behind Don and rubs his neck. Don looks up at her, smiles weakly, and then turns to me.

"When George called and said you'd be coming, I told him to come along. He said, 'Not this time, Don, got a feeling.' He said that and my stomach flipped. And it never flips, does it, Kate?"

She smiles. "That's right. Only one other time I know of."

They both look at me. Long, serious looks. It's spooky, and my stomach flips, too.

"You know your folks and us spent a lot of holidays together? Kate and Lydia grew up together, kept in touch for a long time," Don says.

"I didn't know."

He nods. "We were up the night of the crash."

"Dirk did tell me that."

"George was there." Kate walks in front of us and folds her arms. "Never could pry him away from James. Oh, honey, do you remember how hot Jack was?"

She looks back to me. "Imagine you've heard this enough times from Lydia."

I shake my head.

"You had such a fever," she says. "Your dad went out for medicine."

Don nods. "Just a quick run to the drugstore. It was snowing so hard. Remember how James acted?" Don reaches up and squeezes Kate's hand. "Usually a man says, 'Be right back.' But James didn't say a thing. He gave Lydia a kiss. Not a quick one neither. Darn near made my wife blush."

Kate slaps Don on the shoulder.

"Well, it's true. Then he went into the room where you whimpered, and I swear I heard him cry right along with you."

I stand back up and face the couple. No one seems eager to go on.

Finally Kate shakes her head. "Of all the nights to have a snowstorm. An hour later we got the call."

"Wait. I was sick?" I feel sick now.

Don nods.

"So when did he pick up the woman?"

"Woman," Don says.

"Yeah, and the booze. When he wrapped his drunk body around a telephone pole. They found him with a woman."

Don and Kate look at each other. Kate moves in front of me, kneels, and grabs my twitching right hand. "There was no liquor. There wasn't a woman, Jack. It was George. George went with your father that night. He was with him when he died. The pole is right, but, oh, Jack, no; it was George. He said your dad hung on for hours. That's when he scribbled you the note."

I stare at her.

"Hasn't George given it to you?"

I stand up and cough hard. I need to run. I can't run. My legs buckle, and Don eases me into the chair, wraps his big arm around my shoulder.

"Do you have your dad's letter, son?" he asks.

"Yeah," I whisper. "George gave it to me a few weeks back at graduation."

Don nods. "He called years ago. Asked our advice on that. He knew you had it rough. But your dad made him promise not to intervene until you were older, not if there was another man in Lydia's life. We told him James knew what he was doing, that it wouldn't be right to bust up a family, even one with Bill in it." He exhales hard. "Did we counsel wrong?"

My head is empty and light and I don't know what to believe. But I feel a tug so strong it almost yanks me out of my chair. I'd give anything for George and Don to be right, anything for Old Bill to be what he's always been—a liar. But I've heard his crap so long, and I can't believe anyone would think about *my* life when they're dying.

I lean in to Don's shoulder. "Tell me again."

"What, Jack?"

"Tell me there was no woman. Tell me Dad loved Mom. Tell me what happened."

Donald straightens me and turns to face me. "James died because of a bad storm and an icy road and a telephone pole."

Kate squeezes my hands. "And he died loving your mom more than anyone, except his son."

My arms hang limp, and a tickle worms around my empty head—I almost believe her. I don't know why Mom never told me. I only know that if she were here, I couldn't look her in the eye.

Mom's eye.

The yellow-and-blue one. There were colorful reasons why she kept her mouth shut.

Don breaks the silence.

"Do you think a man knows his time? Like your dad, or George?"

His eyes tell me it's an honest question.

"How could they?" I say.

Don nods. "Doesn't explain this trip you're on, though, does it?"

"No."

The wind whistles and shivers my spine. From far above the windmill creaks.

"Do you know why I'm going to California, Don? Did George tell you anything?"

"He did not." Don pushes himself up. "But if George wants you there . . . where do you go from here?"

I dash to my truck and grab the map. "It's a weird route." I jog back and hand it to Don. He opens it, stares, and grins.

"Ain't so strange. He's sending you along windmill road." He shakes his head and chuckles. "This used to hang in your folks' apartment. I remember these little pictures. It's your dad's old map, but George probably added the names and dates." He points at each sketch. "Your father built each one of these. I've seen this one; it's next on your journey. And mine, of course." He rubs his meaty finger gently over the last two. "But these? Only heard about them."

He hands me the map; it's a different map now. I fold it carefully and smooth out the creases.

Don frowns at my truck and folds his arms. "She won't make it through the Rockies." He walks up to it and traces the lettering with his finger.

"She'll have to." I wipe my face and sigh. Don looks at Kate, who smiles and nods.

"Come on," Don says.

We leave Kate and walk to the second barn. Don lifts the door on a bright orange '55 Chevy. It's beautiful even beneath the thin layer of dust. I circle it, and wipe grime from its number: 55.

"Man." I lean over and peek inside. She's immaculate. "What's it worth?"

Don kicks the tire. "One brown truck."

chapter twenty-eight

LIGHT RAIN FALLS AS NAOMI AND I CARRY OUR bags toward the barn. We leave Don and Kate, arms around each other, standing on the porch. Lizbeth and Mary stomp through farmyard muck. Dirk rocks on the porch swing with arms crossed, his eyes slits. Naomi declined his offer to carry her bags. I said he could carry mine, but patient, perfect Mennonites must have their limits.

"So where's the truck?" Naomi asks.

"There's been a change." I open the barn door. "Do you like orange?"

She gasps and furrows her brow. She turns with a grin.

I load our things in the backseat.

"Let's see if she sounds as good as she looks."

The Chevy roars. I know engines, and judging by the sound, this one's been itching for an adventure. I feather the accelerator, and the car darts forward into the yard.

I let it idle and walk with Naomi back to the porch. With each step I feel lonelier. I turn and take a last look at the truck parked in the barn. It's a great trade, my brain knows it, but my chest is tight. It's like losing George all over again.

The family gathers around us.

"It's traditional to bless all those who stay here." Don says. "You mind?"

Naomi squirms, and I twitch.

"Takin' that as a green light. Dear Father . . ."

Big Don prays long, but it's different from when TV preachers pray. I know Don thinks someone is paying attention.

"You two take care." Kate hugs us and pecks our cheeks. Don follows with bear hugs of his own.

"You're a lot like your dad," Don says.

"I know, twitchin' and all."

He looks sharp into my eyes and softens his gaze. "No. Gentle James lives on in Gentle Jack."

Before I can respond, the girls run up and cling to Naomi.

"You coming back?" Lizbeth asks.

"I don't know." Naomi wipes her shirt. "Depends on Sam."

Dirk strides up to me, extends his hand, and squeezes. Hard. "Drive safe." He moves to Naomi. Hurt, puppy eyes look strange on a tight end's body. He starts to speak, peeks at me, and suddenly lunges toward Naomi. It's half hug, half tackle, and I'm sure they're going down, but Dirk regains his footing. "Come on back anytime." Another glance at me, and he quick reaches into his pocket. He pulls out a note and stuffs it into her hand.

"For me? Thanks!" Naomi turns to me. "Hang on to this for me, will you, Sam? I don't have pockets, and I don't want to lose it."

There's agony in Dirk's eyes as he follows the paper into my hand. Don covers his face with his big paw, but can't hide the chuckle that works his body.

Kate sighs. "If you two are going to make Kansas by nightfall, you better get moving. Give our best to Turk and Trish."

We hop in, and I give the gas a flutter.

Don reaches his head into the car. "South on 81 until 150. Brings you right into Hillsboro. Kansas has weather, so drive carefully."

"Thanks for everything." I take my hands off the wheel. "For letting us stay, and for the car; do I owe you anything?"

"Most people would leave a gift."

Without hesitation, Naomi hops out of the car, jogs up to Big Don, and kisses his rain-soaked cheek. The big guy flushes. She turns to Stu and freezes the poor teen. Naomi finally reaches Dirk, stops inches in front of him. Dirk's eyes grow, he shifts his feet, brushes his hair back, wipes his brow.

And passes out. Falls like a log into the mud. The family kneels around him.

Kate looks up. "That'll do, Naomi."

"Could I see my letter?" Naomi reaches out her hand, but I'm driving and pretend not to see it.

She hits my shoulder. I dig in my pocket for the note. My fingers wrap around it and I want to throw it out the window into the storm. But my arm obeys her instead of me. She has it, reads it, and wears a big smile.

"What does it say?"

She glances at me and back down toward the sheet. "It's my letter."

Minutes later she reads it again. I stretch back, peek over, and try to catch a few sentences.

"Sam!" She folds the paper and scolds me with her look. "Here. Would you mind holding on to it?"

I grab the note and squirm it into my front pocket. It's not fair to be this close if I can't see. Naomi's not fair.

"Were you going to kiss him?" I ask.

"Yeah. Is there a problem with that?"

I turn the windshield wiper to high.

"A kiss is . . . well, doesn't a kiss mean—" I twitch hard. "Is there anyone you *wouldn't* kiss?"

She whips her body toward me. "And what do you mean by that?"

"Nothing, I—"

"Oh, no. You said it. What do you mean?"

My body jumps. Left shoulder, right shoulder. Fingers stretch, face muscles stretch. *What was I saying?* Rain sheets across the glass, and I peer ahead. *Oh, hell!*

"When you kissed me during the snowstorm, didn't it mean anything to you?"

I puff out steam and wait for her rage.

Her body softens, and she sweeps the hair off her face. "No."

"No?" My hand twitches so hard we swerve onto the chopped shoulder. I veer back onto the road. "No? Nothing?" My voice raises over the thunder. "You change my life and don't give it a thought? Well, I did! Plenty!" I wipe sweaty hair from my eyes. "I thought about that kiss day and night for months. Months! So no more casual, oh-what-the-hell-I'll-kiss-Sam stuff. Take your charity affection somewhere else—find a different monster to kiss. One who didn't have a dad who went out in a storm to get medicine—" I'm suddenly exhausted and my muscles still and only the pounding rain has any energy left.

I peek at what I've done. Naomi stares straight ahead. Unreadable.

"Just that," I say, "it mattered to me, is all."

"I wouldn't kiss a monster."

Hours of torturous silence had passed since I spoke.

"You asked if there was anyone I wouldn't kiss." Naomi pauses. "I don't think I'd kiss a monster."

I shoot a glance in time to catch a slow exhale.

"On second thought," she says, "I have."

Her words pierce. She's never mocked me or ripped my Tourette's before. Finally, the cruel truth. I take a deep breath.

Least I know where I stand. A monster.

"I understand," I say.

She slowly turns her head as I make the left onto 150. She looks confused. Ahead, skies lighten behind the Hillsboro sign. Yep, good to know where I stand. Being a creature sucks, but at least she finally said it. So it's a "Beauty and the Beast" type of relationship. Least I didn't lose my "bride" to Dirk.

Don't go getting fantasy and reality mixed up, Sam. Look at her.

I do and my mouth flops open and I can't stop my blurt. "You're beautiful." The car swerves. "Sorry. Stuff pops out."

Naomi lays her head against the window. "Beautiful, huh?"

I slow as we enter Hillsboro. The town appears from nowhere, grows right up from surrounding fields. A water tower and a grain elevator—the only tall stuff there is.

A small sign reads: WELCOME TO HILLSBORO. HOME OF TABOR COLLEGE.

Great, more college guys. If Naomi's still in this car when we pull out of here, I'll call this stop a success.

"Two nights in lovely Hillsboro, coming right up." I drive to a rambler on A Street and stop. "Doesn't look like they have a buggy either," I say, and open the door. A cat runs out from beneath the partially lowered garage door and rubs against my leg. I'm sick of cats.

"Sam." Naomi's eyes plead. "Save time for a walk tonight. We need to talk."

chapter twenty-nine

WELCOME, JACK! MAKE YOURSELF AT HOME. YOU'LL have Aaron's room and the rest of the basement to yourself. Trish is covering the store. I'm with Mom at the hospital. Be back later. Turk

I rip the sheet off the screen door.

"They're not expecting me either." Naomi turns and looks around. "Hope they won't be put off by us traveling together."

"Reckon not."

The evening's hot, the breeze is hot. Ramblers and old farmhouses line streets buckling in the heat. Large trees stretch their limbs over the tiny road, and somehow the grass is green. A steamy oasis in the heart of farm country.

"Let's bring our stuff in." I head down the steps. "Maybe we can take that walk now. According to the map, there's a windmill in this town that I should probably find."

We haul our things into the basement and make our way

back outside. Tree roots lift the sidewalk's concrete squares and make the walkway hazardous. We stroll in silence.

I jerk my neck, and my gaze leaves the uneven pavement. Concrete snags me and I stumble.

"Have you had that all your life?" Naomi asks.

"No." I pull ahead. "Mom says I was normal until six. Woke up one day and, well, this. It's a gift from my dad." A glance at her. "How about you? Been perfect all your life?"

She stops and her hands rise to her hips. "Okay, like that." Naomi stares at me, "Why did you say that?"

I think hard. "Guess I'm making a joke—no, that's not true. I think you're—you seem pretty perfect. Nice and all."

I exhale hard and blink three times.

Naomi grabs my hands, spins, and faces me. She lifts her arms and rests them on my shoulders.

"But you're not trying—when you say that, you just mean—" She lets her head fall to the side.

I stare at my shoes, kick a rock, and my shoulders tense and fall limp. "I don't know what I'm trying to do. Probably everything I say sounds dumb compared to whoever." I peek at her. "It's hard to look at you and say anything that makes sense."

She lifts my chin and gently bites her lip.

"Then look at me some more."

"Jack? Jack Keegan, is that you?" I spin toward the street and nod. A pleasant-looking lady peers out of a white minivan. "I'm Trish! You look just as I'd imagined. And hello to you, young lady." Trish smiles back at me. "How'd you end up with a beautiful girl like this?"

"My name's Naomi." She raises her eyebrows and grins. "It happened really fast. Just last October we ran a race together for the first time." Naomi squeezes my hand. "And then a few weeks ago there he is, standing in the aisle at the ceremony."

Trish gasps and covers her mouth. I cough and do the same.

"We had no idea. Was there no announcement?" Trish sighs. "Of course, it has been years since we've seen Lydia. Friends do move on."

I stand gape-mouthed and stare at Naomi. She winks.

"I'm heading over to the hospital, Jack. Turk called and Mother's taken a bad turn." Trish forces a smile. "This may be awkward, but I know she would love to see you. She loved your father and your mother so much." Trish looks at Naomi. "Not sure how alert Mother is, but she'd love to meet your wife. It was Nadine, wasn't it?"

I raise my hand. "Wait a min—"

"It's Naomi," she says.

"Such a pretty name. Hop in," Trish says.

Naomi grabs my hand and pulls me toward the van. I follow her around to the passenger side. Naomi stops, stares at the handle.

"*What* are you doing?" I hiss.

"Aren't you going to get my door, honey?"

"I—we can't *not* tell them."

"Grandma's waiting."

I reach for the handle and open up to a smile from Trish.

"I remember when Turk used to do that. Young love, so beautiful."

I slam the door on beautiful.

The hospital sets clear across town. A good five-minute drive. Plenty of time for my muscles to work into a frenzy.

Trish hops out, but Naomi sits in the car and waits.

"Get her door, and let's go." Trish smiles at me and heads for the entrance.

I hop out and play the gentleman. "You can't keep this up."

"Me?" Naomi pats my cheek. "It was just a joke. And you could have said something, too."

"*I* could?" I point at my chest. "*I* wasn't the one who said it in the first place."

Naomi steps nearer. "Said what?" She strokes behind my neck, and my brain blanks.

"Whatever we were talking about!" My arm flings to the side, and I clasp hands behind me to keep from whacking her. "Just 'cause I've thought about it don't mean I'd say it."

She pulls her hand from my neck and covers her mouth.

"You think about us being married?" Naomi steps back.

Lie, Sam, lie!

"I think—I think we should get in there!" I pull free and double-time it into the hospital.

It's easy to find the right room. Outside her door, twenty people circle in the hall.

"Come over, Jack, meet some friends of your parents," Trish calls.

"Hey," I say.

Every person in that hall knows Dad and George, and I'm surrounded by stories of those two restoring an old mill in town.

"They made a bunch of trips down here, maybe ten? All before you were born." A bug-eyed man steps way too close. "Probably most of us put them up for a night or two, isn't that right?"

That starts more smiles and nods and stories. Minutes later, it quiets, and Bug Eyes grabs my forearm.

"Lydia ever tell you stories about crazy Larry Epp?" I figure he's asking about himself.

"No. She didn't."

"How about the Wiebes?"

I turn around to eager faces. "I'm sorry."

"It's okay." Larry says, "Rumor has it that her second marriage did strange things to Lydia." He pats my shoulder and it jumps. People smile. "I think I speak for all of us when I say it's a pleasure to meet the next Keegan in line."

I breathe deep. "I would like to know where that mill is—"

"Larry spoke of marriage." Trish's cheery voice rings out. "I'm sorry, Jack, I completely forgot. Where's that beautiful wife of yours?"

"About that—" I say.

"James's son? Married?" The circle closes in on me.

Oh, crap!

"How quick they grow!"

Everyone stares and this is my chance. I can end this joke once and for all.

"Naomi's just—she was right behind me. Hang on." I walk out to the van. No sign of her.

I spend an hour walking the hospital grounds. I try to think of one decent reason Naomi would pull this marriage gag, but I can't and reenter the building.

The hallway is empty, and I reach the room and find a sleeping grandma. Ninety-eight and full of cancer means a lot of morphine. A man is with her, but he doesn't turn, and I quietly retreat into the hallway.

"Are you all moved in?" he asks.

"You're Mr. Penner?"

"Turk is fine. Please come in."

Turk sits on the foot of the bed and stares at the motionless old woman. "Mother will be so pleased you came." He yawns. "I'm sorry you won't get to say hello today, maybe tomorrow."

"Yeah, tomorrow." I plop into the uncomfortable hospital chair. "I met so many people tonight. People acted like they knew Dad pretty well." I squirm. "I should know this, but are you and me related?"

"No." Turk sighs. "You don't have relatives here. But everyone you meet in this town, at least the older ones, likely remember your father and that Old Coot. Mom would best of all." He massages his mother's toes and bows his head. "Your father spent so much time here before you came along." He looks at me, into me, and nods. "It's probably been twenty years, but Keegans aren't forgettable men."

chapter thirty

AN EVENING JOG CLEARS MY MIND. I COULD RUN forever, but I need to get settled. I slip inside the Penners' door and head downstairs to the basement family room. I'm surrounded by a thick kind of quiet.

"Naomi called me a monster." I whip off my shirt and fling it across the room. It flutters onto an oversize cat pillow. "In the car she said it to my face."

I pace the basement.

"So it was clear, right? Her and me was clear. But now—" I rip off my shoes and hurl them against a wall. "It's all messed up again, and she goes right on pretending."

Now the whole town thinks we're together.

A grandfather clock ticks loudly in the corner. In the quiet, the beats are hypnotic. "Who'd be with a monster?" I whisper.

I stretch and make it as far as the couch before I collapse. The clock beats on.

Fifteen, sixteen. I rub my face hard. *I'm as bad as Old Bill.*

In five minutes, all muscles are at rest.

"Sam."

Against the moonlight that streams in the basement's one window, Naomi's silhouette shifts. One large T-shirt. All that stands between me and her smooth body.

I blink hard and reach for a sheet to cover myself, but it's only me on the couch—me in sweat-drenched running clothes. She says nothing, and I swallow hard.

"Sam," she whispers, "did you tell them?"

She steps closer. Her eyes sparkle.

"Tell them what?" I ask.

She eases onto the edge of couch and kneels over me. I shift my legs to make room. I feel bare legs against the back of my hand, and she tosses back her hair. "Did you tell them?"

"No."

Naomi straddles my active body, and bends down. Her hair brushes my face.

"Why not?" she whispers. Her chest presses into mine.

"I—I don't know." Fire scorches my body, and my movements change and soften. "Maybe I—"

Naomi lays her finger across my lips.

"Where's your hand?" she asks.

"I think at the end of my arm?"

Naomi sits upright. She grasps my hand and draws it toward herself. I feel her body tense and relax, and she bends down for a kiss.

A giant fur ball screeches and lands near my head.

"Sam!" Naomi screams, and a mouse squeaks and scurries by my neck. Naomi falls off the couch, jumps to her feet, and trips over the coffee table. I hear her pant.

Room lights flick on and blind me. Footsteps pound down the stairs.

"What's going on? Jack, Naomi?"

Turk dashes into the room. He squints at Naomi, clears his throat, and whips around. He speaks with his back to us.

"I heard screams. Are you two okay?"

Naomi slaps my leg, and I sit up.

"What happened, Turk?" Trish runs down the stairs, the whole time gathering her robe about her. Her gaze darts from me to Naomi and back to me. She spins, too, and stands shoulder to shoulder with her husband.

"We got startled," I say.

Even from the back, I know they're confused. "Come with me, Naomi," Trish says, and reaches her hand back toward us. Naomi looks at me.

"We'll put on some tea. That first year together can be a confusing one, can't it, Turk?"

"I remember well."

"But we're okay now. Sam and I will be fine," Naomi says.

"Nonsense." Trish turns and grabs Naomi. She gives her arm a tug. "I have sense about these things, don't I, Turk?"

"Yes, you do."

"And a talk is in order." Trish pulls Naomi up the stairs. "First off, it's no business of mine what you've done and with whom before you're hitched. But now you must leave others behind. Imagine how Jack feels, you calling him Sam during an intimate situation."

Turk turns. "Trish will straighten her out." He frowns, and offers a sympathetic sigh. "Best *you* can do tonight"—he smiles—"is try and get some rest."

He starts to leave, pauses. "Last time I saw James, Lydia was three months pregnant. James talked a lot about his hopes for you." Turk nods. "With all the pressure on young kids these days, well, he'd be proud that you waited until marriage to work through all this. I know he's smiling down on you right now. Good night, Jack."

Turk plods up the stairs. It's just me and the clock.

I crawl into bed. Muffled voices float down from above.

She won't be coming back down. I swat the mattress. Voices stop, and my thoughts clear.

I exhale hard.

"Are you really looking down on me?"

"Good morning, Jack."

Naomi sits at the kitchen table. I can't look at her. I'm embarrassed and don't know why.

"I suppose Turk gave you a talk, too," Naomi says, and gestures toward a chair.

"Kind of." I plop down.

Naomi lowers her head, tries to catch my gaze. "What's wrong, Sam—I mean Jack." She sighs. "This name change is going to be tough."

My embarrassment leaves. I know why I feel like such a loser.

"I have to tell them."

"Oh no, you don't. Not after last night. Now they'd just think I was trampy. That's why I wanted to see you early, to get stories straight. Believe me, our lack of rings took creativity. I played up the Christmas Eve story, the run wasn't as romantic."

I puff out a blast of air. It's nice hearing her talk about us, even if it's a fake us. Before the trip, I'd have nodded and smiled and gone along with anything. But not now—now I have to look into her smile and doom myself.

"Turk and my dad talked about me. Before I was born, they were talking, and, well, this whole story is crazy, but they believe it, believe me, because of Dad." I run my hand through my hair. "They trust us totally. Doesn't that eat at you a little?"

Naomi's face is blank.

"I need to straighten this out," I say quietly.

"But last night. Didn't you want—"

"It's got nothing to do with wanting."

Her look jumps from hurt to angry. Naomi rises and shoves in her chair. "You jerk." She storms out the door.

I stare at twitchy fingers. It's hard to argue.

chapter thirty-one

ALL FOUR PENNERS LEAVE SHORTLY AFTER NAOMI. Turk to the hospital, Trish to the family bookstore, Aaron to baseball practice, and Nate to a round of golf.

It's my first glimpse of the boys. They have sixteen-year-old faces, but they stand six and a half feet tall.

"Hey," Aaron says, catching me still plunked at the table. "You want to come with me tonight? You showed up at a good time, Frontier Days. All sorts of stuff going on. Rodeo, fireworks, it's awesome."

I grunt yes and watch the kids jostle out the door.

I sigh. "This'll be a long day." I wander the house, stare in the fridge, and peer outside.

Too hot for a jog. Probably fine for a walk.

I open the door and all air sucks from my lungs. I grimace and step forward. Streets are near empty. Ahead, one car crawls by.

Main Street.

I wander the row of shops. They're open, but no one is out. I find shade beneath a large awning and scan the street. Opposite me stands Penner's Book Store.

"Why not?"

I enter the store to the tinkling of bells. Trish looks up from behind the counter.

"Jack! Hoped you'd come. Turk just called. Grandma's better. Your wife's with her now."

My wife. I run my hands through my hair in rapid succession and twitch mightily.

Trish smiles and nods. "So much like your father."

"That's what I hear." I breathe deep and shuffle toward the counter. The store is empty except for Trish, me, and a lie so heavy I can barely move. But I have to. I have to drag it and lift it and show Trish even though she'll probably boot me out of her house when she sees it.

I reach Trish and take a deep breath. "I have to be honest." A book display catches my eye. "I've never read any of these." I jerk a paperback off the shelf, crease the cover, and wince. I'm such a wimp.

Trish shrugs and comes from behind the counter. "Had a good talk with Naomi last night. I know you two didn't ask for counsel, but I can't help but lend a hand when I see a way."

"About what you saw—"

"That lovely lady is bright. You keep treating her right."

I gulp. "I'll try. It's just—"

"She told me how you met. I see why she wants to spend her life with you."

"Will you please let me say—she said that?"

"Oh, and so much more." Trish gives me a big hug. "Have I told you how much you're like your father?"

I wriggle free and step back. "Like, exactly, what was the so-much-more she said?"

"Things need to pass from Naomi to you without me in between. I shouldn't say anything else."

I'm tired of being the only one who has no idea what's going on. I gently kick a CD display with my foot.

"She did tell me how safe she feels in your arms." Trish walks back behind the counter and moves the pot of flower pens to the other side of the desk. "A girl without a father needs that kind of security."

"Go on."

"Like I said, not another word." Trish flips through some papers, pauses, her face all moony. "But your wedding? So beautiful, so romantic." She sighs. "So like—" She shakes her head. "My Turk is one smart man, but he took me to Sears on the way to our honeymoon." Trish raises an eyebrow. "Feel free to share ideas with my oaf."

I can't take it and I won't give wedding advice. Bells tinkle behind me. A lady enters with five small children. Kids fan out and race around, and I don't have much time. I jump toward Trish at the counter, the book in my hands now a pulpy mess.

I check the family once more. Like my limbs, they're everywhere.

I lean over the counter and whisper, "Listen. Oh, crap, how do I say this?"

Trish's eyes widen.

"Sorry, but my damn Tourette's—I mean, well, my—"

I lose arm control and left-hook a tray of pennies. Old Abe clanks off book racks, rolls around the floor. Kids scream for joy and race after rolling coins.

I spin, and my shoulder leaps. The pulpy book flies from my hand and cuffs a boy across the jaw. He shouts and drops onto the floor tiles—his family swarms around him.

"No! Sorry! I didn't mean to throw it." I launch my body in the direction of the poor kid to help him up, to tell him I meant no harm, but my left foot jerks and catches a book display. It teeters. I fling arms around it and knock it to the ground.

"Crap!"

"Children, come quickly!" their mother says.

"Jack, what on earth—" Trish crouches behind the counter.

But there's no stopping me. I reach down and scoop an armful of books. I try to lift the display stand but stumble over it, and stagger forward after the fleeing family.

The mother shrieks, and turns. She blocks my way to the door. She's not moving, but I can't stop. I lurch, slip on a volume, and tumble into her midsection. We plow to the floor.

"Let me go!" she screams, and kicks and claws. Muted wails of children, their noses pressed to the glass, fill the store.

"Get off her!" Trish's hands tug me backward, and I jump to my feet.

The woman stands with a huff, counts her cheering children,

and then jabs a finger into my chest. "I tell you, he attacked my children. He attacked me!"

"Easy—easy now," Trish reassures. "He did throw a book at Jimmy, but it was an accident." She shakes her head. "I can't believe he would deliberately hurt anyone." Trish looks at the books scattered over her floor.

I sniff hard. I want to speak, to defend myself, but the store is a disaster, and I deserve whatever I get.

"That young man is violent. Look around." The woman gestures above her head. "He's a monster!"

"I'm really sorry, Thelma. Go on and calm your kids. Let me have a heart-to-heart with the boy." Trish places a hand on her back and eases her toward the door.

Thelma glares at me over her shoulder. "Heart-to-heart. He needs a belt-to-rear. I don't care how big he is." She flattens her blouse and marches outside.

Trish turns and watches me jump and jerk. "Don't you have anything to say?"

I glance at her and stare down at the book clutched in my hands. It's a Bible.

"I'm not married!"

The story takes a long time to untangle, but I owe Trish the cover-to-cover version. She doesn't make it easy and stands cross-armed, eyes like slits.

"George sent you here," Trish repeats.

"He did."

"You don't know why."

"I don't."

"And the girl is along for the ride."

"Guess so."

"Well, Turk and I never—" She sighs and glances around the store. "This is quite a mess you made." Trish's jaws tighten. "Quite a mess, indeed."

chapter thirty-two

I STACK BOOKS IN PILES ON THE FLOOR. MOST look pretty good, but a few are ripped or creased. Trish doesn't help me—she's on the phone, where her angry voice drops to whispers.

"I won't have—do you realize what they did in our—I don't care if George . . ."

I'll leave town as soon as I'm done. And the way Naomi sounded in the kitchen this morning, I'll travel alone. Then her mom can fly in by Lear jet and take her home, and she'll be happier anyway.

"Leave the rest," Trish says, and sets down her phone. "Turk wants to see you. He's watching Aaron's game."

I look at my hostess. An hour ago she was full of compliments and now she won't look at me. Suddenly I hate being ignored. Look at me angry, look at me and laugh, but please look at me.

"I hadn't planned on lying, but it got going and I didn't—"
Trish raises her hand. "Turk."

I wander in the direction of distant light poles. There's no hurry, and it's too hot to move faster. My trek takes me over nasty stretches of sidewalk, but I've fallen enough today, and I pay close attention.

It's a nice town, really. Folks work in front of their homes, trying to beat the afternoon inferno. They stop and wave as I pass. If I hadn't just wrestled a woman in a bookstore, if I hadn't told the truth, I might say hello. But I did, so I can't.

I cross the highway that runs through town and stop.

The windmill! I've been busy hauling around our lie and forgot about it. *Must be here somewhere. Where are you, Dad?*

I scan for anything that resembles a mill. "Nothing. Probably crumbled years ago." I turn back toward the field and trudge into the ballpark, one big sweat ball.

Seats are filled despite the heat, and the game's in full swing. Turk cheers loudly from his spot on the top bleacher. He quiets when I clang up the bleachers, but he doesn't catch my eye. We sit in drippy silence for two innings. His silence is more horrible than Trish's. I wish he'd holler like Old Bill, but Turk doesn't. He sits quietly and lets me bake to death.

The sun beats down on my hatless head. Turk gulps mouthfuls of water from his gallon jug, but offers me none.

"You're late," Turk says. He looks me over, turns back toward the game. "Is it clear?"

"Wha—" I cough gravel from my parched throat. "Is what clear?"

"What's been done? You defiled our home. Broke our trust. Brought shame upon your name. Wronged Naomi."

I nod until I hear Naomi's name.

"It wasn't my idea. Well, not like I never thought of it before, but she—"

"A man's job is to protect at any cost."

Protect what?

Turk shakes his head. "Putting yourself above her. Weak." He sighs. "I wish James was here."

I blink hard.

"Are we talking about the same thing?" I turn toward him and squint. "Nothing happened. I did screw up with the lie thing, but I tried to make that right. So why come down on me?"

I shake my head violently and almost fall off the stands.

"Take some water." Turk hands me his gallon. I empty his jug.

"She's a beautiful woman, Jack. Either take care of her or leave her to someone who will. Choose."

How can I leave her if I'm not with her?

"Choose!" he thunders, stands up. People on risers turn.

"Please," I whisper, and tug on his T-shirt. "Sit down."

"You disgraced a woman in my home." People stare and murmur. "I was witness. A public wrong deserves a public announcement!"

Have mercy!

"You still refuse to make a choice?" Turk stares at me.

"I didn't refuse," I hiss. "I nodded, I nodded! I don't know what the hell you're talking about."

Turk draws a deep breath through his nostrils. "A simple decision: take care of her or leave her. Simple."

I look around. They stare and whisper and I feel like a zoo animal. Sweat pools at my feet. I've never had such a hot nightmare.

I bury my head in my hands.

"Choose, Jack. Choose. Choose now." Turk bends over, but his voice is just as loud.

The word throbs in my ears. My body twitches to its rhythm. My shoulder jerks—choose, choose.

It makes no sense. Naomi doesn't need defending. And she's the one who should choose. Dirk, me, some other guy. Chant at her for a while.

Turk folds his arms and stares at me with the same stare his wife used.

"Okay!" I stand and hold up both hands. "I'll take care of her!"

Fans nod, satisfied, and turn back to the game.

"Okay, Jack." Turk pats my back. "Let's get home. I left Naomi with Mother, but she's probably home by now."

I stagger after my abuser and get into his van.

"It's a hot one." Turk smiles as if he humiliates young men every day. "If you need air-conditioning, please tell me. You can choose."

"Take care of her!" Words fly out of my mouth on instinct, and I feel like one of Pavlov's dogs.

chapter thirty-three

LUNCH. SUPPER TIME. STILL NO NAOMI.

It's just as well, because the volcano named Trish shakes and rumbles. Fragments of sentences seep out between clenched teeth, and I don't want to be near her when she blows.

Trish pushes lettuce around her dinner plate, but doesn't take a bite. Lucky for me, she seemed satisfied with Turk's handling of my situation.

"Where's that Naomi?" She breathes deep. "We've a matter to settle. That girl looked me in the eyes as she told that story."

No one answers. Seems everyone's afraid of the eruption and beelines out of the house as soon dinner's done.

S'pose I should look for her. I leave a note on the upstairs table—don't want to hide anything else—and jog to the hospital. I pause at the entrance and start to pace. I couldn't see the outside of the place last night. The bricks and small windows. Looks just like the Princeton Medical Center, and now I don't want to go in—hospitals like this make me nervous.

They have since my childhood tests.

"We pop these under your skin. The probes show us electricity in your brain. It won't hurt." My nurse smiled. "Then you need to lie perfectly still for an hour."

"Why? Where's my mom? I want my mom!"

The nurse pressed on my chest, tried to get me flat on the examining table, but I wouldn't budge. "She's in the waiting room, and you can see her when we're done, but now I need you to be still for me."

"No!" I cried, and pushed her hand, the one that held the little needle that she wanted to jab into my head. I kicked at the tray covered with little needles and wires and it clanked to the floor.

My nurse's smile left. Three more nurses walked in, shut the door behind them, and held me down.

"Mom!" I screamed. But she didn't come.

I'm not six years old anymore. I'm here to find Naomi.

My chest loosens, and I step inside. Straight ahead, nurses laugh in a glass room behind the nurses' station. Looks like a party. They probably just restrained a kid and stuck wires in his head. Time to celebrate.

I slip by them and head down a long hall. My head swivels as I read names scribbled on whiteboards outside of each room.

Esther Penner. *Grandma.*

I peek inside. Grandma beams. Her hands fold neatly on

the sheet that covers her, while an IV drip pumps her with a variety of liquids. *Happy drugs. She's out of it.*

"No Naomi," I whisper.

I backtrack into the doorway, and Grandma turns her head. Her eyes, sharp and clear, focus on mine.

"Now, there's a Keegan. Come on in. I know I look old and scary with all this stuff." She picks at the tape that keeps her IV needle in place. Makes me wince.

I walk toward the bed. "No, you don't." My shoulders jump. "Now, that's scary."

"I always liked those little 'hellos' in James. And Francine, of course. They made it easy to locate you Keegans."

"Francine?"

"Your grandma, yes. We'd stay with them whenever we traveled home to California, which, I'd add, was quite often."

"Where in California?" The feeling I had outside the hospital floods me again.

"Oh, we'd visit San Diego, San Francisco. I never enjoyed Los Angeles."

"No." I move nearer to the bed. "Where'd Francine live?"

Grandma looks hard at me, as if she's trying to figure out whether my question is a joke. The confused look stays throughout her answer.

"Why, the same place Francine lives now. Where I grew up and Turk and your father were born. Jerk, of course."

"My own grandmother." I mouth the words and clear my throat. "I'm going to see my own grandmother? And she has Tourette's?"

This grandma watches me pace the room, her eyes calm as calm. I plunk into the visitor's chair, stand back up—I can't stay still.

"You're driving to see Francine?" she asks.

"I'm—I'm driving to Jerk."

She nods. "Does Francine know you're coming?"

"Don't know." I kick a chair.

"Be gentle with her, Jack. She's been through a lot."

I slow my pace. "Like what?"

"She's been through James."

I freeze, and Grandma closes her eyes, yawns, and lets her head fall to the side. "It's hard to be hated by the child you love."

"Hated?"

"But I suppose it's hard to accept the ones through whom diseases come." She yawns again. "Glad you've been able to." Her next yawn ends with a snore.

There is no reason to cry. But tears fall anyway and I feel close to Dad for the first time in my life.

I let Grandma Penner sleep for fifteen minutes. It's all I can stand.

"Grandma?" I pinch her toe. "Hey, wake up."

She opens her eyes, looks tired. "Did I drift off? I'm sorry. I am terribly old, you know."

"Don't sound it."

Grandma nods. "Too old for this earth." She smiles. "But that girl of yours—she looks so young. You look so young. Is she still here?"

"Don't know. That's what I came to find out."

Grandma turns her head and strains to look out the window. Her view is a brick wall and a trash Dumpster.

"Is the sky blue today?" she asks.

"Yes."

"And is it hot?"

"Yes."

She sighs. "In here it's always the same."

I nod. I want to stay beside this woman I hardly know. I could tell her anything and she'd understand—I'm sure of it. It's wonderful, and terrifying.

I plop down beside her. "Mind if I sit here?"

"Can she cook?" she asks.

"What?"

"A good meal. You look well fed."

"Naomi? I don't know if she cooks."

Grandma scowls. "I'll talk to her. How about sewing. Does she do your mending?"

"She didn't tell you." I exhale slowly. "We're not married or anything."

Grandma sighs. "Explains the secrecy. Doesn't mean God can't make something beautiful out of it. Is there wedding talk?"

I roll my eyes. "It has come up lately."

"Needs to, Jack. Baby needs a father like it needs air."

"Baby? We're not—"

Grandma looks past me. I turn. Naomi stands frozen in the doorway with a dinner tray. "They just have chicken tonight." Naomi licks her lips, and her big eyes shift to me. "Have you been here long?"

"Not really." I stand. "Can we talk in the hallway?"

"Why?"

Her response hits me sideways, and I look toward Grandma.

"Such a handsome couple. Don't worry." She reaches for my hand. "It won't be easy, but God will help you through it. New life is so beautiful."

The tray hits the tile with a crash.

Chicken and mashed potatoes cover the floor of the empty doorway. Grandma squeezes my hand, and I glance at her, wild-eyed.

"Now go after her," she whispers.

I back slowly toward the door.

"Can't you run, Jack?"

I nod, leap over the tray, and weave between nurses staring at the exit. By the time I explode out the door, Naomi's a tiny figure that gets smaller by the moment. I throw off my shirt and breathe deep.

"Here we go."

chapter thirty-four

I'D FORGOTTEN NAOMI HAD BEEN TRAINING FOR a marathon.

She runs straight out of Hillsboro. The road is narrow and hilly, without any shoulder, and Naomi runs in the center of the right lane. Cars whiz by us from the front, honk from the rear, but we don't break stride.

I catch her three miles outside of town.

"Na-Naomi. Stop."

She pounds on, legs striding, eyes steeled, as if I don't exist. But I do, and I lean in to her shoulder.

"Naomi!" I reach for her arm. She pulls free and finds extra speed.

I accelerate. "No more!" I grab her arm with both hands and yank. Her body doesn't want to stop. It tugs and swings and flails, and her hand catches me hard across the cheek.

"Are you having a baby?" I move my hands to her shoulders

and straighten her. She glares at me, wriggles away, and backs into the oncoming lane. A car swerves around her.

"No!" She staggers around, throws her hair back.

"Naomi! Are you having a baby?"

"No!" She runs at me and gives me a shove.

"Are . . . you . . . pregnant?"

She doubles over and heaves, but only sobs come out.

"Oh God!" She falls onto a knee. I jump toward her and haul her limp body off the road.

"What a fool I am," I whisper. *It all makes sense. The ups and downs and cries.* "I bet pretending did take it out of you."

We huddle against the guardrail. Each passing semi brings stinging stones and honks and a smelly gust of wind.

I sting inside, too, because we're not married and now I know she doesn't belong to me, but last night she acted as if she did.

I hold Naomi a long time—enough for her to feel several strong jerks. I want to run away myself, run away from myself, but that never works, so I stay and press my back into the metal rail and hope Naomi doesn't stick out her leg at the same time a truck comes by.

Within my arms, I feel her strengthen. She shifts, first those legs, then her middle, as life creeps back into her body.

"You two okay?"

The deep voice floats out from a pickup parked behind us. We both turn, but Naomi shifts her gaze to me. "I am now." She gives me a hug.

"This probably isn't the safest place for that kind of behavior. You sure you two don't want a ride somewheres?"

I raise eyebrows at Naomi, who nods.

The man shrugs, smiles, and drives off. Naomi stands and pulls me to my feet.

"Come on," she says, and bounces toward town. I must've missed something because I'd have sworn that minutes ago she was a sobbing mess. Naomi spins, lifts her arms, and lets them flop against her sides.

My mouth falls open. "There was a girl sitting right there." I point to the guardrail. "She was in tough shape—"

"You don't know how light I feel!" She's got that right. She runs toward me and grabs my twitchy left arm. She tries to steady it, can't, and laughs.

I plod beside her. She's pregnant. My fake wife, fake girl-friend, fake everything, is pregnant. I glance at her stomach. Couldn't have happened too long ago, probably while I worked at her place. Probably I was outside slammin' plants and she and some jerk were inside—my stomach turns.

"I sat there with Grandma and pretty soon I'm talking about my family, and then I'm talking about you, and suddenly I'm talking about it. I almost slipped and let on about the marriage—"

"I told them." My voice is soft.

She stops and thinks. "Well, it doesn't matter now."

I twitch and keep my eyes fixed on my shoes. I want to rewind the day one hour, before I knew, before I saw Grandma. I felt free then. But now I feel stupid. Stupid and pissed. Not sure why. People in Pierce get pregnant all the time—people younger than Naomi. Not all that much to do in a small town. Probably no different in the city.

Naomi bounces forward, turns, and kisses my cheek. "It's
out. Safe with her, safe with you!" She spins around, laughs
some more. "Feels so good to be free, doesn't it?"

"It must," I say. "When someone accepts you even after they
know stuff, see stuff about you, it feels like a burden lifts. I
sorta felt like that in Nebraska; here, too."

"Exactly!" She exhales loud. "I felt like such an idiot after
Andrew left. Andrew—my *free* personal coach." Naomi throws
back her hair. "But it can get so lonely, so when they say 'love,'
you know it's a lie, but right then it doesn't matter. The word
feels so good. Oh, Sam, to know I can talk to you about it!"

I don't need to hear this.

But Naomi tells me all about Coach Zimmerman, how he
disappeared one week after she told him about the kid. She
says amazingly nice things about him considering what he
did, if she were to ask me. But she doesn't.

I stop, turn. Words come fast and easy.

"Why are you going to California with me?"

She looks at me as if it's obvious. "If Mom finds out, I'm
dead. I need time." She starts to walk; I don't, and she turns
around. "What was I supposed to do?"

It's too much. I close my eyes and hear people laugh; the
crowd at graduation, Old Bill as he lies about Dad, Naomi as
she lies about her reason for coming with me. Too much. I'm
sick of her almosts—her little kisses, her squeezes. I'm sick
of everything she says that makes me feel special, makes me
hope. She's a damn pretty liar, but a liar just the same.

There are only three people I want to talk to; two are dead
and one is in a hospital about to join them.

I run. I will not be caught by Naomi, by cheetah, by jet plane. I race into Hillsboro, my name soon a dull echo carried away by the field's rustling. A truck passes me.

Run faster!

Another truck.

Faster!

"What did I say?" Naomi calls.

Dammit, run faster!

There's no room for thought. I peel into town, and knowing Naomi would find me at the hospital, I make for the Penners'. The sun sets as I bound up the steps. Aaron throws open the front door, and I stumble to a halt.

"There you are." Aaron grabs on his ball cap. "We gotta hurry!"

I shake my head.

"You okay, Jack?"

"I don't know."

Aaron looks me over. "You rather not go to Frontier Days? If you need to rest—man, after what Dad put you through—maybe you would rather—"

"Frontier Days." I gasp. "Lots of people?"

"The whole county."

"Can Naomi find me?"

Aaron raises an eyebrow. "Not unless you two arranged a place to meet."

"Let's go."

chapter thirty-five

MY BRAIN IS NUMB AND I FOLLOW AARON LIKE A six-foot sheep. He blabbers about how beautiful Naomi is, and I don't want to hear it. I stop and look around.

"I tell you." Aaron walks on and shakes his head. "You are the luckiest guy alive to ride around with—" He spins. "What's wrong?"

"So much happened so fast, I forgot about it—is there a windmill in this town?"

"Not that I know of. Well, there's the old one behind the museum, if that counts."

"Take me to it."

Aaron frowns and points. "It's that way and Frontier Days is—"

My heart beats faster. "I need to see it."

We reach the community park. He stops and gestures toward a cluster of buildings in the middle of the clearing.

"Behind that museum. That's where it is. Now can we get going?"

"Yep. Let's get going." I beeline for the mill.

"Hey! The festival is this way, you know, fireworks, hide from the beautiful girl, that's all this way."

Aaron's voice fades. I take the left turn and head for the historical museum and the safety of my father. *A dead man can't hide too many painful surprises.*

Footsteps pound behind me. "Hold up. I guess Frontier Days can wait. What's the big deal about an old mill?"

"I want to see my dad."

Inside, I jitter, and the numbness vanishes. I feel just the same before a long run, when excitement and worry beat each other up.

I reach the fence that surrounds the museum and the mill. It's a strange place for a windmill, next to a highway and across from a gas station. Looks old, but not rickety. The thing is solid.

"Yeah, it's all closed." Aaron shakes his head. "The gate's locked."

A white picket fence is all that keeps out intruders in this honest little town, and I step over it.

"You can't do that, Jack."

I walk up to the mill. Unlike the tall towers that poke into the Minnesota sky, this windmill has a plump body and large fins that almost scrape the ground. I pat the base, rough against my hands. A placard stands near it with words almost too small to read.

HISTORIC SITE WINDMILL RESTORATION . . .

Blah, blah. I skim the words, until a name snags my gaze.

RESTORED BY JAMES KEEGAN

"It's true. You were here before me," I say, and step back. "I'm on your heels. You know that, don't you?"

"Your dad did this? Nobody told me that."

I nod. I don't know what he did on the thing. He might have built it all, might have only given it a coat of paint. But his name made the plaque. "You did good." I gently kick the plaque; look his handiwork over one more time.

"I mean it, Jack. Let's go."

"Yeah, I guess." I turn.

"What are you doing there?" An old man shouts from outside the fence. He sounds more confused than angry. "Who gave you permission to go in there?"

I glance at the plaque, remember my map. *Two men, really.*

Fireflies and the smell of gunpowder fill the steamy night, and Aaron and I walk home from the fireworks display. We turn onto A Street.

"I wondered where you boys were," Turk calls from behind. He and Trish speed up and catch us.

Turk tousles my hair. "That was quite a show. I'll bet that rivals anything you have up north."

We reach their home. Naomi waits on the porch.

"Boys. Will you kindly head inside?" Trish says, and turns to Naomi. "Young lady, we have some talking to do."

Naomi's gaze shifts to me. I run my hand through my hair. "No, ma'am. Not tonight." I step in front of Trish. "You can't talk with Naomi tonight."

Trish's jaw drops, tightens. "Did you hear that, Turk? Think of the arrogance. This is a matter that must be made right."

Turk's been staring at me all the while. "Jack?"

I look at him and nod.

"Whoo." Turk exhales hard, nods himself. "Okay. Come on, Trish, boys." He grabs his wife's hand. "There's tomorrow. Let's let these two alone."

"This boy has bewitched you. After what was almost done, and now you side with him over me?" Trish's voice disappears inside. We're alone.

We listen to crickets for a long time.

Naomi forces a smile. "I couldn't find you. I thought you left."

I sit down beside her. "I'm back."

We sit for hours. I can't locate any questions in my mind, and she must not have much more to say. We speak about nothing in short, soft bursts, and fall back into safe silences. But somewhere in the middle, her hand grabs mine, and when we finally enter the house, I know things with us are okay.

We part at the stairs and whisper good night. I thump down the steps and flop into bed.

The night is quiet. Heavy quiet.

"Wake up, Jack."

Turk flicks on the light, and I wince, stare at flashing sunspots. My talk with Naomi ended fifteen minutes ago. There was lots of thinking to do, and Turk caught me wide-eyed.

"I hate to do this. You need to leave," he says.

"Now?" I ask, and prop myself on an elbow. I squint away the red.

"I've lived with Trish a long time." A crash from upstairs makes Turk wince. "Long time," he whispers. "She's in the kitchen."

"Is that bad?" I say.

"No, no, it's fine." Another crash. "Unless it's two A.M. Then it means if I don't get moving quick, life will change dramatically around here."

"You have to get moving?"

He sighs. "You do. Without an apology, she's not letting Naomi off the hook. She needs you two out."

Turk tosses me a shirt and shorts and stuffs my clothes into the open duffel.

"What if Naomi *does* apologize?"

He pauses. "Will she?"

I listen to banging in the kitchen. "I'll get my shoes on."

Upstairs, Trish throws ham sandwiches together while Aaron carries Naomi's things to the curb. Naomi comes running toward me.

"Please get me out of here. They don't want me."

"I know. It's okay. Don't worry." I back into Trish.

"We're going," I say.

She presses a bag of sandwiches into my hands. Trish reaches out and strokes Naomi's cheek. "I don't want you to go. I just can't have you stay." Trish glances at me and turns back to Naomi. "Is there anything you want to talk about?"

Naomi stares down and shakes her head.

"Don't like the ending, but thanks for the stay." I say.

I pull Naomi into the night. Headlamps approach down the street.

"Nate gassed up your car. Now don't speed." Turk walks to Naomi. "I don't know your story. None of it. But whatever you're running from needs attention. Deal with it soon." He turns to me. "And you—choose." He winks.

"Don't worry. I'll take care of her."

Nate turns off the lights, and we climb into the dark car.

Turk slaps the top of the Chev. "Now go, Mr. Keegan. Don't miss any of George's appointments."

Outside, Turk puts his arm around Trish. The two boys join them, and the family steps off the sidewalk. I don't want to leave. George's map says I belong here one more night. Naomi hums a nervous hum beside me, and I need to get going, but I can't make myself pull forward.

Tires squeal and Naomi takes her foot off the accelerator.

"Like that," she says.

chapter thirty-six

WE PEEL OUT OF HILLSBORO. WIND WHIPS OVER the flint hills, catches our car broadside, and shudders the frame.

It makes no sense to drive fast, and I slow to the posted speed limit. Naomi's leg bounces fierce, and I accelerate again. Speed calms her.

"Where next?" she whispers.

"George marked a spot beyond Grand Junction." I point to the map resting on the dash. "Looked at it last night. Hey, it got crazy and I didn't tell you! The windmill George drew for Kansas was big and fat just like the one at the museum—"

"Colorado? I got it!" She slaps my leg. "Amber lives in Vail. It's probably on the way. We can stay there a night."

I was talking about something important.

My stomach tenses. This is my trip. My friend sent me off, my dad's leading the way, and my grandma's on the far side.

"I don't know about leaving George's path," I say.

Headlamps light up my rearview mirror. They approach, pass, and again Naomi's leg jumps. "How fast are you going?" Naomi strains to see.

"We're making good time."

"Please," Naomi says. "She's a good friend. I'd be safe."

I twitch and yawn. "Safe from what?"

She stares as if I'm stupid, as if we have the police on our heels. But there's nothing behind us except a whole pack of lies.

The first rays of sun glint off the "Welcome to Colorado" sign. I zip into the Mountain State on a blue-sky Sunday and loosen inside. Naomi had found sleep hours earlier, and looking at her and the open road, I smirk. Doesn't matter what she did or with whom, out here I feel free. All anger leaves.

I pull over, get out, and stretch. "Mountain State" seems an overrated nickname.

Flat as a pancake.

A tap sounds from the direction of the car. Naomi rolls down the window and pokes out her head. "Why are we stopped?" She looks around, frantic.

"Needed a stretch. It's been a while since I slept." I reach long and slow for the sky. "I thought about what you said, about staying safe and all. There doesn't seem to be anyone out to get us."

Naomi yanks her head in, slides into the driver's seat, and guns the engine.

"Okay, I get it." I shuffle around to the driver's side. "We'll keep going."

"Let me take it for a while," she says, and stares at the road ahead. I straighten. I've seen her winter driving—fast, reckless. But I'm so tired.

I nod. "There's cash in the glove compartment for gas."

"Enough?" she asks.

"Think so." I hop in, click the glove latch, and pull out a wad of bills. "George left me everything. He didn't use credit. I didn't know how much to bring."

Naomi lifts a brow and squeals onto the road. "How much do you have?"

"About five thousand dollars."

"You keep all that cash in the glove compartment?"

I toss the money back in and drift off.

I wake in Denver.

Mountains.

Beautiful. The hood of our car begins up-and-downing. I gaze past Naomi at forests crowning ever-steeper ridges and filling ever-deeper valleys.

She takes the snakelike turns too fast for my gut's liking.

"First time?" Naomi reaches over and squeezes my thigh.

"In the mountains, you mean?"

"That, too."

Naomi's back. I see it in her face, the soft glimmer that blinds a guy, the smile that can mean anything. The mountains seem to settle her, hold her.

"I remember my first time," she says. "Took my breath away."

We're not thinking along the same lines, I hope.

"When we reach Amber's, we can relax."

I breathe deep.

"We're not stopping at your friend's place." I stare straight ahead.

The car swerves and there's not much room to swerve and no place to pull over. Naomi raises both hands. Ahead, the mountain pass turns, and I lunge at the wheel.

"Watch it, Nae!"

"Why?"

"So we don't fly off the damn road!"

"Why aren't we stopping?" She folds her arms, but leaves her foot on the accelerator.

"You trying to get us killed?" I scoot over, plaster both twitchy hands on the wheel, and we whip around the next turn.

"How's it feel? Knowing someone will kill you? That's what my mom will do when she finds out. That's why we're going to Amber's."

I jam my foot hard on the brake and the car shudders. Naomi lifts her foot, and we roll to a stop.

"Get out," I whisper.

She does, and I follow. If another car rounds the bend with speed, we're likely dead, but right now it don't matter.

We stand and glare at each other. She steps closer. We're inches apart. Both of us breathe hard.

"Do you know how much I hate you, Sam Carrier?" She throws her hair back.

"I have an idea." My shoulder twitches.

I want to grab her and shake her and kiss her all at the same time.

A car squeals around the curve; I fist Naomi's shirt and yank. Our backs smack against the mountain. My heart pounds.

She swallows hard. "I thought you understood. When I told you, it sounded like you understood. Don't you ever need a friend to hug you and tell you it's going to be all right, even if they don't know that it is?"

"Yeah."

"And another thing, Amber wouldn't toss us out for doing what we did." Naomi sidesteps nearer and presses into me.

"The Penners didn't boot us for that." I peek down. "It was the lie."

Her body stiffens. "Okay, Mr. Moral. Like you've never lied? Now you *are* sounding like your dad." Naomi fronts me. "What's happening to you, Sam?" She buries herself in my chest.

I stare down at my limp arms that make no move to hug her. *What is happening to me?*

"That's the thing, Nae. I don't know what my dad sounds like." I pull away, and rub my face hard. "But he wasn't a drunk, he didn't run out on me and Mom, and he wasn't a wimp. He looked like me, you know?" I bend forward. "The only thing he left me was this disease, but it got thrown at him, too. He hated it as much as me." I peek into the car at the map on the dash. "And the only way I'll ever find out about the dead guy is by sticking to George's route. 'Cause all I've got of the man are these mills. These damn mills!" I breathe deep and swallow hard. "But they're something. Who knows what I'd miss in Grand Junction if we stop at Amber's?"

Naomi drops her gaze to the ground.

"This is my one shot to figure things out. So I'll make you a deal. I'll drop you off at your friend's house. You keep running from your mom. Play whatever games you want with me. But I can't run from Dad anymore."

Naomi looks up. She wears her thinking face.

"No games," she says. "Not since I told you everything. There've been no games."

I nod. "So how you're acting is how you're feeling and I can believe whatever you do and say?"

Naomi straightens, rubs her cheeks, and tries to look solemn. I don't move, and she raises her right hand to swear it to me. Can't help but grin.

"In that case, may I walk you to the car, Nae?"

"Only if I can stay with you." Naomi stares up at the sky. "You did shove my car out of a snowbank. I'd be an idiot to leave you now."

chapter thirty—seven

"TWO MILES TO ROCKPORT," I SAY. "SHOULD BE someplace to eat there—"

The car lurches twice.

"What's that?" Naomi straightens. "What's that mean?"

Metal grates beneath the hood. "Means I hope there are tools for this gem in the trunk." I steer onto the shoulder, where the engine dies. We roll to a stop.

"Sam?" Naomi asks.

I shrug. "Dead car."

She rolls her eyes. "Think you can you fix it?"

I turn my body and face her square. "Yeah," I whisper. My gaze travels from her waist to her face and back again. I stare on, and panic worms around my head. 'Cause there's a kid in there. A baby who needs watching out for, who's now stuck on the side of nowhere because I was too pigheaded to waste a few days at her friend's.

I replay my heroic find-my-dad speech and wince. Because with a little guy, nothing about this trip is the same. Not anymore.

"What are you looking at?" She squirms.

"Not sure." I twitch hard, open the door, and step out into early morning. There's no hint of sun in the east. Just shadowy mountains all around this flat valley. I whip around, hop back into the car.

"What're you going to do about the baby?"

"Where'd that come from?" she asks.

I don't answer.

She breathes deep, slumps down, and jams a fingernail in her mouth.

"Adoption, I guess," she whispers, and straightens. "It took me a long time to figure this out. Most days, it's all I thought about." She peeks at me, and her leg starts to bounce. Naomi's lips part and shut, and her breath thickens. I know words fight to get out, and I force my muscles still.

"Have you—have you ever been so angry and scared and confused that your brain shuts down and your heart shrivels up and all you want is to disappear?" She hides her face with her hands.

I close my eyes and exhale. *Yeah, I have.* When I next turn toward Naomi, her head is bowed and her hands fidget.

"I wasn't even going to have this thing, Sam. I mean, God, there's a room at Harvard with my name on it, a sports-medicine program waiting for me, a track coach there already planning for me—that school might be Mom's dream, but it sounds like a good one, you know? But how do you do classes, run track, and live a little, with a baby?"

Minutes of silence pass.

"Then George and I got to talking about kids one day, and it all changed. One hour with a gardener—my grandpa—and when he pulled away in his truck, I knew I'd at least have it, but now it's how to hide it, and what to tell Mom, and how to tell the school—I mean, damn! Damn, damn!"

Naomi stops swearing and starts crying. "And it's worse because what kind of person gives away her kid? Who does that? But there's no way I could raise it." She sighs. "I got Mom's life to live, you know?" Naomi quiets. She folds her hands, places them in her lap, and whispers. "So I'll find a place where Mom can't kill me. I could go to Ireland, stay with one of my brothers. I'll have this child." Naomi swallows hard. "And I'll hand it to a stranger." She lets her head thunk against the glass.

I reach out a twitchy hand. She grabs it, squeezes it. "I'm still so scared, Sam."

I want to tell her what it's like to be given away, to never know your parent. I want to tell her about the hole inside that gets deeper as you get older until you'd do anything to fill it, even try to stuff it with an ass like Old Bill. But her hand shakes and she's scared and for once my mouth obeys me and stays shut.

Naomi sniffs and rubs her eyes and breathes deep. I smile at her and she forces one back.

"Well, this car won't fix itself. Let's see if what we need's back there," I say.

I get out, open the trunk, and sigh. "We should be okay." I dig for the wrenches and flashlight and head up front. "Why don't you get some rest? This might take a while." Naomi nods and soon sleeps stretched out across the front seat.

Hours pass, and I think of nothing. My hands don't need my help.

I finally straighten, stretch, and slam the hood. Greasy and exhausted, I lift Naomi's head and slip my lap underneath. I turn the key and glance down at Nae.

"Like a kitten."

My leg jerks, and Naomi opens her eyes, looks up at me. She doesn't smile, but she doesn't sit up either, and I have no idea what she thinks.

"Good morning, Sam. Oh, good. You got it started." She nestles down and closes her eyes, until my next jerk bounces her head off my leg. Naomi sits up, stretches.

"Are we almost there?"

"Yep. Just flew through Grand Junction."

We rumble behind a semi. Gas fumes fill the car and we hurdle forward, windows full down.

Naomi slides toward me and rests her head on my shoulder, her hand on my thigh. I don't know if it's her head or her hand or the fumes, but I get happier by the minute. My thoughts won't stay straight. Dad and Naomi and her kid bounce around inside my head and all I know for sure is that they all feel like family.

"I'm looking for—there, that's the address on the mailbox."

A hundred wind turbines dot the hills that surround the Windmill KOA campsite.

I slow and pull in front of the office.

"We're camping?" Naomi says. "Let me see that map."

"It says Hostetler. Frank and Sue." I frown and look around. "I don't see a home around here. Unless they live in an RV." I point toward the only other campers in the place.

"But those wind things don't match the sketch," she says.

I shrug, and we both slip out of the car.

We step inside the office. It's new and air-conditioned and I plop into a chair.

"You two need a site?" A large, pleasant-looking man steps out from the back room. I jump to my feet.

"I'm looking for Frank Hostetler. Is that you?"

He smiles. "You missed him by, oh, two years. They used to live right on this spot, but they sold out during the drought."

I slump back down. "Do you know where they are now?"

He points toward heaven. "They were good people. So that'd be my guess. Both of 'em, couple months back."

He wipes his forehead. "Sorry to be the one to tell you. You relatives?"

"I don't know," I whisper.

Nobody moves.

"Tell you what. If you need a spot tonight, it's on me." He turns and shouts, "Tony! Set these folks up."

We step over to the rent-a-tent desk. Tony joins us on the other side.

"Your biggest tent," I say.

"And your most comfortable," Naomi adds.

"Honey, if you wanted comfortable, you shouldn't be roughing it with this guy."

I look at Naomi. She thinks hard.

I grab the tent, head toward the door, and pause. "You guys are *Windmill* KOA, right? Those turbines aren't exactly windmills."

"You're right about that," Tony says. "We took the name from the beauty that once stood on Frank's ranch. Stood until last month. Damn storm took it."

I smile and nod. "Was it painted green, red on top?"

"That's the one. So you've been here before?"

I peek at the map. "Saw a picture, is all."

We drive to our numbered fire pit. There are hundreds of choices, and they stick us right next to the RV. I'm too tired to complain.

I drag out the tent and spread out canvas on dirt.

George must not have known that windmill fell. No other reason he would have sent me into nowhere. "But then, you were a believer in wandering."

"You know how to put this up?" Naomi stands over me and chews her nails.

I smile, grab the hammer out of the bag, and whack a stake. "'Course. I used to live in one."

"You lived in a tent?"

I shift to the other side, tug the fabric taut, and pound in another. "Not really *lived* in. More like escaped to. Old Bill'd get hollering and I'd get scared and go sleep in the tent by the barn. Nothing could hurt me." I pause. "My little kingdom."

Naomi sits beside me. "What was it like? At home."

I set down my hammer and sigh. I want to tell someone—I want to tell her. But once I get going, no knowing where I'll stop.

"Had a German shepherd once. Duke. Belonged to Mom first, before Old Bill came on the scene. But Old Bill took to that dog. For some reason, Duke loved him most of all."

I check Naomi's face. She listens, and I breathe deep.

"Duke got into it with a badger. Lost a leg. He was still lovable Duke, hauling around after Bill, trying to keep up. But Old Bill stopped waiting and started yelling. Duke lowered his head and followed. Old Bill kicked him and he followed. Until one day Bill kicked too hard and Duke didn't get up. I saw him crawl toward Bill. I watched Old Bill drop and apologize. Duke's tail flopped all happy like. He lifted his head, rested it on Bill, and died.

"But in my tent, nobody yelled, nobody kicked, and I was king." I blink free of the tent peg. "If I would have known you then, you could have been—"

I shut up.

She squeezes my hand and I glance up.

"I could have been what?" she says.

"I'd have let you inside, is all." I smile.

Naomi scoots nearer, leans forward, and rests her head against mine. "There's tonight."

♦ ♦ ♦

I fasten the canopy to the tent and admire my work.

"Tent's up!" a kid screams from the direction of the RV. In one minute, we're surrounded.

Sounds like a hundred people shouting, but it looks to be only one family. One huge, children-everywhere family.

My shoulder jerks hard, and I catch a kid's gaze. He jumps up and trots over.

"I'm Luke. What's your name?"

"Sam." I grimace back.

"Can we play in your tent?"

"We were going to get settled."

Zip. Kids pour in. I look at Naomi.

"Every king needs subjects, right?" She smiles.

My tent bulges and lists and whoops.

A large woman with a large smile and a large hat bustles toward us. Dressed all in white, she looks like an overweight brown angel.

She stares at the tent, and my shoulder jumps.

"Look'n like you got a fair piece of nervous in you. My kids'll do that to people."

I don't answer.

"My name is Persephone Watkins. And these be my children." She walks to the entrance and peeks in. "Luke, release your brother! Y'all sho' think a heap of yourself, barging in like this after their kindly invitation."

"I didn't really invite—name's Sam, and this is my, this is Naomi."

"Mighty pleased to meet y'all. While's we's on introductions,

that turtle of a man leanin' against the camper is my honey of
a husband, Albert."

I can't see him—Persephone's in the way. But I nod.

"Where y'all headed?" Persephone asks.

"California." Naomi finally speaks. "Sam and I need to get
to California."

chapter thirty-eight

WE SPEND THE DAY WITH SEVEN WATKINS
children. I don't want them here. I want Naomi to myself, but
they won't leave, and come supper time, Persephone, Albie,
their rat-dog, Brutus, and seven kids roast wienies around my
fire pit.

Naomi raises her eyebrows. She wants them gone, too. She
wants me to kick them out. I nod and wait for a lull and open
my mouth.

"Why do you move your shoulder like that?" Luke asks.

My heart thumps. I run my hand through my hair and
want to be small.

"Tourette's," I say quietly, and the fire cracks. Little sparks
float up toward the sky. "I can't help it. Got it from my dad." I
peek at Naomi, who wears a faint smile, and face Luke. "Got it
when I was your age."

"Mom?" Luke squirms. "Could I get that?"

Persephone pushes up from her bench and walks toward her boy. She tousles his hair. "Don't reckon you will." Then she walks to me and tousles mine. "But if you did, it'd suit me fine."

She is an angel. She turns and threads her way back to her husband.

Noise returns. Baby Zeb coos. Three-year-old Sol skips to the table and grabs a bun. Luke shrugs his shoulders, runs, and tackles Sol. Nobody seems to care that I used the T word. They don't understand that now they're supposed to laugh, or mimic, or whisper. Bunch of ignorants, clueless that a kid's job is to make others feel like crap.

I hear my word and Persephone's words all jumbled up, and I shake my head because it can't be true.

Tourette's. Okay. Suits me fine.

The words wash over me like a shower, and I close my eyes and feel years of grimy words smudge, loosen, and disappear. In my mind I see them—Jerky, Loser, Retard—piled on the ground, dissolving. I feel light.

What's going on?

I crack an eyelid. Still nobody mocks, and my heart soars, and falls. How many years I hid, hid that word—the word I hate most in this world that could have set me free.

Exhaustion wallops me, and I slump in my folding chair, feel Naomi's kiss on my cheek, and fall asleep.

The sun is down when I wake. Embers glow in the pit. I feel refreshed but I can't remember where I am. Persephone hums and sews on the opposite side of the fire and her hum sounds like morning. But it's dark and my brain's in a fog.

"Where are we?" I ask. I turn a circle, looking for clues.

"Colorado don't wanna quit." Persephone nears me and together we stare out at a flat plain and the shadows of mountains in the distance.

I turn and see our tent and remember. George. Naomi. Dad. I say nothing.

"I never done asked y'all what business you have in California."

"My grandma lives there, ma'am."

She nods. Kids scream inside the RV. Albie's low murmur follows and soon all is quiet.

Outside, we stand for a long time.

Persephone steps in front of me. Her gaze doesn't give me an escape.

"And you been campin' the whole way?"

"We've been following a map a friend gave me. There was something here I was supposed to see, but it's gone."

"Sho don't sound like much of a friend."

"Ah, no way he could've known. It's not like the old owners could've told him." I chuckle. "George was my best friend. Dad's, too. For graduation he gave me a letter my dad wrote—"

"What you thinking on?"

Butterflies flutter around my gut. "Would have been nice if Dad could have seen me graduate, you know? I think he would have clapped."

Persephone squints, and looks far off over my shoulder. "He live in Minnesota, too?"

"No." I pause. "Died there, though, when I was two."

She shakes her head, says nothing.

"Hated him all my life." I stare at my tense hand. "For this." I look back to Persephone. "He had it, too."

My eyes glaze. But it's dark, and maybe she doesn't see me. "But it wasn't his fault. It's not, you know?"

She keeps looking.

"The more I find out about him." I pinch my forehead between my fingers like George used to do. "I want him to like me. That's stupid 'cause he's dead." My toe scuffs dirt. "Figure his mom'll clear things up. Thing is, if he liked me, wouldn't he have left me something more than a note? I mean, after he died, wouldn't something have come to me? That's what Old Bill says. He says kids always get something. Didn't anything Dad owned sort of belong with me?" *And what if he didn't— didn't think much of me, just when I might like him?*

Thoughts weigh heavy and Persephone is silent. Suddenly I need to run. I back up and start to jog away from camp.

"You done spent too much time listening to this world. Too much time!" she yells at my back, but I don't slow. I run along the road that stretches into nowhere.

Stars shine brighter than any I've seen. They fill the sky, but can't reach down to the horizon. A ring of black mountains rises and eats them. I feel eaten, too, eaten and tiny and surrounded. And a little bit afraid. But I think of Naomi and her baby and keep going. With each step, I sink further into my run until there's only room for the scritch of sneakers and those swallowed stars in my mind.

I've run long enough, and I see him—a dark figure dashing in front of me.

Dad.

He's just a blob, a black-on-black outline racing beneath the stars, but I know it's him.

"Dad!" The shape doesn't stop. I speed up, and hear him inside my head.

Catch me, son.

He calls me "son."

My legs churn, and my face drips with sweat and tears.

Slow down. Please.

He does. Dad stops and turns. He wears a T-shirt and jeans and stretches out his arms. I reach out mine. Though I can't see his face, I know he smiles.

A little farther. Don't stop, Jack. His voice surrounds me.

My voice catches; I'm almost there. I must look dumb running with my arms in front of me, but I don't care. I blink hard.

He vanishes.

"No!"

I skid to a stop. "Couldn't you stay around?" I yell, "Couldn't you stay?"

And I hear a whisper. I hold my heavy breath, spin, and search the night, because I know he's not far away.

chapter thirty-nine

I WALK BACK TO CAMP AND QUIETLY UNZIP THE tent. Inside, a flashlight glows. "Naomi?" I whisper, "Are you awake?"

A body plows into me, and I stagger backward. Naomi's full of hugs and kisses and squeezes. I gently peel her off.

She takes my hand and yanks. "I had an idea you'd be on a run—you idiot!" She whacks my shoulder and backs into the tent. Her hands shoot to her hips. "Stop doing this!"

"Doing what?"

"I don't get you. You're always leaving me!"

"Wait a minute. You were with the Watkinses," I say, and zip the tent behind me. "I was the one who woke up alone by the fire, well, except for Persephone. She saw me leave. Figured you were sleeping."

"Next time you disappear until three A.M. maybe tell me! I thought we had some level of trust."

"We do! I didn't think you'd care if—"

"Oh, I don't care, huh? I blew off Amber for you. That doesn't mean anything?" Her eyes widen and narrow and my gaze drops.

"You *did* do that for me," I say.

"And it was really scary, too!"

"I bet."

It was quiet.

"But you're okay?" I ask.

Naomi's voice softens. "I'm okay, you?"

"Yeah, I just saw—yeah."

The flashlight is out, and it's black in the tent. We settle down and I feel Naomi's warm breath on my neck.

After my run, I'm comfortable. And free. My mind wanders and my mouth loosens, and before I can stop it, the hinge falls off my jaw.

"So, what do you think your baby is, boy or girl?"

Without a word, Naomi jumps off the mattress and disappears into the night.

"Hey!" I call. "It popped out." I plop back down, whisper, "Just wondered if you could tell somehow."

I rise and step out. I circle the tent and spot a shadow pacing on the other side of the RV.

I tiptoe over. "Naomi."

She charges nearer. "What do you want from me?"

I have no good answer for that.

"What are you trying to do? Asking me that . . ." Her body fights itself again, part of it starts to run, part lifts a fist to whack me. I cover my shoulder.

"I was curious. I wasn't trying to make you crazy about whatever I made you crazy about."

"Like I don't feel stupid enough. Like I need another thing to feel guilty about. We're lying there and for once I don't feel like dirt. Because I'm not thinking of the baby or never holding my own child." She stomps her feet and gives a disgusted scream.

"Okay," I say. "I never meant—"

"I mean, it's only this big." She pinches her thumb and fore-finger together. "So why do I feel like trash? Some family will be ecstatic to have it, right? But for me it's a dream killer!" Her voice raises, and I'm sure the whole camp hears. I step back. She steps forward and sticks her finger in my chest.

"I don't want to think about it anymore. I don't want to care about it anymore. I mean, before he left, Andrew called it *garbage!*"

I close my eyes—Old Bill's voice roars in my head.

"You piece of garbage. Ungrateful twitchy garbage. My money buys you food, clothes, and you can't even work the machine." Bob and Joe jumped out of Old Bill's cement truck. Joe ran toward my stepdad, laid a hand on his shoulder. *"The kid can't help it."*

"You believe that? See how still he is now?" My shoulder twitched. *"Stop it, dammit!"* Bill slapped me across the face, and I choked back tears.

"I'm trying. Please. I'm trying to pour straight." My shoulder sprang again. Another slap. Blood oozed from my nose.

"Enough, Bill!" Joe jumped between us, put his hands on Bill's shoulders, and eased him back.

"You're right on that." Old Bill spit. *"I've had enough. Go home, you nothing."*

I turned and let tears flow.

"Never forget that!" Old Bill called, "You're a nothing!"

"And I have to believe him, that it's a nothing. Because I can give away a nothing." Naomi paces. "A nothing that for some reason hurts my heart like a big *something*. Do you hear me?"

"No, Bill," I whisper. "That's a lie."

"A what?" Naomi hollers.

"Piece of garbage, a nothing." I look at Naomi. "That's a lie."

Naomi steps back, surprised, and covers her mouth with a shaking hand. She stands there like a statue, and then collapses into my arms.

"Oh God, oh God!" She pushes me, and we rock back and forth. "It's real. It thinks, it feels—Sam?"

I gather her closer and hold tight. Her body goes limp, and I gently lower to the ground. Leaning against my chest, she sobs and tries to rock, but I sit firm.

"Do you think it knows my voice?" Naomi asks.

One last sob shakes her frame, and I lift her chin, look into her face.

"Let's get you inside."

Her arms shoot up around my neck. I'm not going anywhere. She hums, stops, whispers, "Just hold me."

We both sleep in—way in. Luke and Brutus race around our tent, and I get to my feet. Luke must hear me move.

"Hey, Sam!" Luke can't speak quietly, and it sounds even louder now. "Gonna get up today?"

I join him outside. "Yeah." I shield my eyes from the sun and blink until I can see. "Wow."

Mountains, star-eaters the previous night, are beautiful in the morning.

"Ma said to let you sleep," Luke says.

"Nice of you not to." I tousle his hair, pause with my hand on his head. I've never tousled anyone and it feels really adult, but it also feels good, so I do it again.

"I'm going on a short walk." I kneel down, look at Luke square. "This is really important. When Naomi wakes up, tell her I'll be right back. Tell her I'm walking." Luke doesn't pay attention. I grab his shoulders.

"Can you do that?" I ask. "I'm not running, I'm not leaving, I'm walking."

"What?" He's blank-faced.

Oh well, I'll make it a quick walk.

"I did something!" Naomi greets me with a hug.

"You barbecued the Watkinses' dog."

She whacks me on the shoulder again. It jumps and aches.

"No, dummy." She pulls me inside the tent. "I made breakfast—wait, what's that smell?"

I point at the cast-iron skillet resting directly on the air mattress. The smell of burned rubber overpowers.

Naomi jumps toward the pan and raises it. Gooey strings of melted rubber look like taffy.

"Best eat outside, you think?" I say.

"You could help here!"

I grab the ruined mattress, toss it through the flap, and nod toward fresh air. We walk out and plunk down at a nearby picnic table.

"What was it?"

"Can't you tell?"

I look through the rubbery smoke that rises from the rim of the skillet. Maybe eggs. Possibly bacon. The third clump is a mystery.

Naomi looks at me, waits.

"Was a nice thought." I shrug, grin.

She glances down, frowns, and stares at me. "It *was* a nice thought!"

"Absolutely!" I agree.

"One of the nicer things I could have attempted, really." She stands and walks around to my side of the table.

"More I think of it, the nicer it gets." I say, and rise to meet her.

Again, Naomi hugs me. "You smell smoky." She presses into me, and I tingle. It's a good tingle. "Not that I mind."

I awkwardly squeeze in return. She nuzzles into my neck.

"Do you know that you know everything about me?" Her voice comes from inside my head.

My hands grasp her waist and pull her nearer.

"Uh, no." I glance at the sky. I'm losing my bearings. "I don't know your middle name."

"Lani." Her lips brush my ear, and I'm out of breath.

"And your dad's name."

"Will."

Something gentle shifts beneath my shirt.

My mind rolls as my hands work up her back.

"What would you name the baby—if you kept it?"

All movement stops.

Name of the baby? Twice stupid, Sam!

I wait for Naomi to tense—for her to remove those hands from my stupid skin. For another shoulder slug.

But she stays. She turns her head to the side and presses into my chest. "Last night was the first time I thought about it."

"Forget it, dumb question."

She pulls away, takes my hand, and squeezes.

"It's not so dumb." Naomi takes a deep breath. "You really don't hate me?"

I shake my head.

She nods and scuffs the dirt. "Kids have names, don't they?"

I shrug. "Never met one who didn't."

chapter forty

I NAME NAOMI'S BABY JESS. NOT OUT LOUD, BUT IN my mind. It's none of my business and I'm not the father, but I hate thinking of the kid as an *it*. It sucks to change hands and lose your names, but being an *it* must feel even worse. Besides, Jess is one of those good names that goes both ways.

Probably, Jess will be good-looking, like Naomi. Smart, too. And the odds of Tourette's are slim.

I think about this, take down the tent, and return it to the office.

Naomi leans against the car. I walk back toward her and stop. She could raise Jess. She needs to. 'Cause I can't bear to think of that kid as messed up as I was.

"Where are you, Sam?" she asks.

I blink and see Naomi and almost say something dumb like "I was inside of you." But I clear my throat and move nearer.

"Thinking about Jess." Even dumber.

She frowns. "Who is that—" She must figure it out, because she falls silent, approaches, and lays her head on my shoulder.

Things are different now between the two of us. Gentler, I guess. I know she's not going anywhere, and she knows it, too.

"Jess." She repeats it quietly. "It's a nice name."

"Think so?" I ask.

There is silence, and I stroke her head. She grabs my hand and gazes at me.

"Are you mad at me?"

"No. Stop asking that."

"Why aren't you?"

I jerk my shoulder, and her head bounces.

"Guess because you're still here," I say. She hugs me. I look beyond at tumbleweeds as they skip along the campsite and close my eyes.

I see Dad, the one I never knew. Again, I follow, call after him.

"Are you mad at me? I need to know."

He looks over his shoulder, his face sad.

"No. Stop asking that."

We say good-bye to the Watkinses.

Kids surround us and Persephone covers us with kisses.

"Albie wants to talk to you. Go on into the RV."

I frown and twitch.

"Go on," she says.

I climb the steps and slip inside. Albie sits in the driver's seat and I plunk into the other captain's seat.

"We're leaving," I say.

"Where to?"

"My map says Las Vegas." I've seen pictures of the town. Vegas looks neon and feels thin and hollow and for the first time on the trip I miss Pierce. I wonder about Mom, wonder why I only *wonder* about her. As if she's someone I read about in a magazine.

"I need to make a call," I whisper, "Do you have a cell?"

Albie glances down at the cup holder where a phone rests.

"Could I borrow it?"

Again, he looks at the phone.

I nod. "Okay."

I walk into the bathroom, shut the door, and stare at the keypad. I feel jittery, as if I've escaped from prison and am about to return. I enter my number and stare at the send button. I delete, reenter, and stare some more. Breathing deeply, I close my eyes, press send, and hope for voice mail. It rings.

"Hello?"

Mom's greeting sounds tired, and suddenly I'm tired, too, and slump against the side of the bathroom. I don't know how to act or how I should sound.

"Mom, it's me."

"Oh, Sam." She sounds relieved. It's quiet on both ends. We listen to each other say nothing. She sniffs and clears her throat, lowers her voice. "You're okay. Everything's okay?"

"Yeah. I'm heading for Las Vegas. I'm fine."

"Las Vegas? What are you doing there? Are you alone?" She pauses. "Lots of people have been worried."

I doubt that. I think of where Mom stands in the farm-house, how she leans against the refrigerator. She wears a yellow apron, and her fingertips are pruny, so likely she has me tucked between her shoulder and ear. I stop picturing and can't remember her questions.

"Well, I thought I should check in—"

Mom interrupts. "Don't come home. Not yet. Don't come near here."

I have no idea what she's talking about, or what happened to our friendly conversation.

I hear Old Bill's holler and Baby Lane's cry.

"Please, Sam. I have to get off the phone."

"What's going on? What's Old Bill doing?"

"Las Vegas," Mom whispers. "Your father and George worked on a windmill near there. James wanted me to see it." She starts to cry. "I promised him we'd go when you got older. And then he was gone."

Old Bill's louder now—near the sofa.

"You could go now, for us," she says.

"I think I am."

"Who you talking to, Lydia?" Old Bill's grainy voice comes clear through the receiver.

"I love you, Jack." Mom hangs up.

I don't want to picture Pierce anymore, don't want to hear Old Bill holler or Lane scream. I never want to go back to that town again.

I exit the bathroom and carry the phone up to Albie. He doesn't take his eyes off the dashboard, but gestures with his head toward the empty seat beside him.

"What she say?" It's the second time Albie has spoken to me. Throws me off.

"Who?"

"Your mom."

"How'd you know I called her?"

Albie adjusts his glasses and says nothing.

"She doesn't want me to come home," I say.

He looks at me. Albie's sleepy eyes look like they already know what I should know.

"What's she scared of?" he asks.

"I got Tourette's."

He waits for more.

"Old Bill, that's my stepdad, hates it. I embarrass him and lately, when he gets mad, it's not pretty."

"Nope. That ain't it."

I tongue the inside of my cheek. "Don't know what else she'd be worried about. I've never gotten in Old Bill's face before."

Albie looks at me. "Would you now?"

I'm quiet.

"Oh, that it all right." He chuckles. "Was your dad a good man?"

"Yes, sir. I think so." I pause, and run my hand through my hair. "I'm startin' to see him. When I jog or sit and think. Like he's here, you know?"

Albie smiles.

"But he's dead," I say.

"Sounds like he was waitin' for the right time to show up."

I think about George, who lived two miles from me for eighteen years, about Farkel, seven miles the other way. Naomi, in another world. They all showed up at the same time.

"Maybe. But Mom sounds bad. Old Bill was hollering, Lane was crying, she was crying. Think she needs me to head home."

"Listen to your mama, son. She'll take care of herself. She tell you anything else?"

"She wants me to see something Dad built. It's our next stop." Sigh. "Just hope that one's still there."

chapter forty-one

HOURS OF NOTHING LULL MY BRAIN AND BODY into a partial coma, and we drive through the day without seeing another vehicle.

The engine grating is back, and I don't know if she'll make Vegas. Heat and distance will again leave us stranded on the road. Naomi must hear it, too, but if she does, she pretends not to worry.

"What's this place called?" she says.

I unfold the map. "Keegan Gardens."

"Gardens? Out here?"

I shrug and puff out air.

The Chev gasps, too, but hours later, the car surprises and we reach the city.

I pull into Conoco and make a few adjustments under the hood. Then I ask the Conoco man for directions to a garden, and he points me toward the Millennial Casino.

Minutes pass, and we pull into the parking lot and scoot out of the car. Naomi hops back in and fires her up.

"Where you going?" I yell, surprised.

"This dad stuff. Take some time and get it out of your system. I'll come back this afternoon."

Dad stuff?

I watch Naomi back up and make a slow turn. She presses her hand against the glass, smiles, and shrinks in the distance.

"Okay." I face east. Sun glints off the hundreds of cars in the lot. I shield my eyes and squint. I don't see a garden, but a windmill pokes up a few rows from me. I've seen it before. An exact copy stands in George's Garden Bowl.

I weave through cars, reach the mill. It's working. Blades circle freely.

"Hey, Dad."

Chained to its base are two rusted red chairs—shin bangers.

"Good to see you again, George."

I set a chair upright and plop down. I lean back and think of my friend and the garden that probably was once here and Polaroid cameras. It feels safe.

Until I hear them—graders, levelers, cement mixers. I know each by the sound of their engines, and I want to vomit.

"What are you bustin' up now, Old Bill?"

It's not my stepdad. I know that. But it's his type of business and that's close enough. I hate what was once my inheritance.

I stand, reach out, and touch the mill. White flecks crumble and fall to the ground.

But it works.

"I'm here. Sorry it took so long to get here. I'm sorry for everything." The mill slows as if listening to me.

"Mom can't come. But she wants to, I think. With Old Bill around, don't know if she ever will."

I sit in the parking lot, put my feet up on the mill, and talk to both Dad and George. I don't hear anything back, but it feels good to be near them and I blab on.

People walk by, frown and stare, but for the first time I don't give a rip.

Hours pass and the sun scorches. I slump down, and my head feels heavy. Vision doubles, sharpens again.

"Well, guys, if you don't mind, I'm going to take a little nap."

I dream of working with George. Dad's there, too. We squeeze into the old truck, drive to a fancy house, and unload flowers. George and Dad joke and laugh and we all take shovels and start to dig. We dig deep, I think too deep. Dad puts down his shovel and leaps into the hole. George strokes my cheek and does the same.

I race to the edge and look down. Nobody's there.

"No!" The gravelly voice is my own. I try and sit but Naomi presses me down onto the front seat of the Chevy.

"Here's some water." She raises my hand. My lips quiver, touch the glass. Water streams down my cheeks and neck.

"Sorry," she says, and wipes my face.

I blink and focus. Naomi comes clear. She wears her unreadable face.

"You've been talking a lot. You never told me that you were seeing things—you know, your dad." She bites her lip, but it isn't the cute bite, it's a worried bite and comes with a frown.

"Just dreaming. That's all it was this time." I breathe deep and reach for water. "Dad's different than I thought, Nae."

"You've told me that." Naomi says. There's a distance in her voice, as if she talks about a stranger, but it doesn't matter right now.

"My grandma, you know. She's waitin' at the end of this trip. I can get all my questions answered."

"I know that, too." She sets down my cup and strokes my head. But something's not right.

She helps me sit up, and climbs over me into the driver's seat. I'm beat but I feel close to a big thing. I slump down.

"Why is it that when things go good for me, when I get close to Dad, you get all different."

She looks at me and I can't tell if she cries or my eyes water.

"Because he's dead." She takes her hands off the wheel and whispers, "And I'm not."

Her words hit like a Minnesota October. There's no green, everything's brown, and it's cold enough for a pretty coat of white, but snow won't fall. The world feels stuck, stuck and cold and dead.

"He don't seem so dead anymore. Besides, what does he have to do with you?"

She folds her arms and pulls her legs up against her body.

"Why don't you ask him?" she whispers.

I have nothing to say to that and my eyes fall closed.

◆ ◆ ◆

"We're here." Naomi's voice is soft, and I straighten and rub my eyes. The sun shines. She drove all night.

"You got to be tired," I say. "I am and I didn't drive."

Naomi points to a green sign.

JERK

POPULATION 468

The string of large houses that makes up the town of Jerk sits high on a hill. The address I want hangs on the last mailbox in that string, before the road winds down toward the ocean, which I hear. I close my eyes and it sounds like a snowstorm. Though rhythmic, it's just as wild.

We park at the bottom of a long driveway. I get out and stretch.

"Beautiful, isn't it?" I say. "But I don't see any windmill, do you?"

Naomi steps out, grabs me, and tugs me up the driveway. "Whatever." Her hand squeezes my forearm hard, and her body moves quickly—not the smooth walk I know.

"Naomi." I stop, and she jerks back and exhales hard. "I've been thinking a lot about my dad."

"Oh, really," she says, and pulls forward, but I don't budge.

"And you've gone along with it and that's great. But I screwed up. Again. 'Cause your deal is hard on you, and alone sucks, and you're gonna need . . ." I look her straight in the eyes. Her gaze falls to the ground.

"I'm still here," I say.

She steps back, and I know she's thinking hard, too. "You just . . . you forget about me sometimes. It feels like I could lose you." She watches me. She's trying to see inside.

I nod. "You haven't lost me."

She flings herself at me. I catch her and hug her and lift her off the ground.

"I need all of you, Sam."

Her words make me wince and both arms tense. I'm suddenly angry. I want to kick something hard and I don't know why. I repeat her phrase in my mind and gently set her down.

"What was that you just said?"

"I said I need all of you." Naomi bows her head. "Sounds pretty desperate. I'm sorry. I don't mean to smother you."

I exhale hard. The second time she said it, it felt different. More dumb than aggravating. "Yeah, that wasn't your best line. But I don't think that's exactly what you said the first time."

"It is." She steps closer. "I'm not stupid, Sam Carrier, so—"

I hold up my hand. The fire burns again.

"That's it! No more."

Naomi steps back.

"It's my name." I slap both hands on top of my head. "*Sam* is not it. A thief stole 'Jack' and gave me 'Sam' and I'm sick of it." I pump my fists and laugh hard. It's a full, angry, excited laugh, and sounds strange coming from my mouth. It's a bursting laugh, full of so many feelings I don't try to sort them out.

"And I don't want it anymore!" I turn and tug at my shirt. "I'm ripping it off right now."

Naomi's eyes are big and I laugh again. "George was right. It's *Jack*. No more Sam." I step nearer. "Will you do that for me? I need you to call me by my name. Only my name."

Naomi gently cries but doesn't look away. She steps toward me. "Sam always comes back. He never leaves me." Naomi reaches up and strokes the back of my neck. "I don't know this Jack."

"Trust him," I whisper.

She nods and closes her eyes and leans in to my arms. "Okay . . . Jack Keegan."

chapter forty–two

THE FRONT DOOR FLIES OPEN AND AN OLDER woman steps out, squints.

Naomi releases me, turns, and wipes her eyes with her palm.

"Hello." I step forward and stop. The woman doesn't look anything like me. Maybe the old lady in Hillsboro was delirious.

"Are you expecting me?" I ask.

The woman opens her mouth. Nothing comes out. Her body crumples against the door frame, and it looks like she's going down.

"You okay?" I jump toward her.

"Stop," she says quietly. "Please. Let me look at you."

She folds her arms and gently rocks. The woman stares at me, and I stare back. A slight twitch works her eyes, and she blinks hard.

"My name is Jack Keegan."

"I know!" She rushes me and smothers with her hug. "You have James's voice." She cries into my chest, and I peek at Naomi, who shrugs. "George, that rascal! I thought it was a joke. So much time has passed since your second birthday, and I'd given up seeing you."

She steps back. "Hello, Naomi."

Naomi cocks her head and furrows her brows.

"Oh, I've been hearing about you for years." She looks back at me. "And I've waited a lifetime for you to visit."

My stomach is hollow, like an old, dead log. I should feel full, because I'm here. I made it; this is my grandma. But I'm scared of what she knows—what was kept from me for sixteen years.

This woman sighs. "Do you even know my name?"

"Yes."

"If you knew how many letters that hideous man sent back to me unopened, how often I tried to call." Francine closes her eyes, nods, and lifts her hands to her face. "Tell me you received at least one letter. Tell me Lydia told you something."

I shake my head. I want to say more, but I don't know how to talk to a relative and words come hard.

She bursts into more tears. "You have to believe that I tried."

I watch her cry and think of where I am and the dam breaks. "I know you did. Guess now that I'm here, you'll have to tell me what you wrote in all those letters. At least the good stuff."

She takes off her glasses and wipes her eyes. "I'd love to."

My grandma reaches out her hand. I grab it with my left and squeeze Naomi's with my right. I inhale the same air my father breathed, exhale all my butterflies, and we step inside.

Three items fill Francine's house—plants, watercolor paintings, and pictures of guys. One of them is me. Me as a baby. Me running down the street. Me caught in the middle of a twitch. I'm surrounded by myself, and I plop down onto the couch. Dad is everywhere, too. The other guy is in black-and-white.

"That's your grandpa." Francine catches me looking. She glances around. "Handsome group of men, isn't it?"

I smile and nod.

"Now, where's that Old Coot?" she asks. "I was sure he'd come with you."

My smile goes away—I can feel it. "He was sitting there." I peek at Naomi. "Then he wasn't."

Francine looks to Nae, and then back to me. She pales and slowly shakes her head. Her eyes close tight.

"Yes." The word barely squeezes out of her. She stands and leaves the room.

"That was his last word, too," I whisper.

I open my eyes. Don't know how long I've slept, but it is black outside the window.

Francine's feet appear on the steps, and she walks toward the love seat, steadies herself against the armrest. "Have you driven far?"

"Las Vegas this morning," I say.

"All today? You must be tired. What can I make for you to eat?"

"I'm good." I push up off the couch and stretch. "And I'm not tired now. Naomi, how about you?"

She sits in a big armchair, knees tucked beneath her chin, like they've been for hours. "Same." She smiles weakly at me.

Naomi's gone again. She looked happy hours ago but now she's gone. I lean over and try to catch her gaze, but she's lookin' through stuff. How can I take care of her if I don't know where she is?

"There's so much I want to hear, but I suppose it can wait." Francine smiles. "I'll get your rooms ready." She looks at Naomi. "I'm so glad you're both here."

She walks toward the armchair, leans over, and kisses Naomi's forehead. Francine straightens, turns, and takes one step. Then she freezes, her back to us.

"Was it his heart?"

"Guess so." I say.

"Was he alone?"

My shoulder jumps. I shake my head. "No. He crumpled into my arms."

Francine looks toward the ceiling. Then she turns, clears her throat, and walks toward me. "Bless you." She hugs me again.

"I'll see to those rooms. Feel free to walk down to the ocean. Your dad used to love the ocean at night. When he was young, we'd spend hours staring at the water." She pauses, whispers. "When he was young."

I raise eyebrows. Naomi nods and stands.

"Yeah," I say, and wonder about Dad and Francine. I glance at the Tourette's so evident in Francine's face. I should thank her for letting us stay and being so kind, but her face makes me embarrassed of my own and I look away. I think about it all the way to the door.

I take one more look at the pictures of my dad.

Were you embarrassed, too?

chapter forty-three

THE BEACH ISN'T FAR, BUT THE ROAD WINDS STEEP and narrow through thick trees and feels more made for mountain goat than car. It levels, and we step out into deep sand. A moon, waves that smash against jutting rocks, and forever water steal my words. We pad toward the shoreline and stand shoulder to shoulder in silence.

But inside, my mind tosses, because now is a good time to say whatever I want to say. And what I want to tell Naomi is that I like her. Maybe that's dumb. Maybe she already knows because she seems to know a lot of things before I say them.

But not lately. Not since Dad showed up. Since then maybe she wonders, and I've wondered a little, too. Standing here, I think I'm sure. It's a good time to say it aloud.

"Why do you think my grandpa wanted you to come here?" Naomi says.

My mouth is already half open to tell her my important thing.

"Don't know."

Naomi nods, and she takes my hand. It feels like her hand again, the gentle one. But she doesn't hold on for long. She kicks off her thongs, throws back her hair, and looks at me like she used to. And runs. A steady jog away from me.

I wait until she turns her head. When she does, I give chase.

Moonlight shimmers off the water and lights Naomi's figure in glints of yellow. I could catch up, but tonight following feels right. My gaze shifts from sandy footprints to her form.

I'll tell her when she stops.

I jump a piece of driftwood and land in a footstep. Looks like a size thirteen, my size, probably *his* size. I pull up and shake my head.

"Dad?" *I'm going crazy.*

"Jack?" Naomi runs back, grinning. "Can't catch me anymore?"

I point to the sand and blink. Only Naomi's prints.

"No. I guess I can't," I say.

"You're tired from the drive."

I walk back to the driftwood and plunk myself down.

"Probably more than I thought," I say.

She sits beside me, and we listen to the waves. Again, I want to tell her my important thing, but now I want to say more. I want to tell her that I like Jess, too; and though I've never spoken to Naomi's child, the kid matters, like family matters. It's not Jess's fault that the dad's an idiot, or that Naomi has fancy school plans. The baby is small and helpless and just needs Naomi to say "I love you" and tell the truth.

I breathe deep. "You can't hide Jess from your mom forever. I mean, look at my dad. I ran from him and he turned out pretty good. It'll be tough with your mom, but I'll bet you could face her. Heck, if you wanted to, I think you could even raise this baby."

It's not even close to what I wanted to say, but I thought it, and Tourette's fired it out.

She jumps up and sprints off, her footfalls quickly swallowed by the waves.

"Good job, Jack." I sigh and trudge back down the beach. "Probably should have stuck with 'I like you.'"

We'll patch it up back at Francine's.

The sea is hypnotic. Though night is normally horrible for twitches, this evening my muscles are at peace. I arrive at Francine's driveway out of breath from the climb, but calm clear through. Still, something feels wrong. I look around, pat my pockets, and waggle my head.

"The Chev."

I stand on the spot where we parked the beauty.

Naomi's gone. It's a heavy absence. She won't come back tonight, or tomorrow, and I wonder if she will at all. There's nothing I can do but feel, and thick emptiness pushes my rib cage from the inside out.

I'm alone. Everyone's left me or died. And it's not fair, not anymore. I don't deserve it. Because I'm not dumb or retarded. My hand tenses, and I nod. My name is Jack Keegan, my dad is James. He's proud of me.

I reach the door, bend down, and pick up the note—the one from her.

I'm sorry.
Living parents are harder to face than dead ones.

I fold the note carefully and slip it into my back pocket. I'm sorry for many things, too. And I never told Naomi how much I like her.

"I never met anyone like George." Francine smiles and hands me a lightbulb. The chair I'm on creaks as I take the bulb and reach way into her ceiling fan. My arm jerks, catches a cord, and starts the blades spinning.

Francine laughs. I chuckle, then screw in the bulb.

"While I'm here, anything else I can do?" I ask.

"Sit down."

I recline on the couch while Francine takes Naomi's big green chair. Pads of paper and watercolor paint cover the coffee table between us, and Francine reaches for paper, tray, and brush. She lays the paper across her lap, looks at me, and squints as if she's trying to find something.

"You're as bad as George." I say, "He takes my picture, you paint it."

She puts down her brush. "Not that old Polaroid."

I nod.

"Oh, he loved that thing. Carried it around everywhere." She smiles and splashes streaks of color on her small canvas. "Why did you come, Jack?"

"I don't know."

"Is that true?"

I pause. "George asked me to. I'd talked myself out of it, but then Naomi showed up and—" I run a hand through my hair. "She changed my mind."

Francine keeps painting. "I think it's wonderful. My grandson and George's granddaughter." She frowns at her brush, grabs another. "Where did she go to so early?"

I say nothing.

"When will she return?"

"Don't know."

"Did you fight?" She raises an eyebrow and peeks at me.

The conversation is turning a direction I don't want to go, but Francine's questions are hypnotic like the ocean, and I can't stop.

"I said stupid stuff. She took off."

"I hope she has a shorter memory than your father," she says. Francine's eyes glaze, and she stares over my head. Her brush wanders aimlessly over her pad—back and forth—and turns vibrant color into black streaks.

chapter forty-four

"WOULD YOU LIKE TO TRY?" FRANCINE HOLDS UP A brush. She looks down at her black-streaked painting and sighs. "More black streaks."

I shrug and take the brush from her hand.

We set up in her sunroom. It's huge, with hardwood floors and wall-to-wall windows. The ocean view is incredible, and we stand our easels side by side.

"How do I do this?" I ask.

"No directions, just paint with me."

I dab a little red on my brush, make a pinkish dot on the corner of the canvas. Beside me, Francine goes crazy with color—she has a brush in both hands. She's a wild woman, splotching and streaking until little white remains.

Okay, Keegan, create. I remember my random plot at the Archers', regrip my brush, and make a streak of blue, then yellow. I go for another brush and, along with my grandma, double-fist color all over the canvas. Twitches from both of us send paint onto her floor, onto each other, and we laugh.

"Splatter's half the fun." She steps back to admire her work. "You should have seen your dad."

"Tell me about him."

She looks at me. "What would you like to know?"

"Anything," I say. "I don't think Old Bill let Mom talk about him, so I just have my stepdad's version."

Grandma takes her finger and dips it into her black. She presses it hard onto her canvas. I stare at the spot.

"He is one of the most hateful men on this earth. God might still love him, but whatever he said about James—"

"I know it's a bunch of lies."

"A bunch?" She makes another spot. "That man wouldn't let me speak with you. Imagine a man not letting a grandma talk to her own grandson."

I made my own black dot. "Tell me about my dad's Tourette's."

"It was hard on him. Nobody knew what Tourette's syndrome was back then. School was hard. Other kids were hard." She drops her arms. "I was hard."

I glance at her and frown.

"I didn't want him to have the life I had. But the truth is we embarrassed each other. Too many mirrors showing the ugly parts. Does that make sense?"

I nod.

"He came back to visit. My son, your father, had grown into a wonderful man. But the whole thing stood like a wall between us." She sits on her stool. "He blamed me, and I understand." She whispers, "I'm the one to blame."

My heart thumps. I know what she means. I'm with my grandma, and if I wasn't so covered with paint, I'd give her a hug.

For the next hour she talks, and I make a mess. It's wonderful. But then Francine quiets, and I slow my brush. She's up to the part where I'm sick and I know what comes next.

"They hit the pole. Your father hung on for a few more hours."

A black streak forms across my canvas.

"He was getting medicine for me, right? That's what the Fasts said."

She nodded. "They'd know, being there and all." Francine places her paints in the easel tray, walks over to the glass, and stares. I join her, and she takes my arm.

"I see him, you know," I say. "I'll close my eyes and there he is." I let my eyelids close. Nothing. "He calls me or looks at me like he wants me to catch him even though I can't. But I feel him. Like he's close. Like he's always right here." I hold my free hand inches in front of my eyes. "Am I crazy?"

Francine shakes her head and smiles. "Sounds like the Good Lord's just letting you see what's been true your whole life. He's giving you a picture of yourself. Whose you really are."

I wait for the burning, the painful tingle that pricks my fingers whenever someone goes off on how kind God is. A minute later, I still wait.

"But God's never done anything for me. Why would He start now?"

Francine squeezes my arm. "Were you always right about George?"

"No."

"James?"

I chuckle.

"Me? Your mom?" She pauses. "Naomi?"

"No," I whisper.

"Well, seeing as you've been such an accurate judge of character, would it be possible that perhaps you've been, as the kids around here say, messed up on God as well?"

I breathe deep. "Possible."

"Well, now that you have just taken your first step on another lifetime search, I suppose you'd like what you certainly came out here for."

I frown. "I think I came out here for you."

"That's very kind. But you have to be excited about your dad's gift."

"My gift?"

Her brown eyes twinkle. "Lydia must've mentioned it."

I keep staring at her. *My dad never left me anything. Old Bill said so.*

"That George. That wonderful man." She gazes out the window. "James built mills for a living—"

"I know."

"He never built *me* one." Grandma beams. "But he built one for you."

"He did?"

Grandma laughs and hugs me and laughs some more.

"That's all he worked on the last few times he and George were here. He never felt right being away from you and Lydia for weeks on end, but James wanted to build it beautiful in the most beautiful place he could." She waves her hand toward the ocean. "They'd come in after a day's work. James would say, 'Jack's got to love it. It has to be here. It has to be perfect. It has to speak to him.' You were a baby, but already he was so proud of you."

"He left me a windmill?"

"He did." She puts her arm around me and squeezes. "He planned on giving it to you after graduation, which, if I'm not mistaken, just happened."

"Don't take this wrong." I scratch my head. "It means a lot, him doing that for me. But if he wouldn't have died, and Old Bill wouldn't have been around, we'd have come out here often, right? I'd have seen it and, well, it doesn't seem like a graduation kind of thing, you know?"

She nods. "I told James that. I said, 'Why does an eighteen-year-old need a windmill?' He smiled back and said, 'He won't, but he'll sure need what's inside.'"

"Where is it?" Fingers burn and my leg bounces.

"Well, my dear, you probably ran right by it last night. I call it a sea mill."

I rip off my smock and dash out her door. I tear down the hill, reach sand, and stare down the coast.

"Wow."

Nestled on jagged rock, it rises high out of the water. Don't know how I missed it. I pad nearer until water soaks my ankles.

High tide.

The rocky finger on which it sits pokes up twenty yards out, and waves crash pretty strong. For a moment I think about waiting, but the thought sickens me and I throw off my shoes and slosh into the ocean.

I never liked to swim. I don't like it now, and I wade until water laps my chest.

I'm only halfway there. A wave rolls over my mouth, and I sputter and lose balance. I replace my feet and feel sand. Then I don't.

I'm under, and moving. Don't know if the current yanks me toward shore or away.

The water around me lulls, and I kick and kick and pray I'm kicking toward the surface. I have no more air.

My head pops up and my body sweeps toward a rock. I crash into it, feel it gouge my calf. But I hug it, and work my way around the slippery stone until I find a place to climb. I haul myself ten feet up to a flat place, and crumple onto my side. My leg oozes red, but I'm alive, caught by the only rock that could catch me. I look up. The windmill sets about five feet up on the next plateau. I look out toward the ocean and the waves that wanted to sweep me away.

Thanks, Dad.

I climb to the mill. It looks crazed—blades whip one way, stop, start again. I've never seen a mill like this. Anchored into solid rock, it doesn't look like wood. I reach out and rub my hands over the surface. Rock. The same rock that it sits on.

I bend over and look for bracing. There is none. No crack

along the bottom either. Fifteen feet below me, a wave smacks the rock and showers me with spray.

"This wasn't built on rock. You carved this out of the rock. Man!"

Wind whips off the ocean and nearly knocks me off the spire. I scoot around the mill, careful where I place my feet, hugging it all the way. A windmill hacked out of stone.

Above me, blades whir and stop. They shouldn't withstand wind and water and years, but they do.

This is incredible—what in the world?

A small door is chiseled into the side of the mill away from the wind. It's also made of stone, but fits airtight into the rock around it. I trace my finger over the thin crack that outlines the vault and pick algae from the keyhole.

I peek inside, jam in my pinky until the tip hits metal. "If I could only open you."

I squeeze my hand into my soggy pocket and pull out my keys. I try car keys and farmhouse keys and keys to every out-building on my property.

"Too small." Teeth chatter. "I don't have anything bigger—wait!"

I stuff the key ring back into my jeans. "Hold on, I got one more." I dig out my wallet, and yank out Old Bill's precious key number thirty.

Blades give a furious whirl, but they aren't important to me. Nothing matters but the door my dad hacked and the key in my pocket.

Clouds cover the sun, and I shiver. Numb, pruned hands

struggle to hold Old Bill's key, the one with the etched letters. *JK*, my dad's initials. *JK*, my initials.

I double-fist it and jam it in. Inside, a spring gives, and the door pops open an inch.

My heartbeat pounds in my eardrums. "Okay, Old Bill." I stare at my dad's initials poking out of the hole. "How did you end up with my dad's key?"

I reach for the door and pause. "You took it from Mom, didn't you? My name wasn't enough. You had to steal my gift, too."

I throw open the door. Eight slim boxes sealed in large plastic bags are stacked inside the opening. I reach for the first, and read the word scrawled on yellowed masking tape.

Me

I rifle through the titles.

Ireland
Lydia
George
What you need to know
These crazy jerks

I place the other boxes back into the mill and stare at the one in my hands. Crazy jerks. I open it. Tapes. A plastic tape holder with twelve cassette tapes.

My heart thumps harder.

I yank out boxes and lean against the mill. It would be safer to leave the tapes in their stone tomb, but I'm not letting go and clutch them tight.

I watch the tide for hours. More beach becomes visible, and spray no longer crashes against the rock. I ease myself down. Another hour passes, and lifting boxes over my head, I slip into water that laps my chest.

A friendly current carries me to shore, and I sputter onto the sand.

I start toward Francine's, pause, and turn. I look out over the ocean, like my dad had done. The rumbling of the waves sounds like Old Bill.

All he left you was that disease. Stupid, no-good drunk of a dad—

"Liar!"

I scream at the water, and my scream sounds small. I try again.

"Everything you ever said was a lie, start to finish!"

I shout until I'm hoarse, until every ugly thing I've ever wanted to say to him has been carried away by the sea.

I'm exhausted. But inside I'm light. Clutching Dad's tapes, I haul up the hill, reach the top, and stop.

Naomi sits on the front step.

"Hey," she says.

I nod.

"What's all that?"

"Dad stuff."

She stands and walks toward me. "I'll help you carry it in." She smiles and grabs half the boxes of tapes from me.

"I like you," I blurt.

Naomi stops in her tracks. Her eyes widen.

I straighten and meet her stare.

She bites her lip then, lets out an exasperated sigh. "There you go again! I've been driving around for an hour rehearsing this, and you mess it all up." Naomi smacks my jumpy shoulder and drops a box of tapes. I bend down and pick it up.

"This isn't easy, you know," she continues. "It's not the kind of thing I say, well, ever. And *I* needed to say it first. But now I can't, and I'm stuck, and I wasted my time preparing a useless speech."

I nod slow. "Do you remember the last line of it?"

I can tell she's trying hard to stay frustrated, but she's losing the battle, and her face softens.

"It doesn't matter. It's too late."

"Just the last line," I say.

She swallows hard, and for a minute we stand in silence.

"Forget it." I shift boxes to one arm, stroke her shoulder, and turn toward the front door. "Don't say anything you don't want—"

"Get back here!" She grabs my free arm and drops more tapes. I pick up those too.

"I hate this!" She stares into the sky, exhales hard, lowers her eyes, and locks her gaze on me. "If you knew how horrible it is to be separate from you, or what it's like to see your face every time I shut my eyes. If you knew how I feel when I'm with you, maybe you'd get how hard this is for me! I mean, there's no reason for me to come back here. None!" She pauses, whispers, "Except you." Naomi blinks hard and her breathing slows. She stares at me. "That didn't sound much like my last line."

I can't hug her—we both hold boxes full of cassettes—but I can kiss her. Suddenly there are no tapes between us; they're heaped on my feet. Naomi presses into me. Our lips touch, gentle as an evening's wave, and a moment later I'm drowning in a feeling so wild and free I don't ever want to breathe.

"I don't mean to interrupt," says Francine, her head poking out the doorway. "But you two should get out of the rain."

It is raining. My brain thinks again, and I glance down. "My tapes!"

We scoop them up and dash inside, as heavy rain starts to fall.

I place my gift on the floor, grab Naomi's hand, and whirl toward Grandma.

"Do you have a tape player?"

chapter forty-five

THE THREE OF US TAKE OUR PLACES IN THE living room. Between us, on the coffee table, Grandma places a dusty tape player.

"This is what was inside the mill?" Francine asks.

"Inside," I whisper, and rub my hands.

Naomi draws her knees up to her face. "For how many years?"

"Sixteen," Francine says.

I flip through the sets of tapes. "Guess it doesn't matter what we hear first." I reach for the set labeled ME, and pop out a tape. "What kind of music did he like?"

"Oh, I don't think we'll hear music," Grandma says.

She squirms in her seat, and suddenly I feel anxious, too. A dad who wraps gifts in windmill wrapping paper is unpredictable.

I place my finger on the play button. "Here we go."

Five seconds. Nothing. Ten. Nothing.

"Oh, please," Grandma says.

Nothing? He gave me nothing?

"Hi, Jack." The voice on the tape speaks to me. Naomi leans forward, and Grandma places a trembling hand over her mouth.

"It's James," she whispers.

"Some things a man should say. Likely he'll forget, or won't have the chance. I want to be sure that doesn't happen to me and you. I want you to know everything. Who you are. Where you come from. So I'm saying it aloud, in case you forget. Figure it's my job to remind you."

My heart soars. I spend the next eight hours on the couch. My father's words fill my head and wash away any doubt. The man was smart and funny. He was good and strong. He loved Mom and at the end of each tape I hear it from his own lips:

"I love you, Jack."

It's the middle of the night. The brightest night I can remember. Grandma's asleep on the love seat. Naomi sits wide-awake and stares at the clock.

"I love my present," I say.

"You're lucky to have a dad like that," Naomi says quietly.

I nod and rise. "I am." I walk over and plop down in front of Nae. "This didn't go over well on the beach, but"—she hasn't moved, and I breathe deep—"I need to go home. I've got to look Old Bill in the face, and it doesn't matter what voice he uses on me. And if he calls me Sam, I'll steal my real name right back." I take her hand. It's limp and doesn't resist and tells me nothing.

"I need to set it all straight. Tell Old Bill and Mom that I know the truth."

Naomi's eyes stare vacant, as if what I said means nothing.

"It scares me," I say. "I've hidden from Bill my whole life, but you heard it. You heard my dad. I know it sounds dumb, but I want to make him proud. He believes in me and I can't run anymore, at least not away." I peek back at Grandma, "I finally caught my dad." She stirs.

"Dad ain't out here anymore. He's in here." I thump my chest. "And I got a mom, and a farm, a business and the truth . . . every responsibility I have is back home." I nod. "All but one." I stroke Naomi's cheek, and lay mine on her stomach. "I know you didn't have to come back here to be with me, but you did and . . ." I whisper, "Come with me."

"Where else would she go?"

I sit up quickly and glance over at Grandma. She removes her glasses and rubs the divots. "Is there something I'm missing?"

I scoot back so I'm not between Grandma and Naomi, but both of them keep their eyes fixed on me.

"Jack?" Grandma asks.

"I'm pregnant." Naomi's voice is small, but it doesn't waver. "That's what you're missing."

It's quiet. Just Naomi and me, my grandma, and the secret. I lift my hand onto Naomi's armrest, rest it palm up. It lies there, alone and funny-looking for the longest time. Finally, she lays her hand inside mine, and I squeeze.

Grandma's chin quivers, and she looks from Naomi to me. "Does Lydia know?"

"Mom?" I ask. "Why would—oh, it's, no—"

"It's not Jack's," Naomi says. "It's not his fault." She pulls free of me and buries her face in her hands.

Grandma takes a breath, and I can't tell if she's relieved or not. She stands, walks to the table, and grabs a chair.

"Fault." She sets the chair down by Naomi and eases into it. "That's a tough word to lug around." Grandma sighs, leans back. "I should know."

Naomi peeks through a crack in her fingers.

"I never knew the half of what I just heard on those tapes. James never shared it. I knew I hurt him—the disease, *my* disease, hurt him." Grandma gives a weak smile. "All his agony came through me. It's my fault," she whispers.

"That's so different." Naomi lowers her hands. "There was nothing you could do."

Grandma swallows hard. "I didn't have to have him in the first place. It would have saved us both a lot of pain."

"Yeah, but, look what happened. I mean, I'm sure it was hard, but I just listened to the most awesome guy. Your son was great." Naomi looks toward me. "Jack is great."

Grandma nods. "It's true. Seems the worst situations lead to the biggest blessings. So long as you're not alone. Nothing good comes when you're alone." Grandma strokes Naomi's hair, stands stiffly, and shuffles toward the stairs. "So we stay with those we love, who love us. We take their hand and run as fast as we can toward the people who know us best." Grandma pauses at the bottom step. "And like you said, at first it's hard"—she glances at me over her shoulder—"but it may turn out great after all." She smiles and heads up the stairs.

We listen to footsteps fade, reappear above our heads, and fall silent.

Naomi finally shifts in her chair. "We'd go home together, then?"

"Together."

She runs her hand through her hair and tosses it back. Naomi takes my hand and closes her eyes. "Okay. I'll stay with Jack."

chapter forty-six

I BOOK OUR SEATS ON THE EARLY FLIGHT TO
Minneapolis out of Sacramento. Night passes quickly, and
when dawn breaks, my stiff legs are eager for a run. I walk
into Naomi's room and nudge her shoulder. She rises quickly,
and together we take one last sunrise trip to the beach.

Our jog pauses when we reach my gift.

"It's just one piece? That rock sticking up and the windmill
is all one piece? How'd he do that?" Naomi asks.

I shake my head and smile. "Must've seen a rock and imagined a windmill hiding inside. He chiseled it out of there."
I lean into her shoulder. "But he had help from someone's
grandpa."

Naomi smiles. "George could make anything grow
anywhere."

I start to run, but Naomi doesn't move.

"Do you think George knew I'd come with you? I mean, it

was luck, right? You could have left five minutes earlier. It's all luck?"

I smile at the windmill and finger the key in my pocket. "A week ago, that's what I'd have thought. But no more. Not with Dad or George." I gesture for Naomi to follow and jog down the beach. She quickly catches me.

"They're not done with us yet," I say.

"It's going to be close," Naomi calls from the car. I dash up the steps and into Grandma's house, where she throws together food for our short trip.

"Grandma."

She whirls around. "You startled me. I'll be right out."

"Will you put that down? I need you for a second."

She lowers the crackers and cheese, and leans back against the counter.

"I've been thinking," I begin. "I don't know the whole story with Dad and you. But I get it, I mean, I blamed him for years." My shoulder twitches; so do her eyelids.

"It wasn't his fault." I step closer. "Wasn't yours either. This disease thing ain't your fault. None of it."

She cries but doesn't look away. She cries and stares and vise-grips my hand.

"I guess it would have meant more coming from Dad."

Grandma smothers me in a bear hug. She shakes and sobs and I try to think if I screwed up and said anything dumb. But I come up empty and let her have her way.

She releases me and strokes my shoulders.

"You have no idea . . ."

She's happy, I think, under all that wet.

I point back over my shoulder with my thumb. "Naomi's set, and we're late, so I need to go."

She wipes her eyes with her apron. "Yes, you do. You'll write?"

"I don't write well."

"You'll write," she says.

"Nah." I smile and wink. "You have my car. I'll be back."

The taxi ride to the airport is quiet. That's fine by me. My mind is full of words I'll say, sentences I've squashed for years—Old Bill might not listen, but he'll hear. I glance down at the duffel bag and rest my hand on the binders packed inside.

Our flight is just as silent. Naomi takes my hand. She keeps holding it as my tensing claw pinches and squeezes her fingers. It's not until wheels strike runway that my grip eases, and I pull away my sweaty palm.

I grab my duffel, exit the plane, and wander around the gate. The whole thing feels like a dream. The Fasts, Penners, Watkinses, Grandma—fake people from an overactive imagination. Naomi takes my hand and steers me down the concourse.

"We can do this," she says, and her voice lowers. "Together."

"Together." I nod. It's not as if I'm confronting Old Bill, I'm just saying what's true. Dad deserves that much. I do, too.

"Where ya headin', kid?"

We've walked past baggage claim, through the rent-a-car area, and onto the street.

I shake Old Bill thoughts from my head and find the voice. Comes from a short man who leans over the door of a taxi.

"Pierce," I say, and raise eyebrows toward Nae. She smiles and nods.

I face taximan. His expression is blank.

"Close to Mitrista."

"You're kiddin'. That's a haul and a half."

"Forget it, I'll go rent a—"

"No, no, no." He walks toward me and reaches for my tapes.

My free hand shoots out and catches his wrist. I stare at my hand. Never done anything like that before.

"Duffel stays with me." I let him go, and he raises both hands in the air.

"Easy now. Trying to help, is all." He motions us toward the car, turns, and mutters, "Kids wound too tight these days."

We follow him and slip in back.

"Mitrista, huh? You got money for this?"

I nod.

He rolls his eyes and shoots me a you-better-be-telling-the-truth look in the rearview mirror. "What the heck."

chapter forty-seven

TWO HOURS PASS TOO QUICKLY, AND AS WE TURN in to Bill's turnaround, my chest is tight and my throat raw.

Mom said to stay away. Maybe I should have listened.

I pay the fare and step out, my duffel filled with Dad's tapes clutched to my chest. One step. Then two more. I whip around and stare at the cab. From inside, the driver shoos me on like a fly, and I turn and take a deep breath.

"Do you want to do this?" Naomi softly walks up from behind.

"No."

I scan the porch. The swing I busted sits in a heap, and there's a fresh hole in the screen.

"Yeah. I need to see him."

We walk up the steps. I glance at Naomi. She nods and I knock. Inside, footsteps come nearer. Soft ones.

"Hi, Mom."

She throws open the screen and hugs me. It's not the usual air hug. It's real and long and feels like love.

"You're safe ... and here." She lets go and strokes my cheek with her hand. "And Naomi."

"Hello."

"How do you two know each other?" I ask.

Nae leans in to my shoulder. "I dropped off a jacket for you."

I grin, and remember Mom holding it in front of her face. "Where's Old Bill?"

"He hasn't been here for a couple days." Mom puts her arm around my waist and tugs. "Come in. I want to hear all about it."

We enter a mess. A door hangs cocked on its hinges. Lights have no shades.

"I'm sorry about the place, Naomi," Mom says. "Bill had a rough weekend." Mom sits down and gestures at the table. I shake my head. I can't stand it here. Can't stand the thought of Mom here.

"He's a liar, Mom. Everything he told me about Dad. All lies."

Mom looks at me, her chin quivering. She nods, mouths the words *I know*.

My stomach turns, and my shoulder jerks hard. Naomi rubs that angry shoulder.

"She had to keep quiet." She turns to Mom. "Is that right?"

Mom closes her eyes. "It was wrong. But if you would have challenged Bill on that, I didn't know what he'd do."

"He'd have thrown your twitchy butt out of the house a lot sooner, that's what."

The front door crashes, and Old Bill storms in. He walks straight toward me and stops nose to nose.

He doesn't look right. He's in a daze, a staring spell.

"Hi, Bill," I say.

His eyes widen, and then narrow. The spell breaks.

"Lookee here." He whispers.

Old Bill looks old, which is weird since it hasn't been two weeks since I've seen him. But his eyes focus clear and sharp. He glares with his hard face, the one that used to push my gaze to the ground. I've no urge to do anything but keep staring myself.

Maybe he's always been this old.

He speaks, and the words are low and controlled and terrible. "What are you staring at, boy?"

"I'm not your boy."

Old Bill squints, glances around the room, and his face calms. He steps into the kitchen. "Women here and all. Finish your visit and get out." He opens the refrigerator and starts a search.

Mom and Naomi both peek at me. I don't know what I'm supposed to do. Naomi steps nearer, takes my hand, and squeezes.

"You lied, Bill," I say, and Mom stands up, walks into the bedroom. Old Bill closes the fridge door and turns.

"Maybe once or twice." He talks to me, but stares at Naomi—an up-and-down stare. "About what?"

"My dad. James Keegan."

The sick smirk falls from his red face. He opens and closes his fist, finally using it to grip the counter. "So you believe that dead Coot."

"My grandfather," says Naomi.

Old Bill tongues the inside of his cheek and shakes his head. "No way such a pretty little thing comes from a worthless nut."

I want him dead. I don't care if he's my stepdad, if he married my mother. His words make me sick.

I swallow hard and step forward. "Yep. I believe him. And the Fasts, and the Penners, and Grandma." My legs tremble, and I pull out a kitchen chair and plunk down. "Pretty much everyone but you, Old Bill."

"Get out, Sam."

"Jack. The name is Jack Keegan. My father was James Keegan. My grandma is Francine Keegan." I push up from the table.

"Get out!" he roars.

"My father built windmills. He was smart, he was kind, he was strong."

"Out!"

"He died getting medicine for me. No women, no booze. All lies. Old Bill, you're all lies. And that ends now."

Old Bill walks toward me. I brace my body against the table.

Naomi moves in front of me and lays her head against my pounding chest.

"Move, girl. Move!"

"Together," she whispers.

"I'm leaving, Bill," I say. "Just had to set things straight." I wrap my arm around Naomi. "My dad loved me, and he loved Mom. You didn't do either one."

Old Bill stares at Naomi, curses, and kicks the chair I'd been on, breaking a leg in two.

"I want every Keegan out of this house. Now!"

"Okay, Bill." Mom reappears from the back room, Lane in her arms. "You can have your way. I'm going. We're going."

Mom walks by me, holding Lane close to her chest.

"Lydia! What are you doin'?" Panic covers his face, and he starts to pace. He'll blow any moment, and I whip Naomi out of the house behind my mother.

The door rattles shut behind me, and we hurry down the steps. Inside, glass shatters, and Old Bill crashes outside.

"Lane's my boy! You ain't taking him nowhere." He bounds down the steps as a pickup rumbles into our turnaround. Out steps Farkel, big and imposing, a two-by-four in his hands. He leans over the cab door. Old Bill freezes.

"Got here soon as I could, Lydia. All okay?" He smiles at me. "Welcome home, Jack."

"Thanks." I help Mom, Naomi, and Lane into the cab of Farkel's truck and set all our stuff in back.

"Got room for two more, Jack? Just for a while?" Mom asks as if she really doesn't know what I'll say.

"Plenty." I smile, shut the door, and hop in the truckbed. Four cats scatter.

Farkel backs into the driver's seat, and we pull out. I look back at Old Bill. He stares at me. His big arms, the ones that gave me a Tar-Boy jacket and carried me off Stacy Lake, hang limp at his sides. Strange that I'm not angry, that one minute after he almost clocked me, all I remember is good stuff. I raise my hand. He cocks his head like a man who just lost his world.

"Good-bye, Bill."

chapter forty-eight

NAOMI AND I HELP MOVE MOM AND LANE INTO THE upstairs of George's old farmhouse. I give her some of the pictures stuffed beneath my couch, and that makes her smile. But little else does, and she walks around the farm in a daze.

"I think just let her alone." Naomi and I walk toward my windmill. We watch the blades spin. She puts her arms around my waist and squeezes. "I need to see my mom." I nod and walk her to the shed, where her car still rests.

"Together, right?" I ask.

She's quiet. Naomi starts to speak, stops, and smiles. My shoulder jerks, but who cares.

"I'm glad I met you," she says.

"Me, too."

Naomi traces her finger down the front of my T-shirt. She reaches behind my neck and pulls my head close. She holds it there, my mouth next to her ear, as if she expects me to say something to her, but I don't, and she lets my head go.

Inside, I ache. Our trip was fantasy. Whatever she said or did is gone. Maybe if we hopped back into her car and drove away, we'd be together again. But we're here, in Pierce—with Jace and Heather and Mom and a real baby I named Jess. It's all real and hard and I might not hear from her again.

"I need to go." She gives me a kiss on the cheek and hops into her car. I back away and she pulls out, makes it halfway down my drive, and stops.

I stare at the car, at her inside it. Motionless.

"Am I supposed to follow you?" I whisper.

A minute passes, and the car doesn't budge. Inside my heart swells. I take a step toward it, and the engine roars. Naomi peels out of the driveway.

I stand and watch and stroke the spot on my cheek.

Weeks fill with revisiting customers and setting up my new business: Jack and George's Gardens. I don't know much about gardening, but I love my new truck and I can slam flowers. A bunch of George's customers want to stick with me, and that's good.

I make frequent trips to the Garden Bowl, and each time I stop and see Farkel.

"How's Naomi getting along?"

I take a sip of coffee, set down my cup, and shake my head.

"Ain't that the shame?" Farkel leans back and folds his arms. A cat jumps onto his lap, and he gives it a stroke. "Didn't work out?"

"Worked." I drain my drink and scald my tongue. "Don't know what to do."

Farkel stands. I do, too.

"Hear people make phone calls." He walks me toward the door. "Some even visit."

"Yeah."

"Speakin' of which, you should bring Lydia next time." Farkel steps outside. "She's never seen this garden."

I frown.

"George and you and them men when he died. That's all I let in. Orders. 'Course now, you being the boss, things might be different." He winks, and wraps his big arm around my shoulder.

That night after Lane is asleep Mom and I sit down to write letters. Though I peck badly at the keyboard, I manage to fill up three pages each to Grandma, the Fasts, and the Penners. Mom handwrites novels, but she's making up for lots of years.

Mom stares at the letters on the table, her eyes glistening. "It's been so long."

I walk over, give her a hug, and mention Farkel's invitation. She perks up, and on Saturday she gets a sitter for Lane and we set out together. I pull up in front of Farkel's barn.

"Would you mind if I went in alone?" Mom asks.

"Whatever you want."

I get out of the truck, hand her the truck keys, and pause. "Here." I dig in my pocket. "Here's another one." I hand her Dad's key. "Don't know but you might find use for that, too."

She kisses my cheek, and hops inside the truck. I watch her drive away until she vanishes out the far end of the barn.

Evening comes. I help Farkel fix his pasture fence.

"Think I should go after her?"

"She's a grown woman," Farkel says. "Worry about yourself." He hands me the hammer, but I see headlamps and set my tools down. Mom putters out of the barn.

She drives over to us.

"You ready to go home, Jack?"

"Yeah."

I reach the driver's door.

"Let me drive," Mom says.

I don't know if she used Dad's key. Doesn't seem right to ask. I walk around, say my good-byes to Farkel, and hop in.

"Good day?" I ask.

Mom nods and pulls forward. "It is a beautiful evening."

She swerves, narrowly misses a cat, and pulls onto the road to Pierce. Mom starts to hum—I've never heard that before. I don't know the song, but it's pretty. I lean my head against the window. It's almost a perfect night.

I get up early and slip on my running shoes. Been out of my routine for too long. I step out into morning cool, and shuffle toward the shed.

I lean against it and stretch. The metal door hangs partway open and it's dark inside, but I make out the outline of a bulldozer with Sam's headstone painted on the blade.

Miles later, I'm in my running trance. No one else exists. Then someone does.

Another jogger runs behind me, and then beside me. I'm afraid to look in case it's not who I pray it is.

"You haven't called."

I feel my smile. It's huge, and I can't take it off for a long time.

"You never gave me your number," I say. "Haven't heard from you either. Guess we both had things to do."

Naomi stops. I do, too.

"Will you be staying around awhile?" She bites a nail while she shakes out her thighs and stares at me. "Any big trips planned?"

"No." Again, I smile. "I'm home. Besides, I have a lot to learn about George's business—well, my business. More clients to contact, you know?"

"So you'll come around my place?" Naomi asks.

"If your mom'll have me."

"That's good. That's"—Naomi takes a deep breath—"Jess will need a good man in her life. I mean, I'm not asking . . . I just thought maybe you'd come over and play with her or—"

I pick Naomi up and swing her around until she tells me she'll vomit. Then I gently set her down and shout because I can, because the shout comes out so easily and feels so good. I whoop and holler until she laughs and clamps her hands over my mouth.

"Let's run," Naomi says.

I nod, and she smiles and removes her hands. Together, we jog away from Pierce. The pace is slow, and I have no idea where this run will take us. Wouldn't have it any other way.

jonathan friesen

A Reader's Guide

a conversation with jonathan friesen

Q: Your biography mentions that, like Sam/Jack, you also have Tourette's syndrome. How much of Sam's/Jack's story is your own? What is your personal history with the disease? At what age did symptoms first appear? How did that affect you growing up?

A: Sam's story is completely fictitious, but his internal struggle with Tourette's syndrome mirrors my own quite closely. He is much more honest with himself than I was—I had a hard time accepting the fact that I couldn't stop my movements. Somewhere, I had picked up the idea that I *should* be able to stop them. My symptoms first appeared when I was five. Eye blinks and shoulder jumps. Early on, those movements didn't affect me much. My peers didn't make a big deal of them. But in junior high, those tics (and my dishonesty about them) began affecting relationships. By high school, school was a lonely place. But again, my attitude about TS, and not the syndrome itself, deserves a fair amount of credit for that.

Q: Are there any common misconceptions about Tourette's syndrome that you wish to correct?

A: Yes. Many people's concept of Tourette's syndrome includes people blurting out curse words. Stressing that dramatic aspect makes good TV ratings and humorous movie clips. For a tiny fraction of those with TS, this does occur. But the majority do not swear involuntarily. The other thing I'd like to mention is that I've never met a person with TS who is not profoundly creative or gifted in some way. We're good people to have around!

Q: Sam's/Jack's relationship with George is touching and sincere. George came along just when Sam most needed someone to believe in him. Were there any influential people in your own life who helped guide you?

A: My grandma had the rare ability to build me up and kick me in the rear at the very same time. If you've never had this type of person in your life, it's quite an experience. One minute she would tell me what she saw in me, how proud she was of me. Then, bam! She'd let me have it, and point out all the areas in which I had more growing to do. But I listened to her, because I knew she loved me and I was certain she believed in me. She was a powerful guide in my life.

Q: The romance between Naomi and Sam/Jack is sometimes sweet, sometimes frustrating, but always very

true to life. Was their romance based on any in your own life?

A: Oh, sure. Dating my wife was the most irritatingly wonderful experience of my life. I never knew what was going on. She said things, did things when we were together, that I knew I should understand. It's like we dated in code and I didn't have the codebook. So I got slugged in the shoulder quite often, which didn't turn out to be a bad thing.

Q: Sam's/Jack's story is often heartbreaking, especially when it comes to his difficulties fitting in at school and his lack of meaningful friendships. Sadly, ostracism and even bullying are not uncommon among high school students. Do you have any advice for teens struggling with these challenges?

A: High school ends. A speaker told us on day one of ninth grade, "These are the best days of your life." I heard that again during my freshman year at college. I remember thinking, he better be lying, because this is more nightmare than dream. I look around at my close friends now, years later. I'm not in contact with anyone from high school and only one guy from college, but my life is filled with great friendships—the kind everyone seems to have in high school but few actually do. School ends; the wind blows people every which way. When that wind dies down, there will be someone there for you.

Q: The power of names to define a person is an important issue in the book. What has been the importance of names in your own life?

A: I think a name can shape a life. It can also be a marker in the road. I was born Jonathan, but nobody called me that. I was Jon, or John-Boy, or Jonno, or whatever. I think nicknames are great. They make a person feel special. But after a disastrous college relationship, I wanted to put *everything* behind me. It's as if I wanted to take a shower and wash off everything about myself and who I'd been, including the name I'd been called: Jon. I reclaimed Jonathan. It's my true name, my true self, and reclaiming it made me feel new again.

Q: Acceptance, both of yourself and of others, is a major theme in *Jerk, California*. Tell us why this was an important message for you to convey in writing this novel.

A: If you're a hider, like I was, you build up walls so other people's words and stares can't hurt you. But you also peek over the top of that wall, and judge everyone else. If you feel rotten about yourself, it feels better if you can rip someone else. Then you don't need to look at your own problems. I didn't set out to write a novel about acceptance, but when I revisited the emotions of high school, it was impossible for that not to become a major theme.

Q: There is also a song titled "Jerk, California" (by the band

Halloween, Alaska). Which came first—the song or the novel?

A: The novel came first. The band members read an early copy of the book and came up with the song. I heard it and my jaw dropped because they nailed it—the mood, the feeling. I was shocked. Halloween, Alaska did a great job.

Q: What is your favorite book? Who is your favorite musician/band?

A: My favorite book is *Peace Like a River* by Leif Enger. I read it five pages at a time. That's all I could handle. It was so . . . perfect. As far as music—if money was no object, I'd love to hear Sting play an acoustic set on a small stage. There is something haunting about his music that appeals to me.

Q: Did you always know you wanted to be a writer?

A: No. I always wrote, but I didn't think I'd be a writer. I entered college as a guitar performance major. I played classical guitar, and in bands around the Twin Cities. Writing muscled in and took over, though I still love my guitars.

Q: Where do you find inspiration for your characters and stories?

A: Every story of mine contains an element lifted from real life. I need to understand an aspect of a character, or a piece of the plot. Once I find that interesting detail, my imagination takes over. I stick that familiar piece into a situation or character I know nothing about and start asking, "what if."

Q: What's your writing process like? Where do you write? Do you have any writing rituals?

A: I write in my cave (my office). It overlooks about fifty beautiful acres of Minnesota woods and farmland. I'm a natural night owl, so I'll often write until 3:00 AM, but I'm trying to change that. I don't know if it will work, but I'm trying a grand experiment and now write in the morning. That frees up evenings for the family. My only writing ritual is my pre-writing prayer. I ask God to help me write something that will make Him smile, then off I go.

Q: Who do you share your writing with first?

A: My wife. Always my wife. Every writer needs a brutally honest spouse, and that's what I have! I stare at her face while she reads. It's reached the point now where she doesn't need to say anything when she's done. I usually end up stomping back to my cave for another rewrite.

Q: What's next for you? Any more books in the works?

A: The books will keep coming! I'm excited about my next novel. *Rush* tells the story of Jake King, a young adrenaline junkie who joins a team of crazed firefighters. They rappel out of helicopters to take on California's most dangerous wildfires. But joining The Rush Club, this team's secret society, proves more deadly than any fire, for both Jake and the girl he loves. I'm thrilled with how this story is coming together!

reading group
questions for discussion

1. When we first meet Sam, Tourette's syndrome controls him. What do you see as the biggest challenge to living with this condition?

2. Embracing his rightful name is a turning point for Sam, as is his secret naming of Naomi's child. What role do names play in who people become?

3. We all attempt to hide the obvious, and like Sam who attempts to draw attention away from his Tourette's, we all fail. Have you caught yourself trying to conceal something that you might just need to accept?

4. Sam desperately wants to be with Naomi, yet he can barely look her in the eye. Is it possible to have a deep relationship with another before accepting one's own unattractive features?

5. George doesn't seem to care about Sam's comfort, yet he makes the perfect mentor, and Sam warms to him. Who are the mentors, or "trusted guides," who have affected your life for the better, and why?

6. In the beginning of the novel, Naomi calls Sam her hero. How do Sam's actions throughout the story live up to your definition of a hero? In what ways does he fail?

7. Sam hates Old Bill, yet longs to makes him proud. How can these feelings exist at the same time?

8. What circumstances justify a peace-at-all-costs attitude, such as the one Lydia displays?

9. Sam's journey frees him because he discovers the truth about who he is and whose he is. Has a personal journey ever changed how you view yourself and the world around you?